SPECTATORS OF WAR

by

Luke Swanson

GenZ
The Future of Publishing

Cover Designer: Brandon Fierman
Supervising Editor: Shannon Marks
Design Assistants: Fiona Suherman
Editing Assistants: Sydney Thibodeaux, Alexa Nichols, and Megan Peterson
Publishing Assistants: Amit Dey and Lisa Wood

Please write to the publisher at info@genzpublishing.org

ISBN (paperback): 978-1-952919-83-1
ISBN (ebook): 978-1-952919-82-4

War, like other dramatic spectacles,
might possibly cease for want of a "public."

—Mary Ann Evans,
***The Mill on the Floss* (1860)**

The battle was a raging, deadly storm, with bullets like raindrops and explosions like thunder. It seemed impossible that anyone would come out of it alive.

Two nations, locked in deadly combat. Soldiers were scattered and sprawled across the field. Mere minutes ago, their uniforms had been different colors, but now, they were dyed red with blood.

Those left alive had entrenched themselves on either side of the no-man's-land. Bunkers, foxholes, and machine gun nests were quickly established, and the carnage continued. The sun made its journey across the sky, and soldiers died by the dozen. Neither side gained an inch. They were locked into their positions, and no one saw a way out. So they kept shooting. Shooting and dying.

A young man from Milwaukee crouched behind a stone barricade. Electric adrenaline coursed through his veins, but he couldn't bring himself to move from his hiding spot. If he so much as stood, he would be shot.

He rubbed grime from his eyes. The sun had set a while ago, but flashes from rifles and grenades kept the field illuminated like a demented dancefloor. He looked up—no stars, no sky, just smoke. The stench of gunpowder and singed hair filled his nostrils, along with that of overcooked meat. Everything just smelled burned.

Funny—he wasn't old enough to buy a beer, yet he was fighting for his life. He supposed going to war was a cheaper habit to nurse anyway.

He checked his rifle. One round left. One. What difference could a single bullet make amongst this maelstrom of destruction?

More explosions rocked the barricade he was hiding behind. He braced himself against the stone and cried out. "This is hopeless! We're all gonna die here!"

His legs turned to mush as his fighting spirit gave out. He slumped to the ashy ground and felt like weeping.

It was all too much. The battle smothered the young man like a pillow over his face, to the point that he could barely breathe. He bellowed in desperation. "Nothing can stop this hellfire!"

"I'll give it a shot."

The strong, clear voice rang out over the chaotic violence. A broad-shouldered man slid down next to the young soldier and gave his knee a pat.

The young soldier looked at this newcomer with wide eyes. In that moment, he knew everything was going to be okay. "It's good to see you, Ranger Monroe!"

"The pleasure's mine, Milwaukee."

The younger man lit up.

Ranger's smile could guide ships into harbor on a foggy night. His hair was blond and perfectly ruffled, and he had the physique of a line-backer but the grace of a dancer. A handgun was strapped to his belt, but otherwise, he was unarmed. If there was one man who could bring a stop to this madness, it was Ranger Monroe.

"This is a nice hidey-hole you have here." Ranger grinned and slapped the stone barricade. "All it needs is some jazzy music and a velvet rope, and you could open your own club!"

The young soldier laughed. That was Ranger's greatest power—making people feel at ease, no matter how dire the situation. He could befriend a rattlesnake with one anecdote.

"Say, friend," Ranger leaned in to be heard over the gunfire, "could I borrow your rifle? I lost mine about an hour ago."

"Sure thing, but there's only one round left."

Ranger let loose a charming laugh. "More than enough!" He took the rifle. "It's going to be all right." He readied the gun against his shoulder, said a quick prayer, and leapt out from behind the barricade.

It was like being underwater—the air was murky, noises were bleary, and each moment was heavy with death. But Ranger navigated the field with expertise. He wove between bullets and rolled behind cover at the right moments. Step by step, he crossed no-man's-land.

The enemy's bunker was in sight—so close, yet miles away.

Other soldiers in his army saw Ranger on the move.

"Look, men. It's Monroe!"

"He's not giving up."

"Let's go!"

A flock of warriors positioned themselves behind their gallant leader, gushing with renewed strength. The mere sight of Ranger's square shoulders and determined glare set them on fire.

They all began to chant. "Hah! Hoo! We're coming for you! Hah, hoo, we're coming for you!" Their words nearly drowned out the tidal wave of gunfire.

Nearly.

Enemy bullets rained down on the army.

Ranger blanched. "Cover, now!" He dove behind a boulder, but not everyone was as swift.

Bodies crumpled to the ground, wetting the soil with blood. Men cried to the smoky heavens then fell silent, never to cry again.

The battlefield was merciless, and it broke Ranger's heart to see his comrades torn apart. But he had to push on.

Ranger glanced around the boulder and saw the source of the carnage: a massive mounted machine gun, turning his army into minced meat. He aimed his rifle, stilled his breathing, and fired.

His bullet flew a hundred yards, straight down the barrel of the machine gun. It smoked and shattered, and its operator was left digging shrapnel out of his face.

"Ranger," a voice yelled out, "help me with this survivor!"

Without hesitation, Ranger dashed out from his cover. He and another soldier dragged a downed man behind the boulder. Once they were safe, he assessed his comrade's injury.

"What's the damage, soldier?" he asked while ripping the sleeves off his shirt.

"Got hit in the leg, sir." The man winced through a clenched jaw. "I'll be fine…"

"I'll tell you what you'll be." Ranger wrapped the cloth around the man's bloody thigh. "You'll be home soon." He smiled. "I'm jealous, lemme tell ya. A home-cooked meal, a decent cup of coffee, and a hero's welcome! What I wouldn't give…" He laughed softly, and the other soldiers joined him.

Ranger laughed to mask his concern. The bullet in the man's thigh had shattered his femur. Adrenaline held the agony at bay for the moment. Ranger needed to set the bone so the man could be efficiently evacuated.

He set his empty rifle next to the soldier's leg, then took the remaining strips of cloth and tied the gun along the length of his limb. *Voilà*, a makeshift splint.

"Stay here," he said to the uninjured man who had helped him, "and don't let him lose consciousness. This battle won't last much longer." He drew his handgun and left the safety of cover.

The ground was littered with more and more bodies as he got closer to the enemy bunker. He stepped carefully so as not to trample any corpses, but he needed to move quickly.

"It's Monroe!"

That was the voice of an enemy soldier. Not good.

Ranger's eyes caught sight of an airborne grenade at the last moment. He slid under an empty SUV. The grenade exploded, shattering the car's windows, but not harming Ranger at all.

The flock of soldiers following Ranger was now fully exposed. Another grenade arced through the air, headed right for the heart of the pack. They'd be decimated.

In a flash, the square shoulders of Ranger Monroe appeared from under the SUV. He jumped with all the strength in his legs and swatted the grenade right out of the air—just in time. It exploded, sending Ranger flying back behind the SUV.

Cheers filled the battlefield, but it wasn't over yet.

Ranger staggered out from behind the SUV, covered in ash but no worse for wear.

Just a few strides away, an enemy soldier sneered and reached into the satchel draped around his torso. An incendiary tech. That bag was full of grenades.

Ranger fired three shots into the man's chest. He grabbed the bag and took off running straight for the bunker. He reached into the bag and felt around, all while dodging gunfire. Ten grenades. Perfect. He set one of them to blow, then launched the entire bag through the bunker's outer window.

"Run!" he yelled.

All of the soldiers—ally and enemy alike—fled from the bunker. Three seconds passed in a crawl.

Then.

BOOM.

The bunker lit up like a firecracker, detonating from the inside out.

A hush fell across the battlefield. Men caught their breath. Debris fell from the sky.

Suddenly, three hundred thousand cheers erupted from the stands. What a spectacle!

Massive bulbs flipped on, flooding the entire battlefield with white light. Red, white, and, blue confetti filled the air. The surviving soldiers lowered their guns and heaved sighs of relief. The fighting was over.

The battleground was in the middle of an enormous, roofless sta-dium—one that would put the Coliseum to shame. Ringing the bloodied field were rows and rows and rows of seats, and every single one held a spectator. This stadium in particular could hold three hundred thousand rowdy fans.

Ranger Monroe had fought in battle-stadiums all over the world, and this was definitely one of his favorites. The sheer mass of people it could hold was a big factor. The gasps, the sobs, the ovations...In the heat of deadly warfare, an audience's reactions could have a huge effect on a sol-dier's morale.

Also, the weather was usually nice. San Diego rarely disappointed on that front.

He took a deep breath. Once the stench of smoke and dead bodies passed, it would be a really nice night.

Ranger took large strides onto the roof of the bunker he had blown up, and he waved at the crowd. They waved back, whooping his name. He soaked it all in and glanced at the gigantic screens suspended over the field. His chiseled face was a hundred feet tall, and his smile literally illuminated the stadium.

These screens had displayed every detail of the battle for the crowd to see. Long-range cameras had caught his individual actions, and the small microphone on his uniform had captured what he'd said. The sold-out audience had been there for every sentence, every step, every heroic deed. And they'd loved it.

While the cameras were focused on him, Ranger caught the eye of another soldier and beckoned him forward. The man clambered up onto the bunker and joined Ranger's spotlight.

This was the captain of the opposing army. Was his name...Don? John? Ranger couldn't remember. Didn't matter. Ranger grabbed his hand and held it up, a perfect snapshot of camaraderie and sportsmanship.

A small American flag was sewn onto the shoulder of Ranger's uniform, as it was for everyone in his army. He saw a Finnish flag on the other captain's shoulder and remembered.

"Well done tonight, Erik," he said over the roaring crowd.

Erik, the other captain, smiled. "Good win, Monroe. It won't be so easy next time. I promise you that!"

They slapped each other's arms good-naturedly, and the cameras ate it up.

As was tradition, the generals of the two armies entered the field to take their bows and accept their applause. Ranger didn't know who the Finnish general was, but he seemed jaunty and charismatic. The general Ranger served under, on the other hand...

General Richard Lightfoot shuffled onto the field, looking like he'd missed his appointment at the mortuary. He was ninety-eight years old and clearly miserable. While his uniform may have once fit him snugly, his body had shriveled up like a raisin over the decades, and the jacket and slacks now hung from his limbs. During battles, he spent his time either doing crossword puzzles or napping.

Lightfoot might technically be in command of this army, but Ranger Monroe was the real leader, and the public knew that. As the general waved his bony hand, thousands of voices kept chanting, "*Ranger! Ranger! Ranger!*"

A dozen doctors in white coats stormed the field and began rummaging through the corpses. Every now and then, they'd find a survivor and get to work.

The soldiers milled about, chatting with one another, swapping jokes, making dinner plans. They started to trickle out of the field, into the prep quarters.

"Thus concludes tonight's battle, ladies and gentlemen!" A grand voice boomed throughout the stadium. "The Scandinavian Legion fell, and the Army of Liberty came out on top!" Everyone in the audience went nuts, cheering, clapping, blowing horns, and waving flags. "They'll face off again next Thursday in Helsinki. Tune in or join us live! Thanks for coming out tonight, and drive safe."

The swarm of spectators began filing out of the stadium, leaving behind spilled popcorn, half-empty beer cans, and melted ice cream.

The announcer's voice continued, "Today's battle was designed and executed by Valkyrie Productions, which is based right here in San Diego. Let's give Valkyrie a big round of applause!"

But no one was paying attention anymore. The bloodshed and gunfights were over, and they were ready to go home.

Ranger wiped a layer of sweat and dirt off his forehead and slid off the detonated bunker. He moved with an indescribable quality. He was nimble. He was strong. He was heroic. He walked as if nothing had ever harmed him in his life, not even a stubbed toe.

He trotted over to the busted SUV, where he had evaded the grenade explosion. Lying on the ground, surrounded by doctors, was a man with square shoulders and blond hair.

Ranger's stunt double, Buck.

Ranger had slid under the SUV, and Buck had been the one to emerge and swat the grenade out of the air. That meant he was also the one to take the brunt of the ensuing explosion.

The grenade Buck had swatted away had done some pretty bad damage. His hands and half his face were burned, and his eyebrows were gone. Ranger heard the doctors muttering phrases like "third-degree" and "skin grafts."

But none of that could wipe the smile off Buck's face. His white teeth stood out against the reddened skin. "Great battle, Mr. Monroe."

"Please, Buck." Ranger bent down to grasp his friend's shoulder. "After all this time, call me Ranger." He returned the smile. "You're a star, you know that? A genuine MVP."

Buck glowed like he was having the best day of his life. The docs stuck a tranquilizer in his arm to knock him out before the blinding pain took hold.

Ranger made his way off of the field, and a man clutching a smartphone fell into step beside him.

"You did great tonight, Ranger, knocked 'em dead." This was Rocko, the publicist in charge of Ranger's schedule, persona, and everything in between. "I'm sure we'll have a few notes from the execs tomorrow, but if you ask me, you were first-rate."

"Thanks, Rocko," Ranger said, peeking over his shoulder at the flock of doctors running around the field. "Can you get the hospital room number where Buck will be staying? I want to make sure he's taken care of."

Rocko poked Ranger's bicep and cackled. "Heart of gold, this one! Yes, of course, we'll send him some flowers and a fruit basket." He pecked at his phone then lowered his voice. "Oh, by the way..." He looked around as if he were about to whisper the nuclear launch codes. "An update. We got another offer from—"

"No." Ranger held up a finger that could silence a trumpeting elephant. "No offers from any other enterprises. Tell them to stop. I like Valkyrie, and I respect them. And they like and respect me. I'm staying with them. End of story."

"Okay, champ."

Ranger knew that Rocko had no intention of dropping the issue. Many other battle enterprises were offering Ranger a fortune to come and fight in one of their armies, and it seemed insane to turn down so much money. Ranger, though, was a soldier of loyalty and principle. Why couldn't anyone get that? He'd have to make himself perfectly clear with Rocko...another time.

They slipped through a door reserved for the Army of Liberty, leaving the battlefield behind. The visiting army—in tonight's case, the Scandinavian Legion—had its own designated exit.

The inner bowels of a battle-stadium were often called the "landing grounds." This was the area where soldiers arrived and prepared for the coming conflict. They could convene with their squad leaders, strategize, relax, eat, bathe, get dressed—anything. Once, Ranger had heard a new recruit refer to the area as "backstage"—the young lad had been taken aside and royally chewed out.

Ranger moved through the landing grounds. It was chaos...in the best possible way. As opposed to the violent chaos of the battlefront, this was jovial chaos. The soldiers showered, joked, laughed, chatted, got dressed, and slowly transformed into civilians. They donned their street clothes and left through the back door reserved for those who participated in the battle.

He loved the feeling of fellowship that permeated the air after a battle. It was a mix of testosterone, adrenaline, and gratitude for life. He wished he could hang around, but he was exhausted and wanted some quiet time...and by "alone time," he mainly meant a reprieve from Rocko's endless pestering.

The young soldier from Milwaukee spotted Ranger from down a hallway and called out, "Hey, sir! Hey!"

"Hello to you too!" Ranger waved as he walked, displaying a camera-ready smile.

"Great job today, sir!" Milwaukee shouted.

"Back atcha, friend! Can I grab your name?"

"Marlon Diggs, sir!"

"Good to make your acquaintance, Mr. Diggs. I hope I get to fight by your side again soon!" Ranger rounded a corner and lost sight of Marlon.

Catering services had provided a few snacks. The chicken nuggets were long gone, and only a lonely veggie tray remained. Ranger chomped on a baby carrot as he headed for the exit.

"Hold on, hold on," Rocko put a hand on Ranger's chest. "Give it a few minutes."

Ranger sighed but didn't argue. Rocko was obsessed with the idea that Ranger should always be the last soldier to leave a stadium. He claimed it was because of honor and duty and a few other buzzwords, but it was obviously because Ranger had a huge fan base, and Rocko wanted to give them time to get from their seats inside the stadium to the back door.

The soldiers filtered out of the exit, refreshed and relaxed, until Ranger was the only one left.

Before he could reach the outside world, he had to be surrounded by bodyguards, managers, and agents, like the rings of Saturn. Civilians couldn't get close to him, no matter how hard they tried. Such was the life of a superstar military hero.

Ranger cocked a sarcastic eyebrow at Rocko, as if asking permission.

Rocko swept his arm toward the door. "You may."

Finally, he stepped out of the back door and into the night. A huge crowd waited on the sidewalk. At the front of the pack was a woman—a mother, it looked like, with wide, teary eyes. Worry had long ago enveloped this poor woman and squeezed years out of her life.

For a second, Ranger felt a chill. Was this a protest? A group of people speaking out against war spectatorship?

No. The crowd cheered when they saw him, and he smiled in return. It was just a clump of fans, waiting to see him after the battle. It seemed the mother was waiting for her son to exit the stadium, and since Ranger was always the last to leave, she knew he wasn't going to show. Her son was gone, a casualty of battle. She lowered her head and walked away. Guess she didn't want Ranger Monroe's autograph.

Cameras flashed, tabloid reporters shouted questions, fans called his name.

All the while, he kept his megawatt smile engaged. Cocked and locked.

"Ranger, can you sign my flak jacket?"

"What do you have to say about the rumors that you're dating Maria Nova?"

"Great battle today, Monroe! You did your country proud."

"Hey, Ranger, check out my M16! It's just like yours!"

"Ranger, this way!"

"Ranger, over here!"

He made his way to the car loitering by the sidewalk—a stretch Humvee. He thought it was a bit much, but Rocko had decided it was "on-brand" for a war hero to leave battles in a manly vehicle.

He wondered why, when he saw the big crowd, his thoughts had immediately gone to protesters. It had been a long, long time since he'd seen a picket line protesting the way warfare was conducted. Years, at the least…He scratched his scruff. Had it been a decade? Yeah, it'd been ten years. Sure, people were saddened when their friends and family died in battle, but no one seemed personally or philosophically opposed to it anymore.

"It's just the way things are" was the name of the game.

The next day, on the other side of the country, dozens of people settled onto metal bleachers. Some had brought cushions with seat-backs, but most just jostled uncomfortably on the hard surface. Candy wrappers crinkled, beer cans hissed open, and someone yelled that the hot dogs were fresh off the skewer.

Everyone had eyes on the football field. A group of men gathered in each end zone. They were dressed in homemade uniforms, carrying hand-me-down assault rifles.

Microphone feedback echoed everywhere, then squealed. "I-Is it on?" a meek voice asked. "Okay…Welcome, everyone, to this evening's battle. What a turn-out." The forty people in the audience eyed each other, waiting for the fighting to start. "Tonight, we have the Del City Crushers versus the Lake Arcadia Militia." Fans of both armies showed their support.

"First we'd like to thank Mustang High School for hosting this battle. Be sure to visit the concession stand—all proceeds will go to benefit the marching band's summer trip."

The voice cleared its throat, causing everyone to cover their ears. "Tonight's battle is brought to you by the Mustang Chamber of Commerce, Upsie Daisy Garage Door Installation, and Dennison's Auto Parts. Let's hear it for our sponsors." A handful of claps drifted from the bleachers.

Eventually, the battle began, and the small crowd cheered as the local armies tore each other to shreds.

"Just pin it here?" Jasmine Creedy attached the small microphone to the lapel of her business jacket.

"A little lower," the TV tech said. "Don't want to pick up the sounds of you swallowing and lip-smacking and all that."

Jasmine followed the instructions. It was her first time on television, and she wanted to be as cooperative and friendly as possible so they'd ask her back. She was worried that the mic would pick up her rapid heartbeat, even though she knew that was silly.

The set was simple. Sophisticated. Watercolor paintings on the walls. A couple of flowerpots. Two easy chairs, one camera.

Relax, relax, she told herself. It's just public access TV.

But still.

The key lights shone down on her as the interviewer sat on the chair opposite.

"Now, we're likely going to edit this so that I'm not included at all," he said. "I'll ask very broad questions and follow-ups, so feel free to run with them. Be specific but concise. Educational but interesting." He adjusted the notes in his lap. "Oh, and if you can play up your accent, that'd really help."

Jasmine began to snicker, thinking it was a joke, but the interviewer didn't react. "My accent?"

"Yeah. English, right? Or British? I don't know if there's a difference. Anyway, it sounds distinguished. Lean into it when you talk. It'll give what you're saying more weight."

She shifted in the chair. "I don't think I can sound any more English than I already do. Unless you want me to sip some tea and say 'pip-pip cheerio' every now and then."

"That'd be great."

She'd meant that to be biting sarcasm, but this guy wasn't getting it. She rolled her eyes, then caught herself. This guy didn't matter. She was getting on TV, showing her knowledge, flexing her professional muscles. The right people would see this interview, and she'd go places. Maybe a multi-book deal, or a documentary series.

"Rolling," a voice said from behind the intense lights.

"So," the interviewer started, "introduce yourself, if you don't mind."

She took a deep breath and slapped on a charming smile. "My name is Jasmine Creedy, and I'm a professor of history at the University of London, focusing on the evolution of warfare."

"And..." he gestured with his hand, "take us through that evolution. From the start."

She wanted to crack her knuckles and lean forward in her chair. This was something she truly loved talking about. This was *her* subject.

But she opted for professionalism and covertly flexed her hands a couple times.

"Our modern concept of warfare began many years ago. Sixty-four, to be precise. The United States Army was in the mountains of Afghanistan, on the cusp of attacking an insurgent village. This was not a surprise attack—the Afghani village knew, as did the American public. An East Coast businessman had an idea. Well, it was more of a desire. His net worth was close to half-a-trillion. And that's 'trillion' with a 'T.'"

"That's a lot of crumpets," the interviewer jumped in. He nodded at her encouragingly, as if he was honestly trying to help her push her Englishness.

She pursed her lips and soldiered on. "Indeed. The businessman made it clear that he would like to watch the upcoming battle. He would construct an observation platform in the nearby mountains, and he would pay for transportation, security, and even concessions. Everything out of his own pocket. And he would give the assenting party a hefty sum for the opportunity.

"This billionaire took his proposal to both the U.S. government and the Afghani leaders in question. The Afghanis rejected it outright. The Americans accepted.

"And as easy as that, warfare became a spectator sport. The battle between the Americans and the insurgents was ultimately inconsequential, but the people in the audience were pioneers. The businessman, his family, and his chosen guests got to watch a real-life battle from the safety of cushioned seats.

"The trend took off like wildfire. The ultra-wealthy all over the world wanted to get in on it. They threw their cash at their governments for the chance to watch an actual battle. Can you imagine the stakes? Back then, the closest you could get were fictional films and sporting events. With warfare, though, the tension couldn't get any higher. Real men and women, actually shooting, strategizing, and dying before your eyes. For us, in this day and age, none of this sounds wondrous. I mean, there's a battle scheduled to happen just down the street in thirty minutes—matinee prices too."

The interviewer exhaled, deep in thought. It seemed he'd never considered what it was like to not have warfare readily accessible for his entertainment. Jasmine smiled—she really was good at this! Docu-mini-series, here she comes.

She continued. "But back then? There was nothing like it. People paid a fortune to watch wars. Or, at least, they wanted to. Governments ran into a new problem: There simply weren't enough battles to see. Most warfare was done digitally or via covert espionage. No one wanted to watch a hacker jab at a keyboard. So, next came preplanned warfare. Armies established when and where they would do battle, and their governments sold tickets.

"Before directors entered the picture and started getting creative, all battles took place in wide, open fields. Battlefront-seats and bleachers could be erected quickly, on the cheap. More and more countries from every corner of the globe got in on this new business, and a funny thing happened."

She paused for dramatic emphasis.

The interviewer couldn't take it, even though he knew the answer. "What? What happened?"

"Real wars stopped. Countries stopped going after one another. Except on prearranged battlefields in front of sold-out crowds, of course. But everyone started getting along. When countries did battle each other, it was with a sense of sportsmanship, like the Olympics or the Super Bowl. After millennia of human existence, world peace was finally established on the back of ticketed warfare."

Jasmine took a sip of water and dabbed the perspiration on her upper lip. The lights were killer, but they made her look good, so *c'est la vie*.

"Quickly, the public wanted in on it. The militaries of the world expanded their recruiting office to pull in as many soldiers as possible, so they could enact smaller-scale battles in less-landmark locations. War for the masses, as it were. Armies go through a large number of soldiers, as you can imagine—battles aren't thrilling without live ammunition and real deaths. But wouldn't you know it...People kept volunteering. In fact, army recruitment hit new record highs. No one was ever turned away.

"A new era arrived: that of the celebrity soldier. Real generals, majors, and commanders who were in the military at the time...They weren't cutting it. They were dry. Unappealing. In a word, boring. People who came to watch the battles wanted more. They wanted characters to root for and storylines to become invested in. These were career military men—Patton and MacArthur, not Scott and Peck. The old guard was more interested in winning battles than in wowing audiences. So they had to be phased out.

"When military men weren't up to snuff, movie stars were brought in. Rather than training generals to be charming, they trained actors to be generals. A-list celebrities took to the battlefields, giving speeches, rallying the troops, accomplishing missions. The crowds ate it up and asked for seconds.

"About a decade passed, and a new generation of young and hungry soldiers took over. They had grown up watching battles and aspiring to be just like their heroes. Ironically, they would replace those heroes. Just as some celebrities couldn't make the transition from silent films to talkies, movie stars simply couldn't compete with their replacements, and some retired with grace. Others clung to their last shreds of spotlight glory to the bitter end, getting killed in battle, becoming addicted to painkillers, or any other number of celebrity demises.

"Around this time came the rise of the enterprise system. Militaries around the world began contracting production companies to create their battles from scratch. Now, the creative teams were the ones calling the shots. Enterprises sprang up all over the place, but San Diego became the hub. Film has Hollywood. Theater has NYC. And live warfare has San Diego.

"Producers and directors came in with fresh ideas. Battles that took place at sea, with audience members in buoyant seats. Multi-battle storylines, so viewers could follow an entire war, like they would a film franchise. Spectator chairs that move and rumble along with the action on the field. Meet-and-greets with the leading soldiers from the opposing armies."

Jasmine took a quick look around the room. The whole crew was listening to her and nodding along, captivated. They all knew this information, of course—this was the world they lived in. But she had captured their attention, and she felt like she was levitating in her seat.

She crossed her arms. "And that's largely where we are today. Almost every country on Earth has joined this business, except for a few notable exceptions in the Middle East. Violence has been entirely restructured. Warfare is merely a matter of sport. Humans have always tried to stop war, but all historical attempts ended in failure. A shift in perspective, however, made all the difference. Instead of stopping it, we've found a way to control and re-contextualize it."

Her words hung in the air. The bright lights hummed.

The interviewer cleared his throat. "Oh, you're done? Wonderful. Really good stuff. Now…" he hesitated. "Now, if you could just wrap things up. Sign off with…with what we talked about before? It would really put a button on what you've been saying."

Jasmine sighed quietly, but her winning smile didn't flinch. If this is what would get her in front of an audience, this is what she'd do. She looked right into the camera lens and said, "Pip-pip, cheerio."

The interviewer gave her a thumbs-up. And she died a little inside.

Worst of all, she was honestly craving some tea and a crumpet. She kept that to herself.

The Plaza was hopping. Lots of hustle and bustle. Salvatore Caracas strolled through the open-air mall, hands in his pockets, taking in the crowd. A lot of teenaged couples. Lots of potential today.

He bought a pretzel and sat on a stone bench. He loved people-watching. It was like a microcosm of the chaotic universe in which everyone lived.

The pretzel was a bit saltier than he liked, so he got a cup of nacho cheese to drown out the flavor. He then rested the cup on his bulging belly and enjoyed the snack.

San Diego was full of beautiful people. Always had been. Men, women, and everything in-between. Salvatore had an eye for these things...Ironic, since no one ever looked him in the eye. Maybe it was his bushy unibrow. Or maybe the nacho cheese dripping down his sweater.

Salvatore had a lot of money. Some people would call him well-off. Most people would call him filthy rich. His home on Coronado Island cost eight figures, complete with an underground garage, a handful of swimming pools, and a private gym.

Yes, a gym. Salvatore woke up before the sun every morning, while the birds were still yawning and Father Time had crusts of sleep in the corners of his eyes. He ran two miles, did a dance with the dumbbells, and finished with fifty crunches. Every morning. He liked working out, having dominion over his own flesh. He ate kale and Keto and whatever other dietary "K" was suggested to him.

Also, he chased each protein shake with a beer and a donut. Ice cream, macaroons, pizza...He ate exactly as much junk as necessary to maintain his paunch belly. He slouched when he walked. He didn't wear his golden watches or earrings. He wore horn-rimmed glasses, even though he had twenty-twenty vision. He dressed like the manager of a shoe store— sweater, khakis, hair in a bowl-cut.

Each aspect of his public appearance was designed to elicit a response for a certain type of person. Most people would feel superior to him. Jocks. Educated elites. Prosperous entrepreneurs. People with self-confidence. They would take one look at him, smile inwardly at their own success, and keep walking. They might even feel pity toward Salvatore. Or, even better, disgust.

All of that was just fine. Exactly what Salvatore intended. He didn't need to relate to those sorts of people. He wanted to be on an equal playing field with the dejected, the loser, the pitiable, and the disgusting.

That's what made him so good at his job.

He finished his pretzel and got a gyro. It was a Saturday, so the high school kids were out en masse. It was only a matter of time before he reeled in a big fish.

Ooh, there. He lowered the gyro from his gaping mouth and sharpened his gaze. A boy and a girl were in a heated conversation across the open-air mall. Both pretty attractive. They gestured wildly, like they were putting on a puppet show but had forgotten the dolls. Salvatore could see them clearly, but there was no way he could hear them from this distance amid the noise of the mall.

This was it—the tipping point. The boy threw up his hands and said the two most soul-crushing words in the English language. Salvatore couldn't hear the boy say them, but he'd know the shape of those words anywhere: "We're through."

Ah, yes. A public breakup. Salvatore's bread and butter. Other than actual bread and butter, of course. It was rare for a guy to dump a girl with such...gusto, he supposed was the word. Especially out in front of witnesses.

He leaned forward on the edge of the bench. The girl—the "dumpee"—didn't seem too sad about it. And she was way more attractive than the guy, anyway. Nah, she'll get over his sorry tush real quick. In fact, she was already texting someone. Probably another guy she was on the fence about ten seconds earlier.

Nope. Neither of them would do. He settled back into his seat.

Just then, another kid entered the picture. Or, rather, he exited a department store. Probably sixteen years old, about twenty yards from Salvatore, wiping his hand across his puffy eyes and headed for a bench.

Salvatore tossed the rest of his gyro and stood. He "casually" waltzed around until he "happened to" sit across from the kid.

He looked at the boy with sad, compassionate eyes. "You all right, man?"

The kid barked, "I'm fine. Leave me alone." He pulled a cell phone from his pocket, stared at it for ten seconds, then tucked it away like it was about to bite.

Yep. This was a good one. Salvatore hid his smile, instead nodding quietly. "I'm here if you wanna talk." He softened his consonants and drew out the words, sounding as uneducated as he could. Simple. Trustworthy.

The kid was short and a bit gawky. Not ugly by any means, but in SoCal, he wouldn't exactly book a modeling gig. And that meant his peers in high school probably gave him hell. Unless he surrounded himself with other average Joes, in which case he would constantly be looking in a mirror of self-deprecation and mediocrity.

Perfect.

"I don't mean to be rude," Salvatore started slowly, "but she's not worth it."

The kid flinched but didn't leave.

Salvatore used to be nervous when making this pitch. But he'd done it so many times and had gotten so good at it, he'd eventually stopped worrying. Even now, sitting across from this sixteen-year-old stranger, he knew exactly how things were going to go.

"A few years ago, I had the love of my life," he said, gazing into the middle-distance. If he really got into it, he could tear up, but he had the feeling this kid wouldn't require much prodding. "Her name was Jean. She was my everything. My very first girlfriend. Y'know how objects don't technically have a color until light bounces off of it? She was like the light that created my color. And then one day, she up and left. Didn't say why."

The kid was drawn in, line and sinker—Salvatore didn't even need the hook. He looked the kid up and down: greasy skin, with lines around his wrists from wearing rubber gloves. If Salvatore had to guess, he would say the kid worked at a fast food place.

He continued. "I think it was cuz I was a fry cook, but that's just my theory. And that's the thing! She *never* told me why. All of a sudden, I was alone." He'd said this speech a thousand times to a thousand different heartbroken boys. But he tried to tailor it to each target. "And right then and there, I was determined. I'd show her." He paused. "What's your name, man?"

The kid answered without hesitation. "Tanner." Tears polka-dotted his cheeks.

Despite all the noise in the Plaza, it was like they were the only two people around. Salvatore dug a business card from his khakis and shuffled over to sit beside Tanner.

"I'm Sal. Pleased to meetcha." He held out the card. "I'm a recruiter for Valkyrie Productions."

Tanner gulped and thought for a second. "So you go around and look for people to die?" His face contorted, and he looked betrayed.

Salvatore jumped in. "I look for people who want to prove themselves." He straightened his posture and began speaking in his natural, clipped tone. "Can you imagine it, Tanner? You'd be a part of something glorious. When the gates open and the battle begins, there's you on the front lines. Firing a rifle, vaulting land mines, surrounded by others who respect you. And she'll be watching. She'll see you and think, 'Wow...I really missed out.' That's what'll happen, Tanner."

The kid took the business card with trembling fingers. He blubbered, "I'll p-p-p..." He reordered himself and finished, "What if I die?"

"You'll go out in a blaze of glory." It was a good line. Always worked. Salvatore knew he had won Tanner over, but he sealed the deal with one last sentence: "I never got to show Jean what I was made of. You can show your ex that she made a huge mistake." He tapped the card. "Call anytime."

With that, Salvatore shuffled away, deeper into the mall. He texted his secretary to expect a call from a guy named Tanner within the hour. "A bit scrawny," he typed. "Whatever battle he's assigned to, put him in the first wave. He'll die quickly, and the hero will have to avenge his fallen comrades. Good stuff."

"Forty-eight, forty-nine...fifty!"

Annie Kennedy dropped from the bar and shook the fatigue out of her hands.

The spotter checked the stopwatch around his neck. "Fifty pull-ups in a minute-thirty. Nice job, Kennedy. Take a rest before the two-miles."

"Thank you, sir." Annie grabbed a water bottle and moved to one of the gym's remote corners. She started stretching and limbering up.

Most people would be nervous about the pull-ups and sit-ups and bench-presses and timed runs. But Annie had been through all of that time and time again. No, her physical prowess wasn't a question for her. She knew that she could outpace and take down any opponent put in front of her.

And her shooting was solid, too. Not as pristine as her athleticism, but pretty good. She'd hit four targets out of five—better than most, if she would say so herself. And she would. She had to play up her physical achievements as much as possible, because her personality was "screechy," "unlikable," and "just not enough," to quote a variety of army recruiters.

She started jogging in place.

Kansas had been reasonably good to her. It had been her home for her entire life, and as a descendant of the Arapaho tribe, she felt akin to the land. The Kansas terrain was good for long-distance running, and she'd excelled at that her entire life.

Once that had been conquered, she'd set her sights on sprinting. Check.

Shot-put. Easy.

Archery. Hunting. Skeet shooting. Done, done, done.

Charm. A mountain still to be climbed.

She remembered auditioning for her high school musical. She thought it was *Annie Get Your Gun*. Turned out to be plain old *Annie*. She'd memorized the wrong monologue, but the teacher had heard her out anyway. Once she was done, the paunchy know-it-all had smiled sadly and said she needed to work on her stage presence.

Thus began the story of her life. She finished high school and moved to Wichita, which was as big as cities got in the mid-Midwest. She knew she wanted to join an army and make some people bleed. She'd figured she would have the pick of the lot, given her athletic background. She had imagined she'd have to beat off recruiters and generals with a stick.

But at her first recruiting event, the reality had smacked her like a pie in the face. She'd completed all the physical requirements with flying colors, beating out macho guys half her age.

And then she'd been handed a piece of paper with a sentence typed on it.

"What's this?"

"Oh," the secretary had said. "The recruiters want to hear everyone's take on this line. Feel free to give it a spin, make it your own!"

The line was "Everyone follow me! Once more, into the breach. History is what we make of it!" Corny and over-the-top, in Annie's opinion, but she wasn't in the position to offer notes. So, when her name was called, she'd gone into a little room with a few recruiters and said the line with as much vigor as she could muster.

A week later, she was informed that she'd been accepted into the Great Plains Brigade...as a nurse. She'd never even gone to med school.

That had been ten long years ago. Now, she was long past thirty years old, and as strong as her body was, the sands of time paused for no one.

All stretched and ready to run, she laid on the ground and steadied her breathing.

She liked being a nurse. She really did. She had plenty of friends, and she enjoyed being in any army at all.

The stirring in her gut, though—the one that had driven her to join an army in the first place—had never stilled. She wanted to fight. She wanted to prove everyone wrong.

This was her twentieth tryout in ten years. Recruiters from dozens of armies would gather and take a look at recruits, be they civilians or soldiers who wanted to move up the ladder. She always flew through the physical challenges, and she always bombed the "charisma test."

"Kennedy, time to run!"

And run she did. Two miles in less than seventeen minutes. All that was left was to meet the recruiters face-to-face and read a stupid line.

She showered and dressed in her most commanding outfit. She'd gone through twenty variations of dress in as many tryouts—combat boots, camo colors, wrist cuffs, hair up, hair down, jeans, t-shirt, suit... Nothing had worked so far.

"Kennedy, Annie! Time to talk!"

Annie popped her neck and strolled into the room. Over the years, she had tried being respectful, humble, brash, and antagonistic. Today, she decided to not overthink things. Wing it. Do her best.

Four squatty men sat on the same side of a long table like they were in *The Last Supper*, staring at the stacks of papers in front of them. Headshots and résumés from all the candidates. The guys shuffled through the papers and pulled out her photo.

Guy A had a nose like a ski slope. "Annie Kennedy?"

"That's me, sir." Obviously. They were holding her picture. She resisted the urge to slap herself.

Guy B quickly perused her résumé. "You've been a nurse in the Great Plains Brigade for...ten years, it says?"

"Remind me," Guy C said, "which enterprise owns the Great Plains Brigade? Kaleidoscope? Valkyrie? Millennium?"

She answered, "Born and Bred Productions, sir."

"Born and Bred? I've never heard of them..." Guy C slumped in his chair, immediately disinterested in anyone who came from such a small enterprise.

Guy B continued. "And you're looking to be a captain in an army? Any army?" He said it like a question.

She wasn't sure how to respond. "Yes, sir. I feel my strengths lie in combat." Short, succinct, to the point.

Guy A followed up. "And you know you'd be...leading *actual* battles?"

Annie's answer leapt out of her mouth before she could stop it: "Of course I know that."

"I think what my colleague here is trying to say is..." Guy D ruffled his hair. "Soldiers would look to you for leadership and morale. It's a major responsibility. On top of that, audiences will be following you too, both on and off the field. You're their hero, their..." He searched for a word. "Well, their captain. Like the lead player of a professional sports team and the main character of an action movie franchise, rolled into one. You're fighting for *them* just as much as your fellow soldiers."

"Understood, sir."

Guy D nodded. "All right, then. Let's hear your take on the key phrase."

Annie cleared her throat, swallowed the metallic taste in her mouth, and said, "You're not dying today, soldier. Not on my watch!" She didn't don a personality or put up a front—she said it as honestly as she could. She spoke as Annie Kennedy.

The four recruiters jotted something down.

Guy A simply said, "Thank you."

That was her cue to leave. Not a good sign.

Again, she spoke before she could stop herself. "What do I need to do? How can I get into a stadium as a captain?" Her face was flushed—from embarrassment or anger, she didn't know. Likely both.

Most of the men rolled their eyes or shook their heads, but Guy D looked at her with sympathy. No—pity. She hated that even more.

"Look, Annie..." Guy D searched for more words in his head. "Michelangelo's *David* is a physical specimen, for sure. But it's just a hunk of stone with no charm. And Shakespeare is a master wordsmith, but you wouldn't want him on your side in a bar fight. We need captains who can marry those two things together."

Guy A rubbed his massive sniffer and groaned. "The truth is, hun, I couldn't pick you out of a lineup. There's nothing to ya, no signature, no flair. You're boring. And a little off-putting, to be honest." He raised his eyebrows as if dismissing her. "Now, thank you for your time. We appreciate you serving the Great Plains Brigade as a nurse all these years, and we hope you continue to do good work for them."

Annie spun on her heel and left the room. She wanted to punch through a wall. No—she wanted to punch through someone.

This pancake of a region had done nothing for her. Maybe it was time to uproot.

"Rocko, I'm serious, I don't need you to come."

"But I'm already packed and on my way to the airport!"

Ranger walked through his home, speaking into the air. His walls contained built-in receivers and speakers so that he could talk on the phone anywhere in the house without carrying a device.

He pinched the bridge of his nose. He was scheduled to fly to Helsinki for another battle against the Scandinavian Legion, and he would give anything to be without his publicist for a couple days.

"Listen, Rocko." He quickly thought up a lie. "I have a task for you. Once our series against the Legion is over, I'm going to change my hairstyle—"

A dramatic gasp filled the mansion. *"What?"* Rocko screeched, then began babbling like a dolphin. "This is so exciting!"

"Rocko, I'm not done. I'll change my hair *and* my uniform style. I need you to stay in San Diego and come up with a few options for me to choose from. Remember, the new styles need to complement each other."

"You can count on me, Ranger!" It sounded like he was sobbing. He hung up.

Ranger sighed. That task could keep Rocko busy for the next ten years, but Ranger only needed two days.

The Army of Liberty's private flight over the Atlantic was set to take off pretty soon. Ranger took a few steps toward the front door, then stopped.

Ah—he'd forgotten his toothbrush. He went back to grab it.

As massive as his house was, he only used a corner of it. His mom lived in her own wing, complete with a kitchen, bathroom, and cinema. She didn't get out much, but he always joined her on Tuesday nights for dinner and a movie. They'd been close for as long as he could remember. His dad had left them before Ranger could even remember.

Ranger considered saying bye to Mom before heading out, but she was probably still asleep. Her meds kept her pretty sluggish most of the time.

No need to wake her. He'd see her when he got back.

Mom Monroe and Lil Ranger. When he was four or five years old, he would pretend he and his mom were a team of secret agents saving the world. Or superheroes. Or action stars. They were always a team. They had no options otherwise.

Ranger ran through a mental checklist—toothbrush, comb, extra underwear. Good to go.

His bags were already loaded in the stretch Humvee loitering outside. He donned a pair of shades—and his celebrity smile—and waltzed out of the front door.

Reporters and bloggers waited at the curb, next to the car. They heard the door open and swiveled their cameras straight at him. He waved and cracked jokes, shaking hands and signing autographs when asked.

"Ranger," one man asked, "how goes the war?"

"Well," Ranger replied, "we're heading to Helsinki right now to fight again. We had a great victory the other night, but nothing is certain. That's why we want your input." He stared into a camera lens. "The Army of Liberty listens to the people. A peace treaty is on the table." Everyone gasped and whispered to one another. "If you want us to holster our weapons and stop fighting the Scandinavian Legion, go online and use the hashtag 'PeaceInHelsinki.' Or..." He paused dramatically. "Or if you think we should show them what we're made of, use the hashtag 'WarInHelsinki.' It's up to you, America!"

He finished his announcement and loaded his muscular frame into the back seat of the stretch Humvee. The door slammed shut, and off he went.

"No, no, no!" Danny Carr paced back and forth behind his desk. Back and forth, back and forth. The desk was his drawbridge, and behind it, he was the king of the castle.

The voice on the other end of the speakerphone tried to respond: "Mr. Carr, it's just a few tweaks—"

"Oh, I'm sorry. There must have been a breeze on my end. You didn't hear me?" He dramatically cleared his throat. *"No!* That layout has been pored over and approved by more people than have actually read this country's Constitution. You will *not* change a *thing.*"

"Mr. Carr..." The person on the phone was Maximilian, an executive producer at Golden Eagle Enterprises, based in Helsinki, Finland. At that very moment, the Army of Liberty was on its way to Helsinki to partake in a battle against the Scandinavian Legion. The battle was to be overseen by Golden Eagle, which owned the Legion. The Army of Liberty was owned by Valkyrie Productions, and Danny Carr was one of their executive producers.

Danny huffed and puffed.

This was standard practice, obviously—armies traveled around the world all of the time, fighting on other armies' home-turf. Not an issue.

Another standard practice: Executives sharing outlines of battles with one another. Army positions, obstacles, mines, available weapons, storylines...All of the information that meant life or death for the soldiers was predetermined by directors and producers.

What *wasn't* standard practice, on the other hand, was a rival exec sending over a revised layout for an upcoming battle *at the last dadgum minute.*

"No, Ingrid Bergman, listen up." Danny leaned over the speakerphone like a starving predator. "You might say these are itty-bitty teensy-weensy changes that won't affect the outcome of the battle. A water station here, granola bars there—no big deal, eh? Well, *you* might know that, but *I* don't know that! There could be extra magazines of ammo hidden in that stadium for your Finny boys, or positions that allow them to flank my guys! No! No changes! Executives from both Valkyrie and your Tweety Bird enterprise have approved the layout of this battle, and if you change it at all—*at all*—so help me, Valkyrie will never fight any of your armies ever again. Your profits will go *kaput,* and you'll have to go back to slapping each other with fish to entertain yourself. And not only that, if you touch that layout, I will *personally* send you a kitten, make you fall in love with that kitten, then sneak into your home, take a dump on the hood of your car, and punt that kitten into the ocean!"

He crashed a fist onto the phone, hanging up before Maximilian could respond.

His tirade ricocheted throughout the top floor of the Valkyrie Productions office. He slumped into his leather swivel chair and massaged his temples.

The entire back wall of his office was an enormous window overlooking the Pacific. He couldn't hear the rumbling waves or cawing seagulls, and that was just how he liked it. The outside world could be seen and appreciated, but it couldn't bother him.

Not that he hated the beach. He enjoyed slipping into a Speedo and cannonballing into the water as much as anyone. He lived in San Diego, after all—the best beaches in the world. But when he was in his office, he needed to focus. When he was behind his desk, he was king, and the king didn't have time for sand.

He hit a button on the phone. "Suzanne, come on in. Updates, please." Then he dry-swallowed three aspirin. It was going to be a long day.

Every day was a long day, especially for an executive producer of warfare.

His office door flew open. "How was Max?"

Danny jerked in his chair and grabbed his chest. "Geez, Suze. Be kinder to those door hinges. One day, the whole thing will rip off, and you'll be standing there holding it by the knob."

His assistant Suzanne marched up to his desk, her mega-high heels stabbing the carpet with every step. "The door'll live."

Danny shook off his nerves. His heart rate was spastic, partly from Suzanne's sudden entrance, but mostly from his phone call a minute earlier. He often got too worked up. And by often, he meant repeatedly, always, every day. His doctor had warned him about his blood pressure a few times, but he didn't care. In this business, he had to make it known who was in charge.

"What's the news?" he asked.

Suzanne checked her tablet. "Ranger Monroe has been given more offers. Big offers."

"From whom?"

"Millennium Enterprises and Theater of War. But those are just the two we know about. Undoubtedly, there are many more. Everyone wants him."

Danny chortled. "Oh yeah, for good reason. He's a good star. I'm not worried. We treat him well, and he's a loyal guy."

As he spoke, Suzanne slid a colorful card onto his desk.

"What's this?"

"Recruiter of the year," she answered. "Sign it. Include a nice little message, if you feel jolly today."

"It's not time for that yet, is it?"

"No, but Salvatore is so far ahead at this point, no one can possibly catch up. Figured we'd get it out of the way now. One less thing to think about."

"Smart." Danny opened the card and wrote a note. "Good ole Sal. He works hard for us. Is there a prize?"

"Restaurant gift certificates."

"Eh..." Danny shrugged. "Get a cash bonus for him too. Don't want him switching to another enterprise and recruiting for them. Valkyrie can only create the spectacles we're known for because he keeps us supplied with bodies." He slipped a gold watch off his wrist. "Here. Throw this in."

Suzanne said, "I bet he already has a few of those."

"It's the thought that counts, all right?" He stood and looked out the window. A mass of clouds was sweeping in from the ocean. Within a few minutes, San Diego would actually feel a chill. Stop the presses. "I want to go over the names of Sal's recruits tonight. Send a hard copy of that list to my home."

She drily asked, "Which one?"

He ignored her sass. "Anything else?"

"The treaty hashtags are a huge hit. Both the *peace* and *war* options were trending within minutes, and they haven't wavered from the top spots."

"Love it love it love it. Whose idea was that?"

She checked her tablet. "It was one of our lower-division directors. She mainly works on regional battles, but she sends ideas to us every now and then. Elena Winn."

Danny nodded. He watched a flock of gulls diving into the water. Some came up with fish. Some didn't, and they would be hungry later. One gull, however, adopted a strategy of its own and started harassing beachgoers for their human munchies. It seemed to be the victor, using less effort to bag a tastier meal.

"We should keep an eye on her," he muttered. "She sounds promising."

Just then, a digital alarm sounded from Suzanne's tablet. She tapped the screen and gasped. "Danny, it's happening!"

He spun around to face her, heart thumping again. "What?"

In response, she showed him her tablet. It was open to a news site. *Breaking News: Israel and Palestine on the brink of conflict for the first time in decades.*

Danny clapped and pumped a fist. "Yes! It's go-time." He reached into a cupboard, pulled out a rolling suitcase, and headed for the door. Always packed and ready to go.

Israel and Palestine were two nations that didn't engage in spectatorship. Ever since its inception sixty-four years earlier, both nations had rebuked the art of allowing people to watch their warfare.

At the same time, the two nations followed the rest of the world in not engaging in "real" combat. Not a single bullet or missile had been fired in several years.

Enterprise executives and producers had been watching the Middle East like hawks. Iran, Iraq, Afghanistan, and Pakistan all had armies and public battles of their own—and they made a tidy profit. It was only a matter of time before the powder keg blew and conflict arose.

And the time had come. Fuses were lit. Tempers had boiled over. And all over the world, producers were scrambling. Everyone wanted their own enterprise to be the one to control Israel and Palestine's clash.

Can you imagine? Those two nations made up one of the greatest rivalries in history. Cain and Abel had nothing on Israel and Palestine. A battle between the two of them would sell out ten times over.

Not the mention the fact that a "real" battle would spill into other regions across the globe. That would be bad business for everyone.

Danny yipped at Suzanne, "Check my desk drawer. There's a cell phone number for a guy named Phil. He's the private pilot for Millennium's top exec. He's on his way to the Middle East right now, no doubt. Tell Phil there's a thousand dollars in it for him for every minute that plane is delayed."

"You got it, boss." She pecked at the tablet. "Your plane will be ready to take off in eight minutes."

Danny had been preparing for this moment for years. Nothing would stand in his way.

No one could outflank Danny Carr.

It was a cloudy, humid day in Gettysburg, Virginia. Flies buzzed through the air like they were nervous about the impending rainstorm and desperately looking for shelter.

Hundreds of men roamed around the lush field. A momentous battle was about to take place, but there was no stadium in sight. Vaulted bleachers were set up in the distance, nearly a mile away, so that the audience would get a view of the entire battleground.

Zeke Smith checked his musket one more time. The rain would make loading and firing nearly impossible, given the fact that their lead bullets were propelled by gunpowder. Today's battle reenactment might turn out to be a dud.

Shouldn't be too much of an issue. Zeke cupped a hand over his eyes to block out the hazy sunlight, and he looked at the audience in the distance. Yep, as per usual—the average age was in the upper seventies.

Only old people came to watch historical reenactments. Maybe it was a nostalgia thing. Maybe brand recognition. No matter the cause, it became clear a long time ago that the seating at reenactments needed to accommodate for wheelchairs and walkers.

Zeke sighed and tugged at the collar of his jacket. His entire uniform was made of wool, from cap to trouser cuffs. On such a humid day, he was practically drowning inside his clothes.

The dark blue uniforms of the Union soldiers captured more heat than the grey Confederates. Sometimes he wished he were assigned to the secessionist army, if only for the comfier clothes. It was all pretend, after all. This was a reenactment, a performance, not a real war like they did everywhere else. He wasn't actually a racist rebel, so why couldn't he wear the lighter uniform every once in a while?

At least the boots were equally blistering for everyone. Zeke sat on a log to rest up before the Battle of Gettysburg began.

Each time he looked at his fellow soldiers, he was reminded of how silly it all was. In this modern day, the Union Army was made up of men of all races and ethnicities. Even Zeke himself was Black—he was no historian, but he was pretty sure the Union was made up of mostly White guys.

It was inherently anachronistic, but no one seemed to care. Score one for progressivism.

A middle-aged man lumbered over and waved. "Hiya, Zeke." His smile was framed by a ridiculous mustache. Zeke couldn't believe how goofy people's facial hair had been back in the Civil War. In order to be historically accurate, the soldiers had to look like cartoon characters (even though a relatively small number of them were the right race for the part).

The mustached man sat next to Zeke. This was Jeremiah Roseke, a veteran actor from the Pennsylvania community theater scene. The Union Army conscripted him once a year to portray Joshua Chamberlain in the annual reenactment of Gettysburg. He'd held that honor for decades, and everyone could tell he truly enjoyed doing it.

Jeremiah reached into his wool jacket and brought out a bag of trail mix. He offered the bag to Zeke, who grabbed a handful. The two munched quietly for a few minutes.

While Jeremiah was only a soldier in the Union Army one day a year, Zeke and thousands of others were always under its jurisdiction. They traveled to historic sites and recreated Civil War battles all year round, playing to crowds that were just as geriatric as this one.

"What's on your mind today?" Jeremiah asked. "You're quieter than usual."

"I'm usually pretty quiet," Zeke said.

"Exactly." Jeremiah laughed and tucked away the trail mix. "This is... well, lemme think. I've been doing Chamberlain for twenty-nine years. Never missed. So, if my memory serves, this is your fifth or sixth Gettysburg. Right?"

Zeke bit his lower lip and nodded. He had joined the Union when he was fifteen years old, thinking it'd be a good summer job. And now, all of a sudden, he was twenty (almost twenty-one), and still playing dress-up for elderly audiences.

Jeremiah continued. "These armies see a lot of turnaround. A lot of part-timers. I'm a little surprised you're still with us. Don't get me wrong, I'm very glad. I look forward to seeing you each year."

"I..." Zeke wasn't used to sharing his feelings, but he liked Jeremiah. He was a good guy. "I need to get into a real army. Please don't take that the wrong way."

"Oh, I get it. No offense taken. This isn't for everyone. I'm no soldier. I spend my days reciting Tennessee Williams, not doing drills." He stroked his mustache. "Say, I heard that next summer, they're going to start reenactments in Vietnam. That sounds interesting, eh? You could join that army, see a different part of the world! And I bet the audience would be a little on the younger side."

"I don't think so, Jeremiah." A roll of thunder shook the field. "I might be moving on soon."

The actor offered a hand to the younger soldier. "Then I wish you the best, buddy."

Zeke smiled and clasped Jeremiah's weathered hand in his own.

Buckets of rain fell from the dark sky, and even from so far away, Zeke could hear cries of panic from the bleachers. "Guess they didn't bring umbrellas," he said, and they both laughed.

Danny Carr walked into the president's office. Well, more accurately, he was shoved into the president's office. Two burly bodyguards gripped his forearms and made sure he went only where they wanted him to go.

He had made the comment, "Palestine sure is toasty this time of year," but the two men hadn't responded. He decided it would be best to clamp down until he was face to face with the head honcho.

What a whirlwind. It had been seventeen hours since Danny had heard about the possible conflict between Palestine and Israel. He hadn't slept on the plane. Now, his eyes were itchy, his clothes were rumpled, and his entire body was sweaty. But he'd made it.

Once he passed the door's threshold, the bodyguards let him go. They locked the door and assumed their positions on either side. They looked like they could snap a board in half just by sneezing.

Danny flattened his sweaty hair and adjusted his suit jacket. He carried a briefcase and nothing else.

The room was plain. Brown walls. Wooden floor. Thick windows. A spinning fan, casting shadows over everything. The air smelled like a cocktail of deodorant, bathwater, and fruit juice.

A man sat in the center of the room. President Ahmar, leader of the State of Palestine. He was a dignified figure, powerful in his own right, looking like he had been carved from stone a century before. He wore a black suit, but not a single drop of perspiration was on his skin.

The president gestured to an empty chair opposite his own.

Danny smiled and sat. He opened his briefcase and produced two bottles of coconut water. He'd read this was Ahmar's favorite. He held one bottle out to the president, but Ahmar didn't move an inch. Danny kept his smile affixed and set the rejected bottle on the floor next to Ahmar's chair. He cracked open his own coconut water and took a deep drink.

"Ah," he said after swallowing. "It's toasty this time of year."

Ahmar spoke. "You entered our state under a Canadian flag." His voice was robust and sturdy, like an ancient oak tree.

Danny finished his water. "You wouldn't have let me past the bouncers otherwise."

"Deception is a poor way to start a dialogue."

"Then why are we speaking now? You seem to be well aware of who I am, and you likely know what I'm going to ask you."

"Say it anyway."

Danny could tell that Ahmar wanted him to put in the work. A slow, steady approach would be best—not the blitzkrieg he usually unleashed to get what he wanted.

"Well, sir, I am Daniel Carr, an executive producer from Valkyrie Productions."

"An American enterprise, yes?"

"We're based in San Diego, California, this is true, but we work with armies and directors all over the globe. We even have a number of constituents in this region. The Mediterranean Militia is one of ours, as are the Iranian Jays. I could go on, but I feel you get my point. As historically volatile as this region is, nearly all of them have thrown their hats into the ring of war spectatorship. And many of them have trusted Valkyrie specifically."

"I am not interested in trends or what others believe."

Danny nodded. "I get that. So Jordan and Qatar have armies with us. Big deal, right? Why should *you*, that's the question."

"No, Mr. Carr. That's not the question. There is no question." He rippled like a breeze flowing over a desert. "You are the only person in this room interested in this vile sport. 'Spectatorship.' Perverse. War is not for profit. It is a means to an end, not the goal."

"All right. What's your goal, Mr. President?"

"Righteousness. In this case, we seek retribution against the State of Israel for a decade of sleights. And frankly, Mr. Carr, your presence here is doing very little to assuage my impulse."

And the spinning fan did very little to assuage Danny's perspiration. He was sweating like a pig. He wiped his forehead. "I understand, Mr. President. I'll admit, I'm no geopolitical scholar. There are no fancy letters after my name. But I'm a pretty sharp guy. I know what spectatorship has done for this world. Where once there was chaos, there is now order. And if you begin lobbing rocks at your neighbor, pretty soon the whole region will be on fire. That's just how it goes.

"You have issues with another nation. I won't even use its name, because it honestly doesn't matter which nation it is. What matters is the feeling of anger and tension. You want to strike. But do you truly want war? Full-blown conflict on a global scale? Because that's what's sure to follow."

"Of course I don't want that." Ahmar rankled at the suggestion. "No one does."

"I'm not saying I can solve your problems," Danny pressed. "But I am offering an alternative to pervasive conflict. Spectatorship contains and re-contextualizes warfare in a way impossible otherwise."

Ahmar didn't respond. But he didn't refute what Danny was saying either. That was a big step. Danny felt his confidence building, and he continued.

"My Gramps, he used to tell me about the old wars. Real ones. He was an American soldier decades ago in this part of the world. Sand, sun, bullets, and barbarism. Uncivilized." He crossed one leg over the other, trying to appear lost in thought, as if he were coming up with all of this off the top of his head. "I mean, that's what it was. Men would walk down the street without knowing if they were gonna be blown to pieces. What kind of world is that? Families torn apart left and right..."

The president took a breath. Danny couldn't tell if the man had firsthand experience with any of the old wars, but he was definitely familiar with violence and heartache.

Even the bodyguards by the door shifted a little.

"Back in the day," Danny said, "one of the most popular types of online videos was soldiers coming home from war and surprising their kids. People would get all weepy watching those videos and think they're so sweet. But the reason those videos were so popular was because the kids were genuinely shocked to see their parents still alive. They could've sworn that they had said good-bye for the last time, because war took no prisoners.

Those soldiers had left their kids, fully prepared to never see them again, and the kids thought the same thing. Brutal."

Ahmar took another breath. He still wasn't responding, but his granite face had softened.

Danny reloaded his word-cannon. As long as he was in this room, he was going to keep talking. "But Gramps had other stories about his time in war. The men he served with were all strangers. They walked into the military from all different backgrounds, different religions, different politics. But the looming threat of violence does something to a group of strangers. They fuse together like grains of sand becoming a sheet of glass. A band of brothers, through and through.

"Those are two very disparate aspects of warfare. Carnage and camaraderie. I believe—honestly, in my heart—that spectatorship can get rid of the fear and keep the brotherhood. That's why I'm so passionate about it."

Ahmar stared into Danny's eyes. Searching. Probing. Investigating his heart and words. His face said, *Does this American really believe what he's saying?*

Danny didn't waver—he stared right back. He had honed his skills for years. He could believe anything he wanted to at any given moment.

The president broke the eye contact. "Your words...hold some truth." He exhaled, clearly conflicted. His previous resolve was tempered, but he hadn't formed a new paradigm just yet.

All Danny needed to do now was steer him.

"Let us help. Let me help you usher in a new era for your state. So many nations trust Valkyrie with their armies and soldiers because we're the best at what we do, and I'm the best at what I do."

He bent down and opened his briefcase again. From its belly, he produced a thick stack of papers, which he handed to the president.

"This contract is simple, Mr. President. Any armies created in your nation and fifty percent of the battles those armies participate in will be under the jurisdiction of Valkyrie Productions. From here on to eternity. You and Israel both can set aside your destructive instincts and enter a new age of unity, prosperity, and profit. All you have to do is sign."

The room went silent. The fan squeaked as it spun. Danny desperately wanted to drink Ahmar's unopened bottle of coconut water, but he didn't move. Didn't blink.

Ahmar judged the papers. He didn't read them. He simply looked at them like a captain directing his ship into uncharted rapids. He gulped, withdrew a pen from his suit jacket, and signed his name.

Danny's heart just about exploded from his chest. He let out a shaky breath and wiped his palm on his pants before extending it. "Welcome aboard, sir."

Ahmar allowed himself a small grin, and he shook Danny's hand. "I'm trusting you, Mr. Carr. Do not let me down." He added, "How do you plan on also getting Israel's prime minister to agree to this deal?"

Danny reached into his briefcase one last time and pulled out another stack of documents. Signed documents. "I already did."

The president barked a laugh. He called to one of the bodyguards, "Cigars and brandy, if you please."

Danny cocked an eyebrow at the Palestinian president. "Mr. Ahmar, you cheeky fella."

Ahmar cackled and stood. "Come, Daniel. We have much to discuss and more to celebrate."

❧

Jasmine Creedy was eating dinner when she got the call.

"Hello, Ms. Creedy?" It was a male voice, a little nasally but pleasant enough. "This is Martin from CinemaStream."

She was taken aback. "The streaming service?"

"Yes. We got a hold of the footage of you explaining the history of spectators in warfare, and we were wondering if you'd be interested in producing and hosting a series for us?"

She dropped her fork on the plastic plate. "Really?"

"Oh yes. We were very impressed by your presence. The content and style are to be discussed at a later date, but for now, does that interest you?"

Jasmine was already shoving clothes into a suitcase. She took a beat so that she wouldn't be out of breath when she spoke. "Yes yes yes. Thank you so much!"

"Wonderful. We'll be in touch." *Click.*

She froze. Did that really happen?

Yes. Her hands trembled. She was on her way!

The prison was cold and grey, as if sunlight had been sentenced to life without parole.

Most people would go their entire lives without stepping inside a prison. Salvatore Caracas—Valkyrie Productions' top recruiter—on the other hand, visited every Saturday at noon. He woke up dark and early, worked out, read a chapter of whatever novel was currently on his dresser, ate a carb-heavy breakfast, and drove to the prison.

Gone were his khakis and sweater. Here, Salvatore wore a blazer and wing-tipped shoes. His bowl-cut hair was swept to the side. In this setting, his pudgy belly came across as a sign of opulence—a man who could eat as much as he wanted without worrying about money or calories.

He sat at a metal table in a cinderblock room. Not a lot of color, so he always wore a bright tie.

The door opened, and a guard escorted a prisoner inside. The man in the orange jumpsuit looked confused. He didn't know what was going on.

But Salvatore knew. He had a good relationship with this prison. The warden let him have a chat with all the prisoners scheduled to be released.

"Good afternoon, Mr. Cain," Salvatore said, using a crisp, professional tone. "Have a seat, if you'd like."

The prisoner cautiously sat opposite of Salvatore, eyes wide, muscles tense. He didn't speak.

"My name is Mr. Caracas. And your name is Tommy Cain, correct?" He waited for the prisoner's answer, but when none came, he continued. "You have been in this prison for nearly six years, having been charged with assault and battery. You're set to be released very soon, as you know. You also have hefty debts that have been accruing every day. But you cannot pay off those debts because you are, of course, in here. Is all of this tracking so far?"

"Debts?" the prisoner said.

"Yes. Credit card and mortgage debts you amassed before you were arrested. Six years ago, they were quite manageable, but now...Not so much. Very likely, the moment you set foot out of this prison, you will be bombarded and sued by these companies. And they will win. Unfair, I know."

The man in the jumpsuit looked like he was about to melt. The entire world was piling on top of him all at once.

"I'd like to offer the services of my employer."

"You're a lawyer?"

"No. I'm a recruiter for Valkyrie Productions."

The prisoner put two and two together. "A war enterprise?"

"Yes, Mr. Cain. When you are released, I would be honored if you joined one of Valkyrie's armies. We give all our soldiers room and board, three excellent meals a day, recreation and entertainment, and a weekly paycheck. We also extend legal and financial services to those who are in situations such as yours."

"You...You'd help me?"

"With all legal and financial matters, yes. We take care of our own. To be entirely transparent, Mr. Cain, you're not going to get a better offer than this."

The prisoner looked shell-shocked, going from despair to salvation in less than sixty seconds. "H-How can I get that?"

"I'll just need your signature on a few documents. We'll contact you upon your release, and you'll be a member of the Valkyrie family. You'll be assigned to an army, you'll begin your training, and all your problems will be over. Because you'll be one of our own."

"And..." The prisoner nodded and echoed Salvatore's earlier promise. "And you take care of your own."

Salvatore smiled. "Precisely."

Once the prisoner had signed all the needed papers, the guard escorted him out of the room. Salvatore checked his watch—he needed to be at the inner-city homeless shelter by five o'clock. He always found dozens of soldiers-to-be there.

He said to the guard, "Next, please."

The charity fundraiser was underway. Hundreds of millionaires meandered in the five-star hotel's ballroom, hardly touching the plates of food that had cost them each a thousand dollars. A string quartet played a soothing melody. If asked, no one would be able to say what charity they were raising money for. Starving kids? Building homes? Maybe a combination of the two?

Ranger Monroe marched through the backstage area, adjusting his bow tie as he moved. He never fit into tuxedos very well—his broad shoulders and tree-trunk thighs made him a tailor's nightmare.

Just an hour ago, he had gotten off a plane from Helsinki and been driven here. The war between the Army of Liberty and the Scandinavian Legion was over, and Ranger's army had come out of top. Of course.

Rocko, his publicist, walked alongside him. "Remember, the Army of Liberty could always use more funding, and that ballroom is currently holding a higher net worth than Zambia."

"This fundraiser is for Hands For Healing," Ranger said. "Doctors. They won't be giving money to my army."

"Details, details. If you're nice to a millionaire and make him feel important, he might toss a little extra our way, yeah? So let's see those ivory chompers!"

Ranger didn't respond and kept walking. He wasn't in the mood for Rocko tonight.

But the publicist went over more bullet points. "Just get on the stage, introduce the footage, and get back in the car. You've got a retirement party across town you need to attend."

"I know, Rocko." Then something struck Ranger. "What city are we in?" He suddenly felt very disorientated. His schedule was so hectic, he didn't even know where his plane had touched down.

Rocko laughed. "Portland."

"Oregon or Maine?"

Rocko answered with another laugh and nothing more.

A few minutes later, Ranger bounded into the ballroom and onto the stage, waving and smiling and striking poses like a Greek discus thrower. The attendees went nuts.

Ranger looked out at the audience. Tuxes, floor-length gowns, jewelry, chandeliers, and polished silverware all winked back at him.

He had a quick flashback to his childhood home in Iowa. Dirt road. Huge black cherry tree. Tire swing. Mom in her apron, sweeping the porch.

And then he was back onstage. His current life was lightyears away from that old Iowa porch. He gave a personal wave to a few millionaires closest to the stage, and they cheered louder.

A microphone made its way into his hand. "Thank you, everyone, thank you." His voice rumbled through the ballroom as the diners took their seats. "My name is Ranger Monroe, captain of the Army of Liberty. Thanks to your generous donations, Hands For Healing has provided doctors all over the world with the means to help those who need it most."

A smattering of applause came from the audience, like fat drops of water falling into an empty bucket.

"And as a way of saying thank you," Ranger said, winding up for a big delivery, "the Army of Liberty has something special."

The spectators sat forward in their chairs.

Ranger let the suspense simmer before finishing. "Tonight, you all will watch exclusive footage of a battle between myself and Xi Huang, captain of the Beijing Battalion." Massive screens began lowering from the ceiling. "This is a never-before-seen duel-to-the-death. Two men, one victor, no rules!"

The audience couldn't contain itself. They hollered and babbled and stomped their feet. This was a type of battle they'd never seen before—*mano a mano*. It was guaranteed to be bloody, vicious, and thrilling.

Ranger remembered every second. He and Xi had filmed a one-on-one battle for an occasion such as this, with the understanding that the winner's production enterprise would own the footage. They were locked in an underground bunker filled with tunnels and weapons, and only one man had left alive.

Once the brawl was over, Ranger couldn't walk for a month. The thick scars on his back and torso reminded him of that fight every single day.

He cleared his throat. His knees were suddenly very shaky. "Enjoy." He got offstage as slyly as he could, not wanting to draw any more attention.

Wish granted—all eyes were locked on the screens. The millionaires at the charity fundraiser couldn't wait to watch the two men tear into each other.

⁓⁖⁓

Turns out, Ranger was in Portland, Oregon. His private car took him from the fancy hotel to a mansion that made "five-stars" sound like trash. The house was bigger than the castle at Disney World, taking up more land than a small town. Cars were parked everywhere—in the streets, on the lawn, under pavilions. There was even a helicopter that had landed right in the middle of the party.

Ranger wandered through the masses of people. For the first time in recent memory, he wasn't immediately recognized and mobbed. The whole estate was stuffed with soldiers and celebrities, so he was no one special. He loved it.

Also, every single person had at least one drink in their hands. Most were long past their limits, but the night had only just begun.

Thrumming music almost burst his eardrums. Not even the heat of battle was that loud.

Ranger picked his way across the massive living room, which had been adopted as the dance floor. Sofas, lamps, vases, and chairs had been thrown aside, and anything that wasn't thrown aside was being stomped on by hundreds of drunken dancers. Chandeliers covered in discarded clothes hung from the ceiling.

In the middle of the maelstrom was the man of the hour: Claude von Cloude. Mid-seventies. Crooked smile. Painted fingernails. Thin—almost skeletal. He danced to the music. He spun and spun, letting the feathery boa around his neck and his gaudy leather jacket swirl like a Technicolor tornado. The hair on his brows, chin, and head was dyed bright pink, but his natural grey showed at the roots.

Claude was a major Hollywood star decades ago. He'd been young, rugged, handsome, and strong. He had two Academy Awards somewhere in his mansion, one for acting, one for producing. His face and name were legendary around the world, and the sky was the limit.

Until the sky changed. All of a sudden, film was on the decline and war spectatorship took off. A few producers had the bright idea to train the renowned Claude von Cloude to be a soldier, and he became the captain of the L.A. Archangels. He was a charismatic leader and he won many battles, but more importantly, he drew in crowds. People chanted his name and bought tickets to see how he would win the next war.

Claude was one of the few actors who had successfully made the transition from film to war. But that was a long time ago. His name hadn't been chanted in years. Once he crossed the unspoken threshold of fifty years old, he was booted off the Archangels. He was kept on as a "war consultant," meaning he could offer color commentary during live broadcasts, but his time in the sun was over.

He drowned himself in liquor and became an adrenaline junkie. When he wasn't flat-out drunk on live TV, he was bungee jumping, hang-gliding, wrestling a tranquilized lion.

This party was to celebrate his official retirement. He wasn't a soldier. He wasn't an actor. He wasn't even allowed to commentate anymore. All he had left was loud music, groups of people, and as much booze as he could take.

And Ranger knew that was a lot of booze.

Claude stopped spinning and adjusted the tiara on his head. "Who's that?" he said over the music. "Is that the one and only Ranger Monroe?"

Ranger smiled and hugged Claude. "Good to see you, old friend!"

"It's been years since you've knocked on my door, Monroe. Not counting all the times you've hijacked my dreams, that is." Claude laughed in a way that suggested he may or may not be joking. "Grab a drink. I think I have an extra..." He reached into his jacket's inner pocket and pulled out a bottle of vodka.

"Not for me, thanks," Ranger politely dissented.

"Oh, so you're gonna come into *this* place and *not* drink?" Claude scoffed dramatically. "That's like going to Venice and not riding a friggin' gondola."

Claude began flailing and dancing again. Ranger put a hand on Claude's back to keep him from falling, but the former movie star didn't appear shaky at all.

"How much have you been drinking tonight?" Ranger asked.

Claude chuckled and pretended to think. "Let's see. I started at about 9 a.m., so let's do the math..."

Ranger was surprised. "You have pretty good balance."

"That's what happens when you've been drunk for twenty years. Ya get used to it." He emptied a drink into his mouth and threw his hands up. His rib cage showed through his shirt, and his arms looked like twigs.

Ranger heard his name from within the crowd, and he got caught up talking to a few soldiers he had captained the previous year. And then, a voice screeched over the music.

"Look out below, you whores!"

Everyone looked up, and some gasped, some laughed. Claude stood on a balcony, arms outstretched, a bottle in each hand. He ran a few steps and leapt into the empty air. His feathery boa fluttered like ostrich wings, but not for long. He hooked his legs onto one of the chandeliers and began swinging back and forth, hanging upside-down.

His audience roared and continued dancing. He watched from above, cackling drunkenly, swaying through the air like a nightmarish bat.

And then, Claude unhooked his legs, and he plummeted toward the ground.

Ranger yelled, "No!"

The crowd formed a cushion, and a dozen hands caught Claude's frail body. They hoisted him above their heads, parading him around like a pharaoh.

Claude laughed and toasted himself: "To life, and all its insanity!" The crowd cheered, and he drank deeply from both bottles—he hadn't spilled a drop.

Eventually, Claude got his feet back on the ground. He finished his bottles and grabbed a martini glass. "Whew," he hooted. "Need to catch a breath. Ranger, come sit with me a spell." The withered old actor towed Ranger to a sofa, and they settled down next to one another.

Ranger surveyed the party once more. The people thrashed and convulsed, screamed and floundered. They weren't a crowd—they were a mob. It was more of a battlefield than a dance floor.

As he scanned the room, he realized Claude was watching him intently.

"How do you feel, Claude?" Ranger asked. "Retirement doesn't quite sound like your bag."

Claude ignored the question entirely. He swirled his martini glass and asked one of his own. "Why do you do it, Ranger?"

"What? Fight?" Ranger laughed. "You did it too, in case you forgot."

"Yes, yes, we all fight," Claude waved at the air as if erasing an invisible chalkboard. "But you...You participate in more battles than anyone else in this day and age. You just finished a war in Helsinki, and you're flying out to the east coast tomorrow. You don't need to fight as much as you do." He nodded to himself. "I used to do the same thing. At my peak, I was leading eight or nine battles a week. And I want to know why you do it."

Ranger's chiseled smile melted away. He suddenly didn't feel like socializing anymore tonight.

But Claude took a sip and kept pushing. "Don't get all ruffled. Is it the applause? That's why I did it. The fan clubs. The awards. The lovers throwing themselves at my feet, begging me to walk on them. Applause is addictive. And when it runs out, you shrivel up." He gestured to himself. His gaudy clothes and bony frame.

"It's not like that for me, Claude." Ranger's eyes bounced around the room, landing on nothing for long.

"Hmm...I believe you. How strange." Claude finished his drink and tossed the glass nowhere in particular. "So, fortune and glory aren't what get you going. What is it, then?"

Ranger looked at his old friend. There was something about Claude's glazed eyes, his frail body, and his peacock-ish attire that made Ranger want to be honest. Fully honest. He said, "I could die any second. And that...helps."

Claude narrowed his pink brows. "Helps what?"

"In their last moments, people are at their best. So...I make every moment my last."

For the first time in his life, Claude didn't have a droll retort at the ready. His mouth hung open, but no words came out. Finally, he said, "I don't think I've missed our late night chats." He staggered to his feet and left Ranger behind, searching for more numbing alcohol.

And Ranger sat there, surrounded by people and noise and lights, feeling utterly alone.

Chicago. The Windy City. Not the tallest buildings in the world, but miles taller than those Annie Kennedy was used to in Wichita. Taller skyscrapers, faster cars, louder people, smellier garbage, greasier food...Her entire concept of a big city had been cranked up to eleven.

She had taken a bus north from Kansas, trying desperately to escape the grip of the Midwest. She'd settled on Chicago. That is where she would break through. No questions. No other options.

The sidewalks were jam-packed with pedestrians, but Annie knew how to deal with crowds. Sometimes it was best to weave gracefully between bodies, but sometimes, she needed to throw a few elbows to get where she needed to go.

She reached the recruitment center and stared at the door from across the street. Whereas the recruiting events in Wichita had five or ten representatives from various enterprises, she'd read that the Chicago center would have at least fifty.

Fifty.

Her muscles tensed up. She had never spoken in front of twenty people, much less fifty. If five recruiters thought she was boring or screechy, what would fifty think? What if she memorized the wrong monologue again, like the *Annie/Annie Get Your Gun* fiasco? What this time—*Hamlet* instead of *Hamilton*?

She forced herself to stop thinking and cross the street. She was spiraling, getting too into her own head.

Maybe in such a big city, they'd be more appreciative of her athleticism. It could be that they have too many leaders and not enough people willing to put in the hard work. Yes, there might be a bumper-crop of charisma, an excess of charm, a surplus of stage presence.

She groaned as she pushed open the door. If only.

The Casanovas are the ones who run the world. The class presidents. The orators. Grunts like Annie Kennedy were always relegated to supporting roles.

While sitting on the bus, she had practiced smiling naturally. Another passenger had asked her if she was having a stroke.

She signed in with a receptionist and handed over her résumé.

Charm wasn't her strong suit. That was a simple fact she had to move past.

"Take a seat, hun," the receptionist said. "They'll call you in when they're ready to hear from you." She handed Annie a slip of paper. "This is the line they'd like you to try out. Feel free to give it your own flavor."

Annie gulped. "Already? There are no physical tests first?"

The receptionist took a quick look at Annie's résumé and smiled. "Oh, I see you're from Wichita. This must be your first time in Chicago. Here, the recruiters like to see and hear everyone first. Get a feel for the potential, y'know? Then, they'll choose the top contenders to move on to the physical requirements."

Annie's head felt light. Usually, she could curry at least a little favor with the recruiters based on her outstanding athleticism. This time, however, she was being tossed into the shark tank right out of the gate.

Sifting out the stinkers, she thought. One "um" or "uh," and she'd be gone. Never mind the sprints and pull-ups. It all hinged on the "charisma test." As per usual.

"Thank you, ma'am," she said and wobbled away.

The waiting room was full of men and women waiting to be called into the recruiters' room. Dozens. Maybe hundreds.

Big, beefy men. Gorgeous, toned women. Future stars. Storytellers. Enchanters.

She looked closer at the population of the waiting room. As drop-dead stunning as the women were, there were only a handful. There were far more men.

Hmm.

A vacant seat beckoned her across the room, and she sat. After a long day of navigating the city, if felt nice to take a load off before facing the recruiters.

The guy next to her gave a quick nod, then went back to studying his slip of paper. It was only a couple sentences, but he read it with the intensity of a procrastinating law student.

Annie checked out the line for herself.

"You won't defeat us today. As God is my witness, we will make the world a better place!"

Cheesy, clichéd, and unrealistic. At least she was used to that.

An hour ticked by. Then two.

One by one, the receptionist called out names and escorted recruits through a small beige door. Annie wondered how many of these people were already in an army, like she was, and looking to jump up the ladder. On the other hand, how many were civilians who walked in off the street? Actors, accountants, doctors, middle school teachers...If they could speak well, they were likely to advance farther than Annie, even though she could bench-press any of them.

That thought made her mad, and she sat there steaming as the room slowly emptied. The guy beside her kept his attention fully locked on his slip of paper. He looked quite a few years younger than her—maybe even a decade. Average height, average attractiveness, in average shape.

She said to him, "First time?"

He looked at her as if she'd dumped cold water on him. "Oh, um... Yeah. First real recruitment."

The room was almost empty, and their words bounced off the walls.

He gave her a quick once-over. "You, uh...Do you have any pointers? The receptionist said to put my own spin on this line, but I'm not really sure what that means." He must have noticed how athletic she was and assumed she was a pro at auditioning.

She shrugged and clicked her tongue. "They want to see what you bring to the table, what makes you unique. But I've been going to these things for ten years, and I've never done well, so you might not want to take any advice from me."

The guy shrugged back. "Hey, you know more than me. I'd take any advice you've got."

Annie smiled sadly. "If I had any advice worth heeding, I'd take it myself and stop sitting in waiting rooms." She held out her hand. "I'm Annie."

He took her hand. "Zeke Smith."

"Welcome to the trenches, Zeke. What do you do?"

"Reenactments. Union Army."

"Huh!" Annie said. She'd never met someone who served in a historical army. "That's interesting."

Zeke looked taken aback. "You think so?"

"Not really."

They both burst out laughing. The few people left in the room glared at them, but they didn't notice.

"I'm sorry," Annie exhaled as her laugh petered out. "Honestly, good for you. You're on the battlefront, making things happen."

"For nursing homes and school trips," Zeke muttered.

"What do you mean?"

Zeke just shook his head.

He didn't talk much. Annie liked him.

"Well, good luck, Zeke. I'm sure you'll do well. Don't be afraid to go over-the-top. Audiences love it, and recruiters love what audiences love."

"Over-the-top?"

"Yeah. Don't be sad—be *distraught*. Don't be surprised—be *flabbergasted*. Battle-stadiums are huge, and people in the audience need to be able to follow what you're feeling, even if they're all the way up in the nosebleed-seats."

Zeke smiled. "Smart. Thanks."

"Smart for you. Not for me. That tactic won't work if I try."

"Why?"

Annie groaned. She hadn't intended on pouring her heart out to anyone, but this guy was a good listener. "This isn't my first lap. I know how things go. When dashing young men go over-the-top, they're thespians. When I do it, I'm melodramatic, or shrill, or screechy."

Zeke frowned. "I'm sorry." He sounded genuine, but curt. Not one to waste words.

She continued. "Think back to when this room was full. You could smell the testosterone in the air. Y-chromosomes all over the place. And a handful of ladies. Army regulations dictate that the population of their soldiers must be twenty-five percent White, twenty-five Black," she gestured to Zeke, "and fifty percent *other*." She then pointed at her own bronze skin. "But women don't see much of the action."

"Wow, that's really unfair."

"At my last recruitment, in Wichita..." Annie started, but she reeled herself back in. She didn't want to shove her life story in some random guy's face.

But Zeke prodded her. "In Wichita?"

She grimaced and said quietly, "Eh, they said I was boring. Off-putting. Couldn't engage with an audience. That's why you shouldn't be taking any advice from me."

"I'm sure you always do your best," he said.

Annie set he jaw. "The worst part is, they're right. It's not enough to be able to kick someone's teeth in. Everyone can do that. I need something that they don't have."

"More than that," Zeke said. "You need a narrative. Reenactments are all about clear, concise story threads. They might be old and dusty, but they've lasted this long for a reason." He nodded. "Narrative."

"Huh..." They were both quiet as Annie mulled that over. "Story?"

"I could go on and on," he smiled. "Historical armies drill those principles into your brain. We have whole classes about motivation and story arcs."

The receptionist chose that moment to call out, "Carr, Zechariah!"

Zeke cleared his throat and set his hands on his knees. "Good luck, Annie. Rooting for you."

Annie was caught off-guard by his different last name, but she quickly righted herself. "Um, you too. Thanks."

He stood and walked through the beige door, clutching the slip of paper in both hands.

Annie was suddenly left alone on the far side of the waiting room. Her thoughts buzzed like a highway during rush hour.

Narrative. What did she have that the other guys didn't?

Or...What *could* she have?

A few minutes later, Annie entered the recruiters' room with her head held high. No modesty today. All confidence.

That was the plan, anyway. As soon as she saw what was waiting for her inside, her bravado deflated like a whoopee cushion.

The room looked like a college lecture hall, with seats rising up all around her. She stood below hundreds of seated men, feeling like she'd just been shoved into the Coliseum.

A voice told her, "Whenever you're ready, dear."

They wanted to hear her say the line they'd been hearing all day long. She gave the audience a quick glance—every man looked bored, annoyed, or half-asleep. No one even glanced at her résumé or headshot. They were ready to go home, not listen.

Time to change their minds.

She took a breath and spoke very loudly. Her voice exploded in the spacious room.

"You won't beat us today!" She yelled as if she had to be heard over gunfire and grenades, trying to instill a drop of fear in the heart of her rival captain. "With God as my witness, we will fight, and we will make this world a better place!"

Her voice vibrated in the air. The men looked unimpressed.

She clutched her belly and finished: "A better place for us...and my child!"

That got their attention. Every single recruiter perked up in his seat. They rummaged through the paperwork, searching for her name. They started hissing to one another: "Who was that?" "Now there's some originality." "She's mine." "No way, she has to come with us!"

Word by word, the hissing turned into yelling, which turned into arguing.

They were fighting over Annie Kennedy.

Ranger stared at himself in the mirror. He stood in his prep room deep in the landing grounds of a battle-stadium. His uniform was draped over a chair, his rifle hanging from a hook.

The sounds of footsteps, voices, turning gears, closing doors were all around him, but muffled and distant, as if he were inside a cotton ball.

"Time to fight," he whispered to his reflection. "Time to..."

Time to what? Win? Not lose?

Ranger had never been obsessed with being the best at anything. Not in school, not in his friend group, not in his earlier careers. Medals and promotions held no value to him. No, being *the* best didn't get him going. He wanted to be *his* best. He always held doors open for others. He listened to people and engaged with them. He did his taxes and gave away as much money as he could.

What he had said to Claude von Cloude at the retirement party was the truth. He believed imminent death could turn a scoundrel into a saint. The prospect of dying brings out the best in someone.

So Ranger made sure death was always around the corner. That way, he was always at his finest. People liked him, and he would be remembered fondly. And most importantly, *he* knew he was the best he could possibly be. He had no choice—he could die any given day.

"Good God...Is that really why I do this?"

He moved away from the mirror and started dressing. It was almost showtime, and he had to get moving, but mainly, he didn't want to look at himself anymore.

The roar of the crowd filling the stadium got louder by the second. Likely another sold-out audience. He had a streak to maintain—he'd led forty-nine sold-out battles in a row. One more and he'd get a set of steak knives from Valkyrie.

Focus. Focus. He tried to think only about the battle at hand. Soldiers were counting on him, not to mention the screaming fans. Once he got out on the battlefield, it would be all about him and...

He froze in the middle of buttoning his shirt.

He had no idea what army he was facing. He'd completely forgotten.

Very unlike Ranger Monroe. He shook his head and quickly finished getting dressed. He'd need to go through the battle layouts again before it all started.

The stadium was abuzz. Pensacola was a city of respectable size, but not a ton of national armies visited very often. That day, however, two of the most popular armies in the world were going to square off.

In one corner, the Army of Liberty, led by the incomparable Ranger Monroe. A more famous and respected name didn't exist.

Then there were the Sun Tsunamis, a scrappy little army on the rise. The army had been formed less than a year earlier, but its positive attitude and underdog story had earned it a rabid fan-base.

Might versus spunk. Goliath and David, clashing for the first time. Tickets had sold out faster than the cure to cancer had the previous year.

The Army of Liberty was owned by Valkyrie Productions, and the Sun Tsunamis were owned by Millennium. Fans of the war industry knew that Valkyrie and Millennium had a not-so-friendly rivalry, and they were excited to see these two banner armies duke it out.

"Everyone, keep together!" A group of about thirty students from the local high school lined up at the concession stand to get hot dogs. Tremaine Dodson had attended their school the year before, ultimately dropping out and joining the Sun Tsunamis. He was going to be a field commander in tonight's battle, and some of his classmates had come to see him fight.

Just then, the Ranger Monroe Fan Club rolled in. They blasted air horns, waved flags, and carried life-sized cutouts of their favorite soldier. The Fan Club was based in San Diego, but as many members as possible traveled to every battle Ranger fought in.

"Monroe, our beau!" they started to chant. "Monroe, our beau!"

The raucous fan club passed by a small family clutching their tickets and headed for their seats. A little boy smiled at the cutouts of Ranger—his favorite soldier too—but the shouting made him cover his ears. This was the first battle his parents had ever brought him to. The mom and dad exchanged a quick look, wondering if the gunfire and explosions would be too loud for his little ears, but his smile put them at ease.

Everyone remembers their first battle. The first time an explosion thumped in their chest. The first time they gasped as an unexpected twist. The first time their favorite soldier was killed right before their eyes—the sorrow they felt, then the triumph when that soldier was avenged. What they ate, the shades of the uniforms, the music that played during the presentation of the colors...These details were burned into people's memories.

The National Anthem began to play. It was about to start!

The group of students abandoned the hot dog line. They didn't want to miss a moment of Tremaine in action.

The mom and dad also rushed out of the concession area. This was their son's very first battle—they didn't want one of the memories burned into his brain to be of his parents' tardiness.

Almost immediately, the entrance atrium of the battle-stadium emptied. Candy wrappers and beer cans rolled around like tumbleweeds. All of the loitering spectators hurried to their seats.

Ranger cinched his belt as he moved through the landing grounds into position. He could hear the opening announcements booming in the stadium.

"...Today's battle is brought to you by the all-new AK-48! If you liked the previous model, you'll Kalashnik-*love* this upgrade!"

The landing grounds were empty, except for a few technicians who gaped as he passed. They didn't usually see the hero of the army, since he was supposed to be ready to go long before.

"C'mon," he hissed to himself. "Snap to it."

He wasn't sure why or what or how...but something was under his skin. He felt wispy, like a dandelion that could be disintegrated by the slightest breeze.

Why do I—

Nope. He shut down his inner thoughts before they had time to take root.

Military heroes didn't have existential crises. They led. They inspired. They did their job.

He hitched up his trousers and adjusted the line of grenades slung across his torso.

Time to do just that.

He shook his head and entered the battlefield.

Shrapnel and bullets rained from the heavens. And from hell—death came from all directions.

The Army of Liberty was getting thrashed. More than half of the soldiers had been shot, beaten, bayonetted, punched, slapped, spanked, or blown to bits. The Sun Tsunamis had progressed almost entirely across the battlefield. Only about ten yards of the field still belonged to Ranger and his soldiers.

Of course, that's how the battle had been outlined and mapped out by the executives. It was supposed to be a big come-from-behind victory for the Army of Liberty, and the Sun Tsunamis would look good for getting close to beating such a respected army. Win-win. The crowd would cheer. Fans on both sides would be happy. Everyone would get paid.

Everything was going exactly how it was supposed to.

Except for Ranger Monroe. He was off today. His shots were less accurate than usual. His steps were sluggish. And most off all, his entire demeanor was wrong. There were no roguish smiles, no inspirational quotes that could be put on t-shirts. He hadn't even used any of the quippy one-liners the executives had written for him. (Well, the executives had told the pale writers on the ground floor to come up with some quippy one-liners, but still.)

And now, with the opposing army encroaching, and all hope seemingly lost, Ranger Monroe crouched behind a rock. His rifle was lowered—its safety was even on. He seemed lost in thought.

The audience was losing interest. The gigantic screens usually showed Ranger throughout the battle, but he'd given them nothing. The microphone attached to his uniform had nothing to broadcast.

The Army of Liberty's star captain was acting like a freshly recruited private. And that was *boring*.

The battle managers gave word to have a few explosions go off near Ranger's position. Mines and grenades rocked the entire stadium, and the fire even singed the rock Ranger was hiding behind. But he didn't move.

One of the directors groaned and flicked a switch. "Yo, Ranger! Earth to Ranger, numb-nuts!"

The static in Ranger's ear made him twitch. He slapped at his neck, thinking a mosquito was buzzing around.

"Ranger frickin' Monroe! Hellooooo?"

"Wh-What?" He sighed. "What do you want?"

"Oh, he lives! About time. Have you forgotten where you are, or do I need to sic an air strike on you?"

Ranger snarled, flipped off his rifle's safety, and shot five enemy soldiers clean through the forehead from behind his cover.

The crowd loved it, and they let him know with cheers and chants.

"Yes, more of that, please." The battle director's sneering voice went away.

"You want more?" Ranger whispered to no one as he stood. "You got it..."

He ripped the sash of grenades off his torso and tossed it toward the encroaching army. In a flash, his pistol was in his hand, and he fired a round into one of the deadly orbs, mid-air. The entire line of grenades exploded, sending a concussive wave through the stadium.

Fans of both armies were on their feet. At last, they were going to see some real action.

A section of the crowd started chanting: "Monroe, our beau! Monroe, our beau!" Within seconds, hundreds of thousands of people had joined in.

Ranger Monroe drew a dagger and lobbed it into the mass of enemy soldiers. He didn't even aim, and the blade landed harmlessly on the ground, but he did it with such force and confidence, the crowd practically had no choice but to cheer him on.

He wiped a hand across his brow, not trying to remove grime, but trying to put some on. He needed to look grizzled and sweaty.

No doubt, the long-range cameras were focused on him now, and his chiseled face was plastered on the jumbo-screens.

In one graceful bound, he was on top of the rock he had been hiding behind moments ago. He stood tall and proud, rifle in one hand, waving the other. "Men!" he called out over the rumble of battle. "Soldiers, heed my words!"

Every fighter in the Army of Liberty paused and looked up at their fearless captain. Standing there high above his followers, mightily handsome, speaking with such gusto, clutching his weapon, lights and explosions making his eyes glisten...He looked like one of the mythical Valkyries their enterprise was named after.

"Today we fight not for ourselves. Not for our past and not for our present. But for our future!" He clenched his empty hand into a mighty fist as he prattled off a few empty buzzwords. "A future forged in glory. Honor. Valor!"

The soldiers on the field nodded and whooped. "Hooah!" "Yessir!" "Let's go!"

Ranger could hear his words resounding throughout the stadium. Every person clung to the noble speech he was making up on the spot.

"We won't all be here tomorrow to see the fruits of our efforts," he continued, gaining more and more confidence every second. "But our children will. And their children! Generations will look back on this day! Will we give them something to be proud of?"

He wasn't actually saying anything of worth, but the soldiers punched the air. "Yes!"

"Let me ask you again, soldiers!" Ranger cocked his rifle for effect, even though it was already cocked. "I'm speaking to the *Army of Liberty* right now!" Cheers, cries, howls. "Will we give our people something to be—"

A bullet flew through Ranger Monroe's skull. He stood frozen for a moment, his perfectly coiffed hair dripping red. Then he tumbled off the rock to the dirty ground. He was dead before he knew what had happened.

❧

"Is it on?" A man stood in the middle of the frame, with nothing but a blank brown wall behind him. He wore athletic pants and a baggy hoodie. His head was shaved.

"Yeah, it's on," a voice said from behind the camera.

"...Are you sure?"

"Yes, I'm sure! See the red light? That means it's on."

"Okay, okay, okay." The man on-camera cleared this throat. "All right, I'm ready."

"I'm already rolling. Go."

"What?" The man put his hands over his face. "Edit out that first part."

"I can't edit—we're livestreaming. Just say the bit!"

The man dropped his hands and glared right into the camera. "Fine." He cracked the joints in his neck and dropped his voice a few octaves. "Good morning, America."

The off-camera voice interrupted. "That sounds like a talk show."

"Just let me say it!" he said, forgetting his phony baritone. He quickly got back on track. "We are Invisible Sword. The reckoning that this nation so sorely needs. We claim full responsibility for the electrical blackout that seized Boston last Saturday. We shall strike the heart of this country with precision. We never miss, and you won't see us coming."

He cleared his throat again, and his eyes scanned the cue cards just off-screen. "So...Um, don't forget to like this video and subscribe to our channel. We'll be posting updates here throughout the weeks, as we make our way through the country. If you have ideas for where we should go and what we should do next, use the hashtags 'terror' and 'invisiblesword' so we can see them."

"Hold on," the camera operator butted in again. "Hashtag 'invisiblesword' is already taken. There's a disappearing ink company called Invisible Words, but a lot of people online have misplaced the S and used 'invisiblesword.'"

"That's stupid. Can we still use it?"

"I mean...we can, but it might get confusing."

"Sure, sure." The man rubbed his eyes. "Invisible Gun? Noose?"

"Oh, I like noose."

"Dagger!"

"Yeah," the voice agreed, and the camera shook. "Dagger! Keep it in the blade family."

"Okay," the man looked back into the camera. "We're Invisible Dagger now. Remember to like, comment, and subscribe! We have lots of content coming your way!"

Suzanne and Danny walked briskly through the top level of the Valkyrie Productions office building. The morning sun was just peeking over the glassy ocean. The enterprise's board waited for them in a conference room.

Ranger's death the night before had sent shockwaves through the whole enterprise, not to mention the country and the world. Cities around the globe held vigils and ceremonies all night, honoring their fallen hero.

Social media was ablaze with sorrow, anger, confusion, and every other emotion that had a name. The world's population was in mourning.

Suzanne read from her tablet as the two walked. "The shooter's name is Tremaine Dodson, a field commander for the Sun Tsunamis. The battle in Pensacola last night was his grand debut. We got a hold of his file and bank statements—last week, he was a private, assigned to scrubbing lockers. A few days ago, he was promoted to commander, and a million bucks was transferred to him directly from Millennium Enterprises. Now, either ole Tremaine is the greatest military mind since Patton, or he was given the specific job to shoot Ranger down."

She scrolled through a few pages on the tablet, then continued. "Ranger dying wasn't a part of the battle's approved layout, so Tremaine will be punished. But it'll be a slap on the wrist, basically. No big deal, and his bank account has a few extra zeroes."

"Motive?" Danny asked, the word barely escaping his lips.

"Well, no one *really* knows. The prevailing theory is what I know you already suspect: Millennium has been making Ranger offers, and he hasn't bitten. They figure, if they can't have him, they'll make sure we can't either." She paused, and the only sounds in the hallway were the *thump-thump* of Danny's loafers and her *clack*ing heels. "It's a perfect crime, really—a soldier assassinating another soldier in the middle of battle."

Danny nodded, but didn't respond. Very uncharacteristic.

"So," she brushed a hair away from her eyes, "which newspapers do we give this info to?"

"None," Danny said, and Suzanne gaped in surprise. "Bury all of this. If anyone asks, it's a conspiracy theory. We move on." He swallowed and sighed. "Let Ranger die with dignity."

Suzanne didn't know what to say. Also very uncharacteristic. Eventually, "All right, then." She poked at the tablet.

They walked in silence for another minute. The upper-level hallways were a maze.

"Dirty business..." Danny muttered to himself. Then he thought of something. "Get our designers working on a memorial. We'll have one in San Diego and another in his hometown. Also, put together some scholarships in his name."

Suzanne bobbed her head. "I'll need the president's signature to get projects that big rolling." She held out her tablet to Danny.

Without breaking stride, Danny took the tablet, signed the name *Leigh Gambol*, and handed it back.

Leigh Gambol: ten decades old, shaky, almost deaf, practically blind, afraid to walk out the front door of his retirement community. Also, he happened to be the head of Valkyrie Productions. The big boss, the Executive executive.

Danny had been signing Gambol's name for so many years, his forgery held more sway than the real thing.

Finally, at long last, they reached the door to the conference room, which Danny burst through like a cannonball.

"Morning, everyone!" As if a switch had been thrown, he transformed from the quiet, somber version of himself into his usual loudmouthed persona. "What a twelve hours." He took a seat at the head of the table, Suzanne at his side.

The board of Valkyrie Productions stared back at him. Fifteen men and women sat in stiff leather chairs, wearing power suits, or jewelry acquired by illegal means, or both. All of them were old enough either to remember the olden days of unstructured warfare or to have had parents fight in those wars.

Some were angry, some sad, others baffled—but all were terrified that their leading star had been unceremoniously shot through the head.

Danny cleared his throat. He had never set foot on a battlefield, but every time he spoke to these skeletons, he felt like he was doing jumping-jacks in a minefield. "We're all shocked by Mr. Monroe's death, I know."

One old codger harrumphed. He literally said the word *"Har-rumph,"* then continued. "It wasn't even dramatic. If he'd been dis-arming a bomb or stopping some world-threatening army, that'd be one thing. He'd be a hero and a martyr. We could put his face on lunchboxes for the next hundred years. But he was picked off by some private from a two-bit community-theater army in a bumpkin little town! Useless! What a waste!"

"Now," Suzanne interjected, "the soldier who downed Mr. Monroe was a field commander, not a private. Pretty high-ranking, truth be told."

Danny straightened his necktie. "Mr. Monroe being killed last night wasn't on anyone's docket, but hey." He shrugged and chuckled lightly. "Look, Ranger was a great star. He was. But this is war. We're dealing with live ammunition and green-around-the-gills extras. The tightest script and best director in the world can't account for bad aim."

Not everyone on the board loved him, but he had a few allies, and he'd won them over. Now it was time to work on the stubborn ones.

"Besides, ladies and gentlemen," he sat forward in his chair, "the tide is changing. We have an idea—"

Suzanne butted in again. *"She* has an idea."

Danny waved her words away. "I'm getting there. One of our rising directors, Elena Winn, has had an epiphany. A lightning-strike idea that will revolutionize the way we present the captain of the Army of Liberty to the public."

The old codger leaned back and crossed his bony arms. "Dazzle us." A few other skeptics around the table snorted in agreement.

Danny bit his tongue. *"Challenge accepted, you dusty old dinosaurs,"* he wanted to say. Instead, he smiled. "Can do." And he told them the new plan.

The sun was high in the sky—about three o'clock, Annie would guess. She didn't have a watch, and she'd left her phone in the hotel room. Under a stack of pillows. It hadn't stopped ringing and vibrating and shrieking for what felt like decades.

Seagulls cawed. People laughed. Waves crashed and sighed. She walked alongside the ocean, feet scuffing across the hard sand. This place was called Mission Beach, if she remembered correctly. Down here, close to the water, the sand was dark brown and solid, like she was walking on hardwood floor. Further up, near the buildings and streets, the sand was white and fluffy. Part of her wanted to walk on the soft sand, to feel it between her toes.

But she stayed by the ocean. A wave would crest, then pound itself onto the earth, and droplets of salty water would explode onto her exposed skin. Once the powerful wave was beaten into submission, it would slide across the hard beach and kiss her toes ever so lightly, then retreat, leaving a line of foam.

This would happen again and again: wave, explosion, kiss, retreat.

Kansas didn't have an ocean, so she put up with the hard sand in order to be close to the wild water.

San Diego was pretty nice, she supposed.

Dozens of warfare enterprises had offered to fly her out to the coast in an attempt to wine and dine her. Well, metaphorically "wine"—no alcohol would be served, since she was pregnant and all.

She set a hand on her flat, empty stomach. How long would she have to keep it up?

An answer to her own question drifted in on the ocean breeze: as long as she needed to.

Everyone wanted the "maternal warrior" in their army. It was unique, edgy, and relatable. Imagine it: a soldier carrying life in her womb, wielding a machine gun and taking life from others. The dichotomy was delicious. And every executive was a little bitter they hadn't thought of it first.

As Annie wandered the beach, she passed countless families, couples, and children. Not one of them recognized her. No one made a pitch as to why she should join their army. No one offered her dinner, or a Rolls Royce, or a private island. No one tried to buy her, jockeyed to run her life, or turned her into a commodity, seemingly for sport.

It was a breath of fresh air.

"Afternoon, Annie." A smiling voice made itself known over the noise of the beach.

Annie spun.

A woman stood further up the beach, on the soft white sand. She was modestly dressed, but she wore sharp earrings that looked like they could slice someone's throat. In fact, everything about her was sharp—nose, cheekbones, chin...eyes. Her eyes were frighteningly intelligent.

Annie squinted against the sun. "So, what enterprise are you with?"

The woman said, "Eh, that doesn't really matter to me."

"It does to me." Annie moved away from the water to get closer to the stranger. "I like knowing who I'm talking to." She stopped a few feet away so they could talk without yelling over the waves.

The woman nodded. "Smart. I'm a director with Valkyrie Productions, but that's far at the bottom of the list of things that define me. My name is Elena Winn." She offered Annie her hand.

Annie didn't particularly want to shake hands with the enterprise director who had somehow found her on the beach, but her military instincts won out. "Afternoon, ma'am," she said as they shook hands. "Annie Kennedy...although you already know that." She let go of the hand and crossed her arms, flexing her impressive biceps and shoulders.

Elena gestured down the beach. "Care to take a stroll?"

"I don't like it when someone tracks me down in public."

"Happens often, does it?"

Annie began walking through the soft sand, the stranger keeping stride. "This would be the first."

Elena chuckled, and Annie was surprised her teeth weren't razor-sharp like a werewolf's. "Annie, I'm here to make my pitch to you."

"I figured."

"Currently, battles are overseen by people like me: overworked, under-paid directors with too much overhead and not enough creative control. For instance, I directed a battle for Valkyrie in Tacoma last week. I wanted to incorporate the nearby bay, have waves come rushing into the stadium, drown a few soldiers, and have the captains battle it out on pieces of float-ing debris...But that was too convoluted for the men on the top floor. The executives had the battle mapped out, and I couldn't deviate from that. I was less a director and more of a crossing guard, just keeping things moving."

Annie had heard of this before. As a nurse in the Great Plains Brigade, she'd worked with hundreds of directors over the years, and not one of them was happy with the amount of creative control they had. Annie had chalked that up to the fact that artsy people were never satisfied in general.

"Battle by battle," Elena continued, "director by director. Any given war can be overseen by hundreds of different directors! Character moti-vations and storylines are all over the place. Audiences deserve better. A careful eye, a dedicated hand."

"And that's you?" Annie took a guess at what the woman was building to.

"You bet your tight little *tukus* that's me." Elena beamed like a fox about to snap the neck of its next meal. "Rather than a director being assigned to a battle, I propose that one be assigned to a star soldier. It'd be a symbiotic relationship. They could work together to craft storylines and character moments in each battle. Press conferences, wardrobe, pub-lic appearances—"

Annie groaned inwardly. "So you'd be my publicist?" That was the last thing she wanted.

"No, no. I'd be so much more. You're the paintbrush, I'm da Vinci—pointless when separated, earth-shattering when together."

"And the higher-ups approved this? They're okay giving up so much power?"

Elena shrugged. "The board took some convincing, but Daniel Carr swayed them. It's signed, sealed, and delivered—I'm yours."

As much as Annie wanted to scoff at the idea of someone telling her exactly where to go and what do it, she had to admit, it sounded good. All her past attempts at impressing the recruiters had ended with rejection. Only when she had come up with an interesting concept had they been remotely interested. But they loved the storyline of a pregnant soldier, not Annie Kennedy herself. If she was going to succeed, she needed someone in her corner at all times.

A Frisbee flew through the air right in front of them, and a shirtless doofus in desperate need of sunscreen jumped to catch it. Annie threw out her arm to stop Elena from walking, and the beach bum flopped onto the sand. He would've tackled Elena if Annie hadn't stopped her.

The guy staggered to his feet and ran back to his friends, not apologizing, not even noticing the women he had almost crushed.

"Nice reflexes, Ace," Elena smirked. "It's like you've done this before."

Annie looked out at the water, and Elena looked at Annie.

"I've read your file cover to cover," the director said. "You're practically a Greek goddess. You could thrash any soldier put in front of you, then run a marathon. Peak physical shape."

Annie clenched her jaw. "If you've read my file, you know why I've never been selected for battle. I'm not...camera-ready. Can't say my lines with...vigor."

Elena grabbed Annie's jaw and turned her face toward her own. Annie almost snapped Elena's neck then and there—she didn't like people touching her.

The director stared at her with sly, devious eyes. They were eyes that knew something you didn't. Eyes with a plan.

"I think you've already figured this out," Elena said. "It doesn't matter what you *say*—it matters what you *do*, and what you *do* stems from who you *are*." She gestured to Annie's stomach.

Annie bristled, oddly offended but trying very hard to not show it. "This one thing about me isn't all I am."

Elena responded, "For now, it is." She tilted her face up toward the sun, absorbing its rays, like a flower naturally drawn to light. Her sharp earrings glistened. "The world *loves* pregnant women. And now a *pregnant soldier*? Brilliant. I wished I'd thought of it. You're going to have Midwestern conservatives drooling."

Annie shook her head and started to walk away.

Elena kept pace. "You're right—it's time to get to work."

Jasmine sat at her desk in her midlevel apartment. She typed a password into her personal computer, and suddenly, a man's finely-trimmed face filled the cracked screen.

"Oh, hello! I'm in," she said to the face. "Can you see me? Jasmine here."

"Yes, Jasmine, we see you," the man said with a somewhat nasally voice. It was Martin, an administrator at the world-famous streaming company CinemaStream. "Just so you know, a few other higher-ups are watching and listening to this video call. Is that alright?" He said it as if it wouldn't matter whether she said yes or no. Which, of course, it wouldn't.

"Absolutely!" Jasmine cleared her throat and prayed to the Wi-Fi gods that the call wouldn't drop. CinemaStream's offices were in New York, while her small apartment was in London. She desperately wanted to make a good impression, and explaining that she'd bought her wireless router at a thrift shop didn't really strike the tone she was going for.

"Okay, Jasmine," Martin said. "We've received the video files you sent us, but we haven't watched them yet. We're going to do that now and offer you immediate feedback. Sound good?" Again, she couldn't really object.

"Perfect." She took several deep breaths. Wow...This was the real deal. Make or break. The moment of truth.

She felt good about what she'd filmed. She really did. It was candid and authentic. Plus, it was full of her presence and style, which is what Martin said had drawn CinemaStream to her in the first place.

They'd like it. They had to.

Martin hit a few keystrokes, and the screen switched to a video-playing app. Jasmine nearly hyperventilated, but she quickly pulled herself together. She was a professor, for crying out loud. She'd been published, and she dealt with judgment every single day. This was no different, she told herself. And told herself and told herself, rocking slightly in her chair.

Her footage started playing on the screen.

Establishing shot: a drizzly night in the Enfield borough of London. Streetlamps made the lines of rain look like fairies shooting through the air.

Jasmine's narration: "Warfare spectatorship has taken the world by storm, rewriting history, creating a new chapter of its own. Each and every day, millions of people participate in this new global pastime. Economies have flourished, unemployment is at an all-time low, and the population has never been more entertained."

In her small apartment, Jasmine smiled and settled deeper into her chair. This was really good. The camerawork, her writing...it had all come together really well. She'd played up her accent too, trying to sound more sophisticated. Maybe she'd actually pulled this off.

Her narration continued: "But what does spectatorship leave in its wake? What becomes of the veterans in this new chapter of warfare?"

The video moved through the streets of Enfield, slowly revealing a squat, gray gymnasium in the thick rain. It was a great shot.

Next: inside the gymnasium. In the big empty room, there was a circle of folding chairs facing each other. A half-dozen war veterans met there for a weekly support meeting.

Jasmine planned to get to the emotional core of the entire warfare establishment. Or, at least, she tried to touch upon it.

The footage went on for thirty minutes, allowing the vets to recount their triumphs and horrors. In the film, Jasmine acted as a willing ear, an active listener. Every now and then, she ushered the conversation along or asked a prompting question, but the film belonged to the vets.

And what they had to say was riveting. They told stories of carnage and joy, agony and ecstasy. Jasmine imagined that the editing wizards at CinemaStream could cut together some intense footage dramatizing the yarns the veterans spun. It would be a hit for sure.

At one point, Jasmine asked a woman, "I'm sure you learned many, many things while in your army. What lesson do you carry with you every day?"

The woman was about sixty years old, with frizzy hair that made her look like she had just stuck one of her chewed fingernails into an electrical outlet. She gulped and thought for a moment, then her face got a little whiter. "I walk down the street, or in the aisles at the grocery store…" Her voice went up and down like a seesaw. "And I can't look at a man without wondering what he's capable of. I look at someone, and I imagine all the people he's killed. It's a useful skill. Keeps me on my toes."

Next was a young soldier, male, closer to twenty than thirty. He had fiery tribal tattoos snaking around his massive biceps. "People who love their lives are weak. They have something to lose." He busied himself opening a pack of cigarettes, avoiding eye contact. "I thank God for those battles. War made me strong. I don't fear death anymore. It came for me time and time again, and I survived. I can do anything now."

The footage made its way through all of the veterans in the support group, scoring profound soundbites from each of them. It was pretty amazing how they all opened up and poured out their souls to the camera, as if speaking to a lifelong confidant.

The truth was Jasmine had been meeting with this support group every week for nearly ten months—long before CinemaStream had contacted her—talking with them, building trust, trying to understand the culture of warfare. That was how she'd gotten them to open up to her. She hadn't mentioned this in the footage, though. She didn't want to give the impression that she was vain or proud.

The footage drew to a close. The last image was the oldest veteran in the group. He was shriveled, skeletal. He wasn't angry, he wasn't sad. He looked like he hadn't felt a genuine emotion in decades. His sunken eyes looked into the camera.

"There's nothing worth fighting for anymore. It's all common."

And with that...Cut to black. The end.

Jasmine exhaled and nodded quietly to herself. Oh yes...This was very good. Informative, raw, real, powerful.

With the footage over, the video call automatically popped back on her computer. Martin wasn't looking at her—instead, it seemed he was whispering to someone just off-screen. The volume was muted from his end.

"H-Hello?" she said. "Martin?"

He kept bickering silently, thousands of miles away.

Finally, after what felt like a year but had probably only been a minute, Martin turned his volume back on and faced her. "Hey, Jasmine." His nasally voice was wearing a mask of faux positivity.

Jasmine had heard that tone many times in her life. It was the voice of a drama teacher telling a child that "Villager #3" was a very important role, or a coach saying that an athlete has a lot of potential.

Sure enough:

"I see a lot of potential in your footage, Jasmine. I really do. As do the others who saw it."

"Okay..." Jasmine breathed and reoriented her internal expectations. "Yes, yes, yes, I see, I see. So...when you say potential...that means you're unhappy with its current form."

"Not unhappy, Jasmine, certainly not." He was saying her name a lot. Bad sign. "Believe it or not, this is just as we planned. We wanted to get a handle on your filmmaking talents, then talk about tone and content."

She nearly rolled her eyes at the "according to plan" line, but she remembered at the last second that this was a video call. "So all that footage I worked on isn't going to be used?"

Martin scratched his beard and paused, thought for a moment, then answered. "Jasmine, we're not looking for an exposé or a heavy documentary. We want to put viewers on the battlefield, experiencing warfare in a way they likely never will. We want them to get out of the spectators' seats and be right in the middle of the action."

She mulled that over and again said, "Okay..."

"You're not fired, we're not letting you go. You're still the creative engine behind this series. But we need you to...up the ante. That's a saying in England, right?"

"I know what it means," she said, perhaps too briskly.

"Great." Martin nodded once. "Also, one teensy-tippy-tiny detail. We'll want you shooting in America. Just one of those things. Our viewers aren't going to be riveted by the soldiers of Stratford-upon-Avon, y'know? So we'll get you on a flight out here, pair you up with one of our camera crews, and we'll talk more then. Alright? Cheers!" And his hairy face disappeared.

Jasmine stood up from the desk, her limbs numb and wobbly. She'd been so certain of that work. It was emotional and honest.

Coffee was in order.

No—screw it. A cup of tea. With lots of honey. She didn't care if it was agonizingly English. *She* was agonizingly English. She hadn't poked fun at Martin's Brooklyn accent or anything.

She shook her head to dismiss the thoughts.

Like it or not, they were her employers.

If they wanted her to up the ante, that's exactly what she'd do.

Salvatore entered the dark, dingy bar. It was about three in the afternoon—anyone drinking at this time of day either had a very good reason or none at all.

A low, droning, twangy song about a man losing his pick-up truck made Salvatore want to rip his ears off, but he soldiered on. He slouched his way to the wooden bar and sat down.

Today, he wore his thick glasses, ill-fitting khakis, and discount sneakers. He was going for maximum pathetic-ness. He needed to relate with those getting drunk while the sun was still awake.

And there he was, wilting at the bar. The man Salvatore had come here to talk to. The man was a few dozen pounds overweight, balding, wearing a Hawaiian shirt. He nursed what seemed to be his fourth beer, staring into the glass as if the winning lotto numbers were at the bottom.

Salvatore ordered a vodka tonic but didn't drink any yet. He looked over at his tipsy neighbor. "Oliver, is it?"

The rotund man stiffened, recognizing his name, but he didn't look at Salvatore.

"Oliver, my name is Sal, and I'd like to help you. I'm a recruiter for Valkyrie Productions—that's a global warfare enterprise, if you're not familiar. Now, your wife Kelsey had an affair, yes?"

"...Ex-wife." Oliver took a long drink.

Salvatore knew that Oliver and Kelsey had divorced. In fact, they had signed the papers just an hour before. But he'd wanted to make Oliver say it.

"And your ex-wife Kelsey, she had an affair with a man named Joe? Joe DeMarco?"

Oliver finally looked at Salvatore, jaw clenched, eyes blazing. "Oh yeah, wise guy? You wanna chat about my ex-wife and the dude she snuck around with?" He was actually frightening when he was mad. The vein in his forehead looked like a hungry snake. "What do you know about it, huh?"

Salvatore replied calmly. "I know enough. What I *do* know is that Joe DeMarco recently joined an army called the El Capitan Cobras. And the Army of Liberty, which is owned by Valkyrie, is going to fight them in two weeks." He paused as Oliver absorbed the information.

The sad, half-drunk divorcee slowed his breathing. His eyes went from fiery to icy. Sinister. Plotting.

Salvatore nodded. "If you signed up today, you'd be able to go through the process in the nick of time to..." He chose his words carefully. "...have your shot at Joe DeMarco. It'll be a chaotic battlefield. No one will notice if you target one man in particular."

He took a sip of his vodka tonic—which was just water. He came to his bar often, and the bartenders knew how he liked his drinks while he was working.

"I'll leave my card with you, Oliver. Think about it—"

"I wanna sign up now." Oliver finished his beer and looked Salvatore straight in the eye. "Give me a gun and put me within a hundred yards of that skunk...He'll be sorry he ever met me."

Salvatore pulled out one of the recruitment contracts he always carried with him. "I've no doubt, my friend."

❧

Annie sat in the back seat of a massive suburban. SUV? Humvee? She wasn't really into cars.

It was quiet except for the whirring engine and the occasional sniffle from the driver. Must be allergy season.

She was covered in bruises and scrapes from her intense workouts. It had only been a week since Elena Winn had found her on that San Diego beach, but it felt much longer. The handful of days had been filled with nothing but dozen-mile runs, deadlifts, and raw egg smoothies. She had thought she was in the upper echelon of athleticism, but now she knew there was quite a ways to go before she would become a Greek god in the eyes of the public...like Ranger Monroe had been.

The car was on its way to a battle stadium in southern California. Her first round of combat as captain of the Army of Liberty was only a few short hours away.

Elena's words crested in Annie's head again and again. "Tonight, you'll introduce yourself to the world."

The world. Annie wanted to throw up.

She'd stayed up several nights, studying the battle's layout over and over, as if her life depended on it. Because it did. It wasn't in the plan for her to die tonight...but Ranger getting his brains blown out hadn't been scripted either.

"Trust Elena," she whispered to herself. "Trust her."

Yeah, right.

Annie liked Elena. But she didn't trust her, and she likely never would.

Elena Winn was wickedly smart, and smartly wicked. She had a knack for envisioning battles like a painter filling a blank canvas. And only a person with zero regard for human life could do that as well as she did. A master chess player doesn't have an emotional attachment to her pawns— that's just how it is.

As such, Annie was nervous. Not only was her public career and reputation in the hands of Elena Winn—so was her life.

The driver sniffed again and rubbed his nose raw.

Hot cocoa usually helped Annie when her allergies turned her head into a bag of hay. But she didn't know this guy. She was terrible at small talk, so she hadn't said anything when she climbed in a half-hour ago. It would be weird for the first thing she ever said to him to be about hot cocoa. So she kept her mouth shut, and they drove on in silence.

Eventually, the car rolled to a stop. Annie's door opened from the outside, and a worker with a clipboard quickly ushered her into the stadium. The door slammed shut, and the car revved away.

Annie was shoved through the stadium's landing grounds until she reached a massive concrete anteroom. The whole of the Army of Liberty milled about, dressed and ready to go. On the far side of the room was an opening that led directly onto the battlefield. The ceiling was tall, and the army's hundreds of voices bounced around like metal tennis balls.

She panicked for a minute. Was she supposed to be in uniform, ready to take the field?

But her panic subsided when she saw Elena approaching. Elena knew what was going on, as always.

She twiddled her fingers at Annie in a mischievous wave. "Evening, captain."

"Hello, Ms. Winn." Annie didn't have a snappy response prepared, so she stuck with a professional one.

Elena smirked at Annie's stiffness. At least, that's what Annie thought Elena was smirking at.

"You're never going to call me Elena, are you?"

Just then, a wiry man wearing a bow tie started screaming at the army. "Everyone, everyone, shut up and listen, okay?!" He was partially bald, but it seemed he hadn't been that way a few days ago. He wiped his sweaty forehead and fanned himself. "Gather around now, you brutes!"

Annie began congregating with the rest of the army, but Elena put a hand on her shoulder. "Nope," she said. "You hang back with me."

"Who is that?" Annie asked.

"That pocket-protector in human form is the director of the overall battle. Don't listen to him. He's not that important. *I'm* important because I'm in charge of *you*."

Elena drew Annie to the side of the anteroom, and they went over the battle layouts one last time.

Tonight, Annie Kennedy was making her debut as the Army of Liberty's captain, and she was going to lead her men against an army named...

"The Demons Ex Machina."

Annie groaned. The name was so overly masculine and cheesy.

Fittingly, the army itself was also overly masculine and cheesy.

To prepare for the battle, Annie had spent the last week researching the Demons' strategies, generals, and persona. The Demons prided themselves on their villainous reputation, and they did everything they could to cultivate it. Their uniforms were leather and covered in chains. The general held press conferences in garbage dumps and trash-talked their opponents. Their insignia was a red skull with chainsaws instead of crossbones.

Every detail she learned made her hate them more. They were the perfect enemy for Annie to thrash right out of the gate.

"And there's a twist," Elena said with an arched eyebrow. "A grand finale to your grand debut."

"A twist?" Annie said. "Can we change battle layouts this soon?"

"I don't know who this *we* is, but *I* can." She pulled out a sheet of paper and showed Annie. "I made a deal with the Demons last week, and they recruited this guy. Within a few days, he was promoted to general. You're gonna kill him to end the battle, and the Demons will vow vengeance or something stupid, and we'll spin a grand story over the course of many battles to come."

Annie read the sheet with wide eyes. "Good Lord..."

Elena cackled. "I know, right? The people are gonna love it. You'll be the biggest star in military history in a matter of hours."

The ground seemed to tremor beneath Annie's feet. Was that the audience in the stadium shaking the whole foundation? No one else acted as if anything were wrong. Maybe she was just a little off-balance. She needed to sit for a second. She needed air...

"Places, everyone!" The bow-tied director yelled at the army as he waved his arms. "Three minutes!"

A few soldiers muttered in response, "Thank you, three."

Annie rolled her shoulders in an attempt to loosen up. She donned her uniform jacket, buckled her belt, and strapped on her weapons and ammo. Altogether, the ensemble was heavy, to be sure, but not nearly as heavy as she'd expected. Her nurse's bag and equipment had been more cumbersome.

Elena noticed her surprise. "Your uniform is designed to hinder you as little as possible. We wanted full mobility that wouldn't put any undue stress on your condition."

Oh. Right. Annie set a hand on her stomach. "Thank you."

Microphone feedback echoed throughout the anteroom. A man wearing a suit sauntered into the center of the army, waving and slapping backs and laughing at jokes. The soldiers clapped and waved back.

The man stopped and adjusted the wireless mic taped to his face. "How's my favorite army doing tonight?" The concrete room erupted in cheers.

"For the new fighters with us, my name is Danny Carr, and I'm with Valkyrie Productions. Basically, my job is to make you all look *great*. How am I doing?"

The Army of Liberty went nuts, practically chanting Danny's name. Annie had never seen soldiers so enamored with an enterprise executive producer.

"I just want you all to know..." Danny fanned the cheers down, adopting a somber tone. "I can't thank you enough for stepping up tonight. You are carrying the flag Ranger Monroe gave his life for. Annie Kennedy... Where are you? Annie!" He dramatically looked around the room until his eyes locked on the new captain. "Annie, the Army of Liberty is a shining city on a hill, and you're its mayor now! Serve this army well, and it'll serve you."

Annie could see why the soldiers loved Danny so much. He had an undeniable charm, as if he had traveled across the world to talk to no one else.

"And to all of you," he addressed the army as a whole again, "I'm sure you know...Annie has a bun in the oven! Yes, yes! Protect and serve her as your captain, of course, no doubt. But also protect and serve her child. We have a Niece or Nephew of Liberty on the way. We're this child's family...and family members would die for each other, right?"

The entire army nodded. Some had tears in their eyes. Annie couldn't believe it. Somehow, these complete strangers had just agreed to die for her unborn child, if need be.

In that moment, she felt like the most powerful person in earth. It was terrifying. And thrilling.

"Also, my son recently joined this fine army, so watch his back while you're at it. And so!" Danny clapped once. "The world is watching. Give them a new hero!" He pumped his fists and jogged out of the anteroom.

The army was electrified. They vibrated in place, whooping and hollering like the Spartans about to make their last stand.

"Wow," Annie breathed.

"Eh," Elena shrugged, "he's a putz. Don't buy his snake oil."

Something tapped Annie's memory on the shoulder.

Danny Carr's son was in this army? Why did that name sound so familiar? She hadn't even heard of Danny until a minute ago. She'd been in Kansas her whole life, working for Born and Bred Productions.

An alarm blared and a red light flashed. Time to go. The army began surging through the opening, into the stadium's battlefield.

She had been in Kansas her whole life...except for her audition in Chicago. Where she'd met a guy named Zeke Smith...who the secretary had called "Zechariah Carr."

Bingo. Zeke must be Danny's son.

She craned her head all around, searching the mass of bodies for the familiar face. Zeke was in her army somewhere, and for some nebulous reason, she trusted him. She started to call out, "Zeke! Hey, Zeke—"

But an explosion drowned out her words and killed ten of her men. The battle had begun.

⁓⁓⁓

While Annie Kennedy was making her debut on the battlefield against the Demons Ex Machina, the sun was setting in West Amana, Iowa.

Vast plains. Few roads. Happy citizens. Usually, the sky would change from deep blue to rich violet, the fireflies might do their dance if they felt frisky, and night would take over peacefully.

Not anymore.

Massive floodlights illuminated the center of the tiny town. A granite obelisk stood watch, taller than most of the town's homes. There was a waist-high fence around the obelisk so no one could touch it or get too close. A man's face was etched into the stone—handsome yet relatable, stern yet tender.

The Ranger Monroe Memorial drew hundreds of thousands of visitors from every corner of the globe...and that was just on its opening day. Many citizens of West Amana had never even left Iowa, much less imagined the ocean of press, tourists, and mourners that had poured into their village over the past few days.

Vendors set up stalls to sell t-shirts and chili dogs. New businesses and hotels cropped up overnight. West Amana was hopping, and it likely would stay that way until Armageddon. It suddenly had to adapt to its role as "the home of Ranger Monroe."

As soon as the sun kissed the horizon, megawatt lights lit up the memorial so everyone could get a good shot of it for social media. Families got off a tour bus. Some were crying. Most were ooh-ing and aw-ing and taking selfies.

The last person to get off the bus could hardly walk. He wore a long coat and a hat pulled over his face. If someone looked closely enough, they could see pink hair sticking out from under the hat. But no one looked that closely.

Claude von Cloude staggered through the crowd. He could barely stay on his feet. The former soldier had more alcohol in his body than blood.

He approached the memorial and climbed over the short fence. Still, no one paid much attention. A few moms grumbled about drunks ruining their vacation.

The night was cool. Breezy. Claude took off his hat and dropped it as he walked. He wanted to feel the wind in his unwashed hair.

He stopped next to the obelisk and put a shaky hand on the granite. He reached his other hand into his coat and pulled out a nickel-plated Colt pistol. The one he'd used in battle for decades.

"I'm thinking of better times..." he said to the breeze.

He put the barrel under his chin and fired.

Left, right, left, right...

Annie had to focus on running. If she didn't, she would curl into a ball and wait for the hellfire around her to go away.

She had been in battles before. Plenty of them. But there was something different about being a soldier, carrying a gun, and being the target of another army's wrath.

Bullets filled the air. Dirt exploded from the ground. The coppery stench of blood burned her nostrils.

A man in a leather uniform leapt in front of her and unleashed a war cry. One of the Demons. He had a red handprint painted on his face, and his hair was spiked to be shaped like a middle finger.

"Hello from Hell, Madam Kennedy!" He pointed his rifle at her and pulled the trigger.

Instinct took over. She dropped to the ground and rolled to one side, splaying her legs as she moved. She kicked the Demon's ankles, and he tumbled over.

She stood over him and drew her handgun.

At that moment, she knew all eyes in the stadium were on her, either directly or via the jumbo screens. The microphone on her uniform was undoubtedly live.

What should she say? This was her introduction to the world. Should she be witty? Powerful? Benevolent?

She realized she'd been standing still for nearly ten seconds. The Demon looked up at her with crazed eyes.

"What?" he giggled and spat. "The hormones making you all mixed up? Huh, mommy? I think I left my maternity blanket back home—"

Annie shot him in the mouth, sheathed her pistol, readied her rifle against her shoulder, and moved on—all without saying a word.

The crowd was split. Some didn't know what to make of this stoic, non-speechifying warrior. But most loved it. They cheered and hollered, and across the country, hundreds of fan clubs were formed.

One of her men called out to her, "On your six, captain!"

She spun around to find a Demon behind her, whom she quickly dispatched. She held up a fist to communicate her thanks, and she kept moving closer to the center of the battlefield.

A pack of six enemy soldiers descended upon her, cackling and crazed. "Found her!" They all slung their rifles across their backs and grabbed auxiliary weapons from holsters on their calves.

Annie wasn't sure at first what was going on. But once she realized, she couldn't help but roll her eyes.

The six Demons flicked their weapons on. *Brringinginging*...The soldiers hollered and waved mini-chainsaws around like they were new toys opened on Christmas morning.

The buzzing sound made Annie's ears ring. She tried to put a Demon in her rifle's sights, but the group fanned out, encircling her. A cyclone of death.

Literally. Annie had watched tapes of previous Demon battles, and they dubbed this very tactic the "Cyclone of Death."

Overly masculine and cheesy to a T.

The best way to overcome this maneuver, Annie had learned from her research, was for two soldiers to stand back-to-back and blast away. Unfortunately, Annie was very much alone. And the Demons relished it.

"Need help, little lady?"

"Ready to die?"

"You never *chainsaw* this coming, didja?"

That last one elicited boos from the audience, but the Demons drank up the hatred. It seemed to make them even rowdier. They hopped around and babbled like they were possessed.

But while they were distracted, intoxicated by their own idiotic egos, another soldier leapt into the middle of their cyclone. A soldier with an American flag on his shoulder.

He got his bearings and stood back-to-back with Annie. He nodded sharply and said, "On your mark, captain."

Annie smiled. This guy had done his homework too. "Fire."

The two soldiers of liberty gunned down the chainsaw-wielding Demons. The crowd's cheers were even louder than the bullets and the buzzing.

"Well done." Annie turned to her companion and found the familiar face she had been looking for.

"You got it, ma'am." Zeke Smith grinned at her and saluted. He fell into position beside her, weapon at the ready.

Annie checked her clip. "Thanks for the assist...Mr. Carr."

Zeke shot her a look. Even with a battle erupting all around him, someone using his real name gave him pause. Then he smirked. "All right, Sherlock. We can talk more later."

"Cover my flank." She gave him another smile, then dove into the action one last time.

She was near the middle of the stadium. This is where the layout said she was to meet the Demons' new general and end the battle.

A grenade rolled across the dirt near her feet, so she dashed behind a barricade. After the explosion, she peeked over the short concrete wall... and something happened.

A small patch of ground in the dead-center of the field opened up, revealing a vertical tunnel leading down into the ground. Out of the tunnel rose a platform, and on the platform was a square-shaped man in a general's uniform.

Annie looked closer. The man's eyes were cast downward, so she couldn't get a good look at his face. He swayed on his feet as if he had just disembarked from a months-long boat ride. Despite the explosions and earsplitting carnage all around him, he seemed unfazed.

She caught a glimpse of his face. Yep...That was him. She recognized his mug from the sheet Elena had shown her.

Mac Donaghy. The Demons' newest recruit-turned-general. He had been enlisted specifically to face off against Annie Kennedy.

A death-row inmate. Imprisoned six years ago. For murdering a pregnant woman.

The long-range cameras zoomed in on Mac, and the jumbo screen flashed his stats for the audience to read. Seconds later, thousands of fans reacted in horror. They screamed, booed, hissed, and threw popcorn and beer cans.

All the way from the nosebleed seats, someone yelled, "Kill him, Annie!" The words rippled through the crowd, and before Annie knew it, a chorus of *"Kill him! Kill him!"* engulfed the stadium.

It looked like Mac had been drugged to keep him docile and compliant. Annie stood up from behind her hiding place and aimed her rifle.

The chants and jeers finally roused Mac from his stupor. His eyes were bloodshot, and he looked at the general's uniform on his own body like it was a leech. He couldn't catch his breath, seemingly gagging on air.

She flexed her finger around the trigger.

Mac's red eyes landed on her. "You..." he hissed. He must've been briefed by the Demons. Maybe he'd been told that if he killed her, his sentence would be reduced. Or maybe he'd been brainwashed into attacking her and only her. Or maybe he just wanted to cut loose and flex his murderous muscles for the first time in six years.

Maybe maybe maybe. Who knows?

Didn't matter to Annie. No matter the reason, Mac Donaghy charged straight at her, roaring and flailing, eyes flashing with the intent to kill.

But she had a rifle and he didn't.

She fired a round into his chest. Mac staggered for a few more steps, clutching his wound.

A thought crossed Annie's mind: She could shoot him one more time in the head or the heart to finish him off. The crowd wanted as much bloodshed as they could get, and they'd love her for it.

But she felt that one shot was good enough, and, even though Mac was still standing, she shouldered her weapon. A single bullet would do the job.

And moments later, Mac pulled in one last shuddering breath, then fell to the ground.

She walked off the field without so much as a speech or a snappy one-liner.

The audience applauded and cheered and hailed their new hero. A legend was born.

Annie Kennedy. The maternal warrior.

General Richard Lightfoot sat in his favorite recliner, eyes closed, listening to the Bee Gees. It was his favorite recliner for two reasons: One, it reclined very far back, to the point that his feet were elevated above his head; and two, there was a cup-holder built into both armrests, so he could have two servings of black coffee at the same time. He wasn't hard to please.

He usually fell asleep very easily. His third wife called him the Quickest Snooze in the West. He didn't find that very funny, but he was usually half-asleep when she said it, so he let it slide...until one day he didn't, and his third wife became his third ex. He was on his sixth wife now, if his memory served.

Anyway, he was usually a quick sleeper, but not tonight. Tonight, the roar from the stadium kept him up, so he'd flipped on the Bee Gees music and enjoyed that instead. He had no idea what was going on out there, but the audience clearly liked whatever it was.

Pop culture had passed him by decades before, and he'd stopped trying to keep up. He drank his coffee black, did his crossword puzzles, sat in his chair, listened to the hundred-year-old golden-oldie music he knew he liked, and waddled into the stadium whenever someone with a headset told him to. He took his bow and went home, trusting that he'd get his check the following Friday.

He still got checks every week. He didn't trust "digital money," whatever that was. And he liked signing them upon depositing.

Speak of the devil. A lady approached him and caught his attention.

"The battle is concluded, General Lightfoot."

"Right-o." He clicked a button, and the diagonal recliner whirred as it righted itself. It took a minute, but he eventually got back on his feet.

The lady led him through the landing grounds, into the bloody, thunderous stadium. Bodies covered the ground, and he had to take a circuitous route to get to the middle of the field. His legs weren't what they used to be, so he couldn't step over the corpses. But he didn't complain. That was one thing he was very good at—not making a fuss. He hated it when old people complained all of the time.

When he reached the center of the battlefield, he found himself face-to-face with a porcupine. No, wait...It was a twenty-year-old chump with more piercings in his face than a voodoo doll. The chump stuck his tongue out at Lightfoot, then spat in his palm before offering it to the Army of Liberty's general.

"Put 'er there, Foot-Fungus," the rival general sneered.

"Oh, right. Morons," Lightfoot muttered to himself. He'd forgotten they were fighting the Demons today. He would've brought some disposable gloves. But he shook the other general's hand, waved to the crowd, and walked away—no fuss.

Usually, the crowd had quieted down by now. But not tonight. They were still whooping and wailing, trembling in their seats with enough energy to power a city.

Something special had happened here. For the first time in his memory, Lightfoot wished he'd watched the live feed of the battle.

He squinted a little to see which set of soldiers was his. Once he caught sight of the little Stars-and-Stripes on the shoulders, he hobbled toward his fighters. He wanted to ask someone what had happened.

The soldiers were just as excited as the people in the stands. They pumped their fists and fired celebratory shots into the air. Each crack of a rifle sent them into a tizzy, and they let out a cheer: "Hah! Hoo! Annie's coming for you!"

Lightfoot recognized that as one of the Army of Liberty's typical battle chants. But why were they saying that *after* the fighting was finished?

He moved through the army, and as he got closer to the center, the air vibrated more and more. An electric current filled the atmosphere, as if he'd shuffled across a carpet while wearing his slippers.

At the heart of the army stood a woman. A largely unremarkable woman, if Lightfoot wanted to be honest. She wasn't the most muscular, nor the prettiest, and her persona didn't radiate charm or likability. While the soldiers hollered and laughed and whirled all around her, she stood still, almost frozen, taking it all in with steely eyes.

And that was what struck General Lightfoot. She sparked enthusiasm, even as she herself was rigid and solid. This woman was a lightning rod.

He fought the tidal wave of bodies and stood in front of her. "Good win tonight. I'm Richard Lightfoot," he said, trying to be heard over the yelling. He offered his left hand, the one that didn't contain the Demon general's spit.

A hush fell over the Army of Liberty.

The woman shook his hand, and a wry smile tugged at her lips. A smile that suggested she knew the whole army was waiting to hear her voice.

"Captain Kennedy, sir. Annie Kennedy."

The subsequent cheers were deafening.

Lightfoot had seen a lot in his ninety-eight years on the big blue marble called Earth. He'd caught snowflakes on his tongue on the peak of Kilimanjaro. He'd cradled a tiger's head in his lap as the magnificent beast died of old age. He'd been to almost every country, influenced global events, and met close to a million people. And he'd fought in wars—real wars, before the fancy bureaucrats and show-business people got involved.

Even after all that, he had never witnessed such a reaction. He'd never heard an army cheer so loud. He'd never seen soldiers so enamored with a commanding officer. And, thus, he'd never met a captain with such power over her army.

The factory was dark. Quiet. Empty.

Made sense. It was three in the morning, after all. The whole city was dark and quiet.

Jody crept through the shadows, feeling a quiver in his stomach. A tingly combo of nerves, excitement, and pure adrenaline. He let out a childlike giggle, and the noise rippled throughout the metal and concrete building. It was likely his Invisible Dagger cohorts heard it, from the rafters to the storage closets.

He shone his flashlight around and saw a steel column, running from the ceiling to the floor. He wasn't an engineer, so he figured that was as good a spot as any. He set the bomb he was carrying at the base of the column and walked away.

The leader of the group had assigned him the southwest corner of the factory. If in twenty minutes, when all the bombs exploded, the southwest corner was still standing, Jody would get a stern talking-to.

He ran his hand over his shaved scalp as he walked through the dark factory. And he smiled. He may not be an engineer or a tactician, but he was a good talker. He was the face of Invisible Dagger, the hottest domestic terror group in the U.S.

Even in the darkness, he was wearing the outfit he wore in all their online videos: a loose-fitting hoodie and athletic pants. He was trying to make these clothes, along with his bald head, his *thing*. His buddy Staten, though, said that baldness and a hoodie weren't enough to be a *thing*.

"You need a face tattoo of a bloody knife," Staten had said one day while they were simultaneously working out and brainstorming iconic looks, "or a double-hook-hand, or earrings with medieval flail balls dangling from them." And then they'd all started laughing at the phrase "medieval flail balls," and the conversation was sidetracked.

Jody thought the elegance was in the simplicity. Everyone could copy his look, if they so chose. Anyone could be part of Invisible Dagger if they owned a razor and lived near a thrift shop.

Besides, online fans had already posted photos of them dressing like him. Shaved heads, hoodies, and sweatpants. Boom. Easy. He'd seen dozens of photos on the internet—people dressed like him showing off their rifles, people dressed like him setting crap on fire, people dressed like him mooning governmental buildings. His look was catching on.

And Invisible Dagger was just getting started. He couldn't imagine what their influence would be like at their peak.

Speaking of which.

He'd almost forgotten. He dug his phone out of his baggy pocket, flipped on its flashlight, and held it up so he could film his own face as he walked. With a few button-taps, he was streaming live to Invisible Dagger's hundreds of subscribers.

"What's up, Daggsters? It's your main man Jody here!" He cheesed for the camera.

The group had debated for hours on end about what to call their fans. Jody liked "Daggsters" the best—quick, snappy, easy to understand. Roderick, who was the group's resident marketing guru, preferred the nickname "Vizzies." Other prospective names included "Stabbing Squad," "Level Reds," and "Lil Terrors."

But Jody was the face of the crew, and as far as he saw it, what he said was what their subscribers heard.

"How's everyone doing tonight? Or is it this morning? Whatever. If you're watching live right now, that's because you're a part of our VIP inner circle, and you've picked up the clues we've dropped online. Well, congrats, Daggsters! You figured out we'll be up to no good on this day at this time, so I've got a treat for you."

He flipped the camera to front-facing and got a shot of the dark, silent factory. The lighting wasn't great, but it only served to enhance the mysterious aesthetic, which made the viewers at home feel like they were privy to a secret, like they were co-conspirators along with the Invisible Dagger crew.

"Here we are at Curtail Manufacturing, in Baltimore, Maryland. One of the country's leading producers of..." His mind blanked, and he was glad the camera was still facing the factory, so the viewers couldn't see his flat expression. "Umm, I think, maybe auto parts? Microchips? Vending machines...?" He trailed off—he couldn't remember. Didn't matter. He improvised for the audience. "Regardless, this factory is a pillar of this nation. One we aim to knock down, and usher in the reckoning it so deserves!"

In a pinch, he could always fall back on buzzwords. Roderick had drilled the word "reckoning" into everyone's brain, so that Jody sometimes jolted awake muttering it. He wasn't exactly sure what it meant, but he had a close enough idea.

"In twenty minutes," he continued, flipping the camera back around to himself, "this factory will be blown to bits! It'll be a sight to see. If you're in the Baltimore area, come on out. Snap some pics and use the hashtag 'reckoning.' And as always, let us know where you think we should go next!"

He signed off and made it to the center of the factory, where the rest of Invisible Dagger waited for him. Four men, including himself. Just a handful, in the grand scheme of things, but that actually made Jody even more confident. They were small but swift—daggers.

Plus, they couldn't convince any of their other friends to join them when they'd first had this idea. And now that they were suddenly successful, their leader had decided to keep their ranks closed, like an exclusive nightclub.

A slim man with a hideous scar from his right temple to his left lip sighed at Jody. He crossed his arms. "C'mon, Jody, we have a schedule. If we're slow getting out of here, we'll be late setting off the charges."

This was their leader, the brains behind Invisible Dagger: Holland. He was probably the smartest guy Jody knew. Holland always knew where to go and what to do. Jody had no idea how, but Holland was the guy who could get things done, no matter what. He had assembled them into a team. He supplied them with guns and ammo. He got the vehicles they needed. He'd mapped out the plan for the Boston blackout, and he'd even come through with the technical gadgets they needed to pull that off.

Holland, the brains.

Staten, the muscles.

Roderick, the eyes.

Jody, the voice.

Together, Invisible Dagger.

"I know, I know," Jody huffed.

Rod spoke up. "It's good to keep the viewers updated, though. Make 'em feel included."

Staten nodded in agreement.

"It's more important," Holland said, "to be on time. Reliability will lead to loyalty." He started walking out of the factory.

Staten nodded in agreement at that too, and they all followed their leader out.

The bright moon greeted them, unobscured by clouds. It must have seen Jody's livestream, and it wanted a clear view of the explosion that had been promised.

The four terrorists wound their way through the city streets on foot, so as not to draw any attention on traffic cams. Once they were far enough away, they stopped in an alley, and Holland withdrew an electronic trigger. He stared at it longingly, but eventually handed it to Jody.

Jody, in exchange, passed Holland his phone. Staten and Rod used their flashlights to illuminate Jody.

Holland cleared his throat and pointed the phone's camera at Jody. "Okay, three, two..."

Jody once again donned his on-camera persona, smiling impishly and talking like he was trying to be heard over a windstorm. "What's up, Daggsters? It's—"

"Stop, stop," Holland shook his head. "There's graffiti on the wall behind you."

Jody turned to look. Yep—on the bricks behind him was a crude drawing of a wiener. Holland had insisted from the beginning that Invisible Dagger's content be PG-rated, so that parents would be okay letting their kids be fans. Jody moved a few feet down the wall, then started again.

"What's up, Daggsters? It's your main man Jody again. Lookie at what I've got!" He held the trigger up so that it was lit up by the others' flashlights. "That's right—the button that'll blow the Baltimore factory sky-high." (He perfectly avoided the fact that he'd forgotten the name of the factory.) "I bet you want me to push it. Well, so do I. Buuuuuuuut...Only if this live video hits a thousand likes, and our channel gets five hundred new subscribers!"

"Three hundred subscribers," Holland corrected from behind the camera.

"That's what I said," Jody kept on rolling. "So wake up your friend, send 'em this link. You want to see these fireworks, don't you? Smash that like button and get everyone you know on the Daggster bandwagon!"

Within minutes, they hit their goals, but Rod motioned for Jody to keep selling. Couldn't hurt to wring a few more subscribers out of the situation.

But Holland shot Rod a piercing glare, the scar on his face like a coiled snake ready to strike. *"Reliability,"* his eyes seemed to say. *"We need to keep our word!"*

So Jody set his finger on the button. "Aha! Looks like we've hit our numbers! Way to go! Now, count down with me. Three...two...one!"

He pressed the button, and the cases of explosives set in the Curtail Manufacturing factory detonated. The whole building turned into a massive fireball, shattering windows and cracking sidewalks for blocks.

Baltimore woke up. Police sirens blared, and cars zoomed toward the destruction.

Invisible Dagger watched it all on the news in their motel room.

Annie opened the front door and stepped into the empty house.

Her legs and shoulders were still sore from the battle last night. Actually, to be more accurate, her legs and shoulders were still sore from the immense party following her debut battle last night. After the battle, the entire stadium had been invited to stay (except for the Demon army, of course), and the celebration had gone until the sunrise. Music blared, booze flowed, and soldier and civilian alike rejoiced the arrival of their new captain.

Insane, marathon parties like that really weren't Annie's style. She had put in some face-time, taken selfies with hundreds of drunk fans, and given a five-word thank-you speech before calling it a night. On her way out, she'd looked for Zeke among the throng, but no such luck.

Now, she massaged her neck as she tiptoed through the house's barren halls.

The idea of living in Ranger Monroe's home in San Diego made her shiver, but Elena and Danny Carr had insisted. It was all part of the image—the new captain of the Army of Liberty symbolically taking the fallen hero's place.

The house was sleek and chrome, and it made Annie feel like she was in the kitchen section of a hardware store. She half-expected to see price tags on everything and a sales associate asking her if she needed help.

Swimming pools and hot tubs. Massive closets and plush mattresses. Wall-sized TVs and ear-splitting speakers. Storerooms, grills, and ten-foot-tall fridges. Guest rooms, guest baths, and even guest garages. It was staggering.

She had never seen a place as nice as this with her own two eyes, much less had the key in her pocket. Being a war hero had its advantages.

Her footfalls echoed in the big empty house, like heartbeats in outer space. Luckily, the press and bloggers didn't know she'd moved in yet, so she had some peace and quiet for at least a few hours. She could unpack, unwind, maybe try out the three-sixty-degree shower in the master bathroom...

But then, more feet joined hers on the buffed flooring. *Clip-clap, clip-clap*. Elena Winn rounded a corner, appearing from within the house, as if she had been there for hours and had been expecting Annie much sooner. Her gait was as smooth as a snake's—her sharp earrings barely moved as she walked.

"Morning, Annie," she smiled.

Annie had spent years trying to iron the emotion of shock out of her instincts, so she merely nodded. "Ma'am."

"Your debut against the Demons last night was..." She kissed the tips of her fingers like a chef. "Marvelous. We'll debrief more in the car."

"The car? Why? Where—?"

"We have a meeting with Danny Carr at the Valkyrie Productions office in an hour."

Annie had wanted to try out that shower before the day got too crazy, but it looked like that wasn't going to happen.

Elena seemed to read her mind. "I'll have some big brawny men unpack your things and get the place arranged, so you can enjoy it tonight." She took long strides out of the ajar front door, and Annie followed. "And I'll call in some cleaners. It'll take tubs of bleach and air freshener to get that old-lady smell out of there."

Annie cocked a brow as they approached a limo waiting for them. The doors popped open automatically. "Old lady?"

"Yeah," Elena exhaled as she slid into her seat and shut the door. Annie got in too, and the car took off.

Elena took a slip from a hydroflask, then finished her thought. "Monroe's mother lived in her own wing of the house. She was relocated to a nursing home nearby. El Cajon, or some such place."

A lump of guilt roosted in Annie's gut. She didn't like the idea of kicking a bereaved woman out of her home...her *son's* home. But Elena didn't allow enough time for the guilt to take root.

"So how far along are you?" Her eyes flitted to Annie's stomach.

Annie opened her mouth to answer...but only air came out. No one had asked her that question yet, and she hadn't prepared a BS timeline of the pregnancy. She stammered, "I, a couple, uh..."

Elena chuckled coyly. "I see. Let's say..." She looked out the window at the city zipping past them. "Six weeks."

Annie went on the offensive to cover up her gaffe. "What do you mean 'let's say'? I'm *seven* weeks along, for your information."

Elena winked. "Sure you are. Whatever you say."

Annie wanted to fight, to argue, to keep up the façade of her pregnancy, but it was clear the jig was up. Elena obviously knew the pregnancy wasn't real, a mere prop in her warfare career.

But she was going along with it anyway.

Elena began to think out loud, making notes to herself. "We're gonna need to have a gender reveal party soon. Get all the bloggers and reporters to cover it. Then we'll start a social media campaign to name the kid."

"No." Annie put her foot down. "I won't have random people on the internet decide my baby's name."

Elena looked at her with a knowing glint in her eyes. Without even opening her mouth, she managed to say, *What, you want to be the one to name your fake baby?* She looked Annie up and down, then nodded. "All right. You can name it. But we have to build it up, make it a big deal."

Annie let out a breath—part frustration, part relief. "Fine." She felt a moment of panic, and she craned her neck to look at the driver's seat. She hadn't even thought about there being a witness to this conversation...but the seat was empty. There wasn't even a steering wheel.

Elena bobbed her head. "My limo is self-manned. No one ever overhears what I say in here. It's like my own confessional booth, where I'm the confessor and the priest." She laughed.

And Annie smiled too. Elena gave her the willies, to be sure, but Annie was very glad they were on the same team.

Danny's day was already starting off strong.

He bellowed into his phone. "Is it cleaned off?"

Last night, during one of the greatest triumphs in the Army of Liberty's already-triumphant career, something had happened in Podunk-Nowhere, Iowa. An old army veteran from a bygone era had blown his brains all over Ranger's brand-new memorial.

Cable news had been speculating for hours about the possible motives of the suicidal man, but no one had presented any theories beyond the usual conspiratorial fluff. Everyone was abuzz—blood had a way of doing that, especially outside of an arena, where it wasn't "supposed" to be.

For the record, Danny didn't know the man's motives either. Nor did he care. He just needed the memorial to be open to the public. The day after Captain Annie Kennedy's heroic introduction, there were bound to be thousands of people flocking to Monroe's monument, either out of hatred for the woman who had taken his place or out of excitement for the Army of Liberty's future.

But he was currently on the phone with the manager of the memorial in Iowa. Apparently, a local church had reservations about opening the exhibit to the masses so soon after a death had occurred on the premises.

The manager cleared his throat and answered Danny's question. "Well, yes, Mr. Carr. The...mess has been cleaned off the obelisk, and the whole area has been disinfected."

"Then I don't see the issue!" Danny paced behind his desk. His drawbridge. "Those people want to pay their respects to a *hero*. A *legend*. The one and only Ranger Monroe. And there's no way in hell an elderly, no-name veteran with mental health issues who happened to splatter his depression all over our new memorial is going to stop them."

"The man had mental health issues?"

"As soon as I call into a few cable news shows, yeah, he did." Before he hung up, he had one last idea. "Crank up the price of admission to the memorial today and say the proceeds will go to a charity TBA." He hung up and flopped in his chair.

Little known fact: Valkyrie owned and operated an organization called "To Buy Ammo." "TBA." Anytime they publicly said funds would go to a charity TBA, their stockpile of ammunition got that much larger.

And his end-of-year bonus got a little bigger too...which meant he was that much closer to adding another penthouse to his collection.

Suzanne strolled into the office, brandishing her almighty tablet. "Your eight-thirty is here."

Danny nodded absently, but then paused. "Wait, who? I don't have a meeting until ten."

"Yes you do." She showed the schedule on the tablet's screen to confirm. "Elena Winn and Captain Kennedy."

"I didn't set that up. Did you?" He stood and straightened his tie.

"You would know if I set something up." She tapped the screen and turned to leave. "I'll send them in."

"Hold on." Danny came around his desk and stood next to Suzanne. "Stay." Something about the Winn woman made him want backup.

Suzanne nodded to her boss as the two visitors entered the office.

Winn and Kennedy, side-by-side, lock-step. Danny sized them up but couldn't get a clear reading. Kennedy's face was that of a Roman statue—solid, militaristic, and intimidating. And Winn—well, based on Danny's previous two meetings with her, she was always inscrutable.

"Morning, ladies," he said. He kept his tone light, despite the fact that he deeply disliked the idea of this meeting appearing without his say-so. "To what do I owe the pleasure?" Winn opened her mouth to speak, but Danny quickly cut her off, addressing Kennedy instead. An old trick he'd learned long ago. "Oh, Captain Kennedy, before I forget, well done last night! Thrashing those D-holes really set the right tone for what's to come in your career."

At the edge of his vision, Danny saw Winn ripple and grimace. Bingo.

To her credit, Kennedy politely redirected. "Thank you, sir, but I'm only as victorious as my fellow soldiers, the battle directors, and my personal director, Ms. Winn." She passed the verbal baton to Winn.

"Early this morning," Winn began, her eyes boring into Danny's, "while the world celebrated Captain Kennedy's introduction, something happened. Something sinister, which slipped under the radar."

Danny sighed. "What, you're all broken-up about the suicidal vet too? The memorial is cleaned! What more can we do?"

Clearly, neither Winn nor Kennedy knew what he was talking about.

Winn shook her head a little, as if batting away an annoying moth, which Danny didn't like at *all*.

She continued. "In Baltimore, at three-thirty a.m. local time, multiple bombs detonated inside a factory, leveling it to the ground. No casualties, but not for lack of trying, it seems."

Annie asked, "What does that mean?" Danny had the same question, but he was glad he hadn't been forced to be the one to inquire.

Winn explained, "There were more bombs planted in the factory's basements and storage, intended to collapse the surrounding streets. Other buildings and apartments would have been affected...but they didn't go off. One theory in the media is that the destruction of the factory proper created a sort of shelter around the bombs, shielding the world from their blasts. But the truth is, it was flat-out incompetence. Knuckle-dragging, good-old-fashioned idiocy."

Suzanne *tsk*'d and shook her head. "A dumb bomber is probably worse than a good one. Police would be able to predict a good one."

"Well, we don't need to be able to predict these guys."

Danny groaned. "Guys? This is a group we're talking about?"

"Can we sit down?" Winn gestured to the easy chairs next to the window overlooking the ocean. She gestured downward and shrugged. "Weak ankles."

Another old trick—rapidly changing the subject and asking for something right when a conversation got interesting. Danny didn't believe for a second that any part of Winn was weak, but he acquiesced.

As soon as they all settled in the plush seats, Winn asked Danny for a bottle of water. Again, being a gracious host, he complied by asking Suzanne to grab one. Suzanne, in turn, tapped her tablet, and ten seconds later, an intern appeared with four bottles of chilled Swiss water.

"So," Danny said as Winn took a sip, "why have you come into my office on this early morning to tell me about moronic factory-bombers on the other side of the country?" The unspoken question: *Why are you bothering me with things I don't care about?*

Winn finished her drink, then dug out her cell phone. She selected a video and turned the screen for Danny to see. Annie, who seemed to be entirely in the dark about this meeting, craned her neck to see as well.

"Meet..." Winn paused for dramatic emphasis. There was a reason she was such a successful director. "...Invisible Dagger."

Danny watched in dumbstruck amazement. A bald dingus named Jody spoke directly to the camera—or, more accurately, to the "Daggsters," fans of the group—as he bragged about blowing up the factory.

The guy had a soft face, and his voice had all the charm of an animatronic bear at a children's playplace. He was, in Danny's professional opinion, what Salvatore Caracas would call "first-wave fodder."

Winn set aside her phone and took another drink. "This is just one of fifty-eight videos Invisible Dagger has posted online. Their website has almost two thousand subscribers."

Suzanne thought aloud, "That's not that much."

"That number has doubled in the past week. They're gaining traction."

Danny rubbed his eyes. A viral domestic terrorism cell, posting online and gaining fans. As if there weren't enough crazies in the world. "What sort of lowlife loonies would be fans of terrorists? I mean, they're killers."

"Actually," Winn corrected, "they haven't taken any lives yet."

Quickly losing interest, Danny asked another question. "What's in the other fifty-seven videos?"

Winn answered, "The electrical blackout in Boston and this factory explosion in Baltimore are their two biggest hits. The rest are Q-and-A's and day-in-the-life kind of stuff. There are four of them: Jody, Holland, Roderick, and Staten, although Jody gets by far the most screen time. We don't have to worry about predicting them, like I said, because they post vlogs and updates everywhere they go."

"Hold on." Suzanne held up a finger, remembering something. "I saw someone on the beach wearing a shirt that said 'Invisible Dagger' a couple days ago. He had kids with him."

Winn nodded. "Their fans are very widespread. Data says the videos are watched on every continent."

Danny deadpanned, "Even Antarctica?"

"Penguins *love* these guys." She wasn't deadpanning—she seemed serious, which put Danny on edge for the first time. She added, "Their merch store sold out of shirts and keychains this morning, following the bombing. The website says they'll be adding bumper stickers and bullets with their faces on them."

When Danny checked his watch, he made no effort to hide it.

Suzanne took the more tactful route. "Ms. Winn, this is all very informative, but we have to ask...So what?" Well, at least the start of her sentence had been tactful. She even set down her tablet, signaling she had no intention of taking any action as a result of Winn's words—the ultimate Suzanne affront.

"Mr. Carr," Winn addressed Danny, ignoring Suzanne, "I'm not just the overseer of armies, battles, or marketing strategies anymore. I am in charge of Captain Annie Kennedy."

"Yes," Suzanne said, "we know that. We gave you that title."

"Think of your favorite action movie, Mr. Carr. Fistfights, foot chases, vehicles flying all over the place. How would you like to witness that before your very eyes? *And* you would never know when it was about to erupt. Full-scale immersion. A real-life thriller."

Suzanne sighed. "Yes, and the point?"

"The point is, that is what's next for spectatorship. Captain Kennedy's next mission is to take on Invisible Dagger."

Kennedy whipped her head to stare at Winn. "Thunderstruck" would be an understatement.

Danny couldn't contain a rough chuckle. He had never heard of anything like that, and for good reason. It was ludicrous. Impractical. Uncontrollable.

Part of him was mad he hadn't thought of it first.

Suzanne was the first to speak. "How is this possible? And by 'possible,' I mean 'legal.'"

Winn raised one sharp eyebrow. "I have a contact with the FBI. He says Invisible Dagger is all ours."

Danny scoffed. "You have a *contact* in the *FBI*? Pray tell, who?"

She only laughed. "I never pray and tell, Mr. Carr. And by the way..." She took Danny's bottle of water and sipped. Very slowly. Making him wait for her to finish her sentence. "...I'm not asking for permission. Don't worry, Captain Kennedy will still participate in your little wars, and she'll take photos and do interviews. But that will all be miniscule in comparison to the epic tale I'm going to weave. And if you get in my way, the public will eat you alive."

She stood. The meeting was over.

Danny wasn't used to being told the score—he usually made it himself. The experience left him a little winded, somewhat puzzled. But he liked it.

Kennedy, on the other hand, looked like she was going up the first hill of a roller coaster she just realized she didn't want to be on.

He gave her a reassuring smile, silently convincing her this was all a great idea. Partly because she was a good soldier, and he needed her to be confident. And partly because he couldn't wait to see if Winn's idea would work.

❧

General Lightfoot parked his car in the lot, cut the engine, and sat quietly for a minute. Towering trees surrounded the lot, and he enjoyed listening to the birds' music.

He ended up losing track of time. Finally, he hoisted himself out of the car, grabbed the grocery bag from the backseat, and shambled toward the Front Porch Retirement Center's entrance. He hit the *lock* button on his key fob—everyone kept telling him he needed to get an automated vehicle. Nowadays, they could drive and lock themselves, and the news said they were far safer than human-operated models. Lightfoot respected the data enough, but not the machines. There was no way he'd trust a computer to drive him around.

When he said things like that, people always had one of two reactions—they either scoffed and muttered something like "Crusty old man," or they sighed and muttered something like "Poor old man." Lightfoot wasn't a fan of either response.

Ever since war spectatorship sank its claws into the global culture, he'd noticed a severe decline in the elderly population. Most were cooped up in facilities like Front Porch, glued to their TVs and wearing extra-thick diapers. Lightfoot still lived in a house, with his current wife, and if there ever came a day when he too needed a nurse and a catheter, he was prepared to swallow a bullet. Being so feeble and infirm sounded like the lowest level of hell to him.

He waved until the automatic sliding doors did what they were supposed to do, and he moved through the lobby. It reminded him of a televangelist's bathroom, all chic tile and funky lighting. He reached the front desk and signed in as a guest.

A receptionist smiled at him. "Hello, General Lightfoot." She over-articulated every syllable, as if speaking to a deaf toddler. "I hope you're having a super day."

He nodded politely enough, then walked away.

She called after him. "Know where you're going?"

Again, he nodded. He'd been here dozens, if not hundreds, of times. He hated it when people treated him like he was senile. Helpless. Old.

The center smelled too clean. Regular places had residual odors, just from everyday living. Not here—it had a negative smell, as if all life had been sucked out of the air.

Retirement centers. He wanted to spit.

Room 117. He knocked once and went right in. If he waited for a response, he'd be standing there until he died...which admittedly could be at any point.

As usual, the room was dark, all lights off and shades pulled shut. He set his grocery bag on the counter and called out, "Leigh, where are ya?"

A wrinkled face peeked out of the bathroom. "Wh-What?" The man's voice tremored with the fear of someone who hadn't stepped outside in years. "Who is that?"

"It's Rich." Lightfoot pulled two bottles out of the bag—one jug of pineapple juice, another of Jack Daniels.

Leigh Gambol shuffled fully into view, wearing a plush bathrobe. The ten strands of hair he had left stuck out every direction, and he still had some of his breakfast stuck to his chin, but Lightfoot didn't make fun of him. The guy was even older than Lightfoot and almost blind, so grooming wasn't his priority.

Gambol was the president of Valkyrie Productions and one of the richest men in the country, but Lightfoot was his only frequent visitor. The rest of his family was either dead or off somewhere enjoying his money.

Decades ago, before either of them had made it big in the world of spectatorship, Richard Lightfoot and Leigh Gambol had met at a wedding in Monte Carlo. Gambol had been getting married to the sister of Lightfoot's second wife, and the two men formed a fast friendship. Even though Gambol was Lightfoot's ex-brother-in-law-in-law, they were closer than ever.

Lightfoot offered Gambol the fruit juice. "Bottoms up, buddy."

Gambol grasped the bottle with two skeletal hands. "I'm sorry? What is this?"

They eased onto a sofa, and Lightfoot said, "It's good for you. You drink that, I drink this, we're all happy." He tipped the whiskey into his mouth and sighed. "We're all happy."

"Okay..." Gambol quietly complied and drank. Despite having a porous memory, he'd learned to implicitly trust what Lightfoot said.

The two men sat in the dark room, and Lightfoot recounted the battle from the previous night. The battle that featured the most electrifying captain he'd ever seen. "Kendell. No, her name was...Kimmy? Aw drat, what was her name...?"

A line of juice dribbled down Gambol's chin. "Whose name?"

"Never mind, never mind." Lightfoot waved away the detail. The fact remained that the soldiers and audience had reacted to her in a way he'd never experienced before, and that's what he told Gambol. He loved telling stories to his friend—he could forget or make up anything he wanted, and Gambol would never know.

The National Museum of Combat and Carnage attracted thousands of guests daily. It routinely ranked as one of the foremost tourists destinations in the country. It was best known for its premier exhibit—the Top Ten Bloodiest Battles in the History of the World. Most of the museum was dedicated to highlighting those conflicts. Tanks from Normandy, stained uniforms and swords from Stalingrad, various cannons from Antietam...

Annie passed a glass case that held an old American rifle. The plaque claimed this was the very same gun Robert E. Lee had used in the infamously bloody Civil War battle in 1862, but Annie doubted the general of the entire Confederate Army had actually fired a shot himself. Still, that didn't stop a group of mullet-sporting tourists in denim jackets to drool all over themselves as they ogled the gun.

A voice crackled over the PA system: "*Attention guests, attention guests. The meet-and-greet with Captain Annie Kennedy of the Army of Liberty will begin in fifteen minutes! And don't forget, next month, we will be displaying authentic Roman crucifixes, on loan from the European Museum of Torment. This is a ticketed exhibit, so grab yours today!*"

Elena led Annie through the museum corridors. Annie had never been here before, and every few feet, she was either sidetracked by an interesting exhibit or she got lost in a dead-end of displays. The place was designed like a maze. Elena, on the other hand, looked neither to the left nor the right as she walked—she must have been here dozens of times.

"Remember," Elena said to Annie, "keep each interaction under thirty seconds, if at all possible. We're expecting many attendees, lots of photos and autographs, so we'll want to keep the line moving. But be gracious too, of course."

"Of course," Annie muttered. She took in the carnival-like atmosphere of the museum. "I thought I was going after Invisible Dagger?"

Elena nodded, as if she'd anticipated Annie's question. "Those buffoons are laying low right now. They haven't made a peep in a week. What would be the point in fighting them someplace no one will see? No, your battles need to be in a public square, or an airport, or maybe even airborne. I'm still working out the details. So for now, you need to be loved. You've already introduced yourself as an adept soldier, but you also need to be the people's darling." She smiled shrewdly. "Their surrogate mother."

They entered a wing of the museum dedicated to "Peace in Our Times"—thus, it was mostly empty and used for presentations or gatherings. A long table sat under the Army of Liberty's flag, and a *Meet Captain Kennedy* banner hung from the ceiling.

Scores of fans were already waiting for her, along with a mob of paparazzi. Strangers who had never known her name until a few days ago cheered when they saw her face. She smiled and waved, but she felt robotic. Unnatural. She quickly reverted to her strong, stoic persona. It played to her strengths...or rather, it hid her weaknesses.

Elena walked her to the table and whispered, "Have fun." She patted Annie's shoulder and took her spot a reasonable distance away, giving Annie some room to feel like she was running the show.

Annie took a breath. Then another. Her heart hammered against her sternum like a piston. Leading a charge during battle was one thing, but engaging in playful small talk with fans would be the death of her. She could do pull-ups and run sprints all day, but taking selfies and chatting with random groupies sounded like hell.

Things went okay for a while. A group of Indigenous American girls told her all about how they felt "seen" and "represented" on the battlefield, now that Annie was a captain. A man asked her to sign his bicep. She took a photo with the county chapter of the Second Amendment 2.0 Action Committee. A pregnant woman said she was going to name her unborn child after Annie.

As she walked away, the woman remembered a question she'd forgotten and turned back. "What are you going to name yours?"

Annie froze for a second, then patted her own stomach. "Not sure yet. But I'll let everyone know when I do."

The woman smiled and nodded, as if she and Annie were in a secret club only future moms knew about.

Annie exhaled. For the past few days, she had focused on the idea of her own pregnancy until she was certain she wouldn't have a public flub. She'd even stared at herself in the mirror until she thought she saw a bulge in her belly. Elena had caught her in her lie once, and Annie was determined to never let anyone do that again.

She scanned the line of people. Many wore t-shirts with her face on them. How did those get made so fast? Some had their own rifles, either for her to sign or simply for show.

One man caught her eye: a lanky guy wearing a ballcap and leather jacket. Annie was no fashionista, but she'd never seen that combo together.

But she couldn't focus on that guy for too long. The next man in line approached the table. His face was red and puffy, as if he'd been weeping for a year straight. "Captain Kennedy!" he cried out. He fell to his knees in front of the table so that he was eye-to-eye with Annie.

She jolted in surprise, but quickly got her bearings. "Yes, hello, hi. Nice to meet you. Can I get your name, sir?"

"Rocko," the man answered. "I...I *was*..." He swallowed the lump of pure concentrated sorrow in his throat. "I was Ranger Monroe's publicist. Bless that dear man's soul." He slowly stood back up, seemingly relieved to finally be in Annie's presence.

Annie felt it was right to stand as well, so they were on equal footing. "Thank you for coming to meet me, Mr. Rocko. I'm sure Mr. Monroe appreciated your service." She took note of his distraught appearance and added, "And your friendship."

"When I heard you would be here, I had to see you. I-I-I..." He sniveled and sputtered like an old engine. "I found this in my things." He reached into his coat pocket and withdrew a single white sock. It had no pattern and looked like it smelled a little, but he held it out as if it were the Shroud of Turin.

Annie wasn't sure what to do, so she nodded at him politely.

Rocko pushed the sock closer to her face. "This was his. Ranger's. It must have gotten mixed up in my things. I came across it and...so help me Paltrow, I broke down. Sobbing like crazy." He looked close to reenacting the scene. Tears brimmed along his eyelids. "I thought you should have it."

Her mouth automatically said, "Thank you," and, even though she didn't want to touch a dead man's old sock, she took the piece of laundry.

The bystanders and paparazzi ooh-ed and aw-ed, like they were witnessing a historic moment. She had no idea how to respond. "I'll...make sure it gets to the right people."

"Oh, well," Rocko chuckled sadly, "it's for you. I thought, since you and Ranger were as tight as tight can be, you'd appreciate having it."

"Mr. Monroe and I never actually met."

Rocko gasped and staggered back. "Y-Y-You and Ranger never met? But you're his successor! His...well, I *thought* you were his confidant and friend." His cheeks started to flush, and his jaw clenched. "You mean to tell me, the current captain of the Army of Liberty *never* met the greatest man to hold that post?!"

Spectators gawked at his outburst and murmured to their neighbors. Annie held out a hand to try to calm Rocko as if he were a braying horse, but he bucked all the harder.

"You're nothing compared to Ranger Monroe!" He kicked the table and started to reach across, his hands going for her throat.

Annie could've easily broken his wrists, socked him in the jaw, thrown him through the air...but that wouldn't have solved anything. Rocko was clearly broken enough already, and assaulting a man in broad daylight wasn't on her to-do list.

Still, Rocko climbed onto the table, ready to pounce. "You're not as great as him, and you *never will be!*" Hot tears streaked down his contorted face.

Hands grabbed Annie's shoulders from behind and yanked her away from Rocko. Elena escorted her to the side. "Museum security guards," she scoffed to no one. "What're they good for?" Then to Annie: "Let's get out of here."

As the tardy security guards wrangled Rocko, Annie did her best not to notice the hundreds of eyes and camera lenses directed at her. She could practically feel the blog posts and opinion pieces being written about her at that moment.

Annie Kennedy, the maternal warrior, reduced a fan to tears.

Is Annie Kennedy kind enough to be a mother?

Annie Kennedy did nothing to stop her attack—she's far too soft to lead an army.

And so on. Ad nauseam. Forever.

As she and Elena circumnavigated the crowd, her eyes purposefully avoiding the onlookers, she noticed a flicker of movement out of the ordinary. Someone charging. Toward her.

The guy in the leather jacket and ballcap. He snarled and bellowed, "For peace! Down with death!" And he drew a long, wicked blade from within his jacket.

A protestor. A zealous one.

He lunged forward, swinging the blade like it was a conductor's baton.

Annie ground her teeth together. She'd had enough for one day.

She rammed her shoulder into his chest, knocking him off-balance. Then, in less than two seconds, she punched his throat, then his kidney, then his throat again. He gaped at her, frozen on his feet, choking on air. He dropped the blade and clutched his chest, desperate to breathe.

The paparazzi were, predictably, snapping photos every second. Onlookers recorded the whole thing with either their phones or their memories.

Annie could have finished the guy off with a one-liner or at least a knock-out wallop. But instead, true to form, she walked away without another word, leaving him for security to mop up.

As she left, she could feel the crowd's cheers vibrate the entire museum. In a matter of sixty seconds, she had taken the audience on a roller coaster of emotions. And they had *loved* it.

Everyone except Rocko and the leather-jacket-blade-wielding guy, both of whom left the museum in the back of a police cruiser.

The Army of Liberty's private gym was quiet at dawn. Zeke thought that was strange—when he was in the Union reenactment army, at least a few men were up early every day, working out or practicing their formations. And that was a *reenactment* army, where the soldiers were more focused on staying spry and fit, not becoming muscle-bound poster-boys.

Zeke silently scoffed as he trotted on a treadmill. Well, if no one else was going to work to better themselves, he would have to push himself even more.

He moved to the dumbbells next.

After five long years of wearing a wool uniform and lancing blisters off his feet, he was determined to make a name for himself in a real army.

Not just any army. The Army of Liberty. The most prestigious army in America. He was only twenty years old...almost twenty-one, he reminded himself. He could climb the ladder of success and reach a rank to be proud of if he worked hard and pushed himself past his pre-disposed limits.

And...

His arms couldn't handle any more. The thirty-pound weights nearly slipped from his fingers, and so he returned them to the rack with a *thunk*.

And if Annie Kennedy—the woman he met at the Chicago recruitment, his new captain—thought he was something special, he wouldn't try to convince her otherwise.

Fighting alongside her against the Demons Ex Machina had been one of the highlights of his career in warfare. Also, they'd gotten along so well in the waiting room in Chicago. At least, he thought they'd gotten along. He desperately hoped she remembered him fondly too.

He couldn't get her out of his head.

So he grabbed the forty-pound weights and went to work.

His phone buzzed. As he pumped the dumbbells, he checked the screen.

It was his dad.

He ignored the call.

Annie paced in her living room—her large, empty living room, which had previously belonged to Ranger Monroe—the *greatest man to hold the post of captain*, to paraphrase Rocko.

An idea nagged at her. A question that hadn't allowed her to sleep last night.

She spoke the name, "Elena Winn," and the hands-free phone built into the walls of the house started dialing.

Elena answered, "Captain, you're up bright and early. What can I do for you?"

Annie jumped right into it. "Did you set that up yesterday? The man with the knife at the museum. Was that you?"

A deafening pause filled the house as Elena thought before she responded. "Why would I do that?"

"Proof of concept. Me fighting an assailant in 'real life,' in front of an unsuspecting audience. Your brainchild of a real-life action movie needs to be verified, I'm sure, before you can get funding for all those car chases and public fights you have in mind."

Elena responded, "Annie..."

Annie stopped pacing. For the first time since Annie had known her, Elena sounded heartfelt, fully honest.

"...The attacker at the museum yesterday was *not* set up by me. Listen, this is very important—I will *never* put you in danger without your knowledge and approval. I'm a director, but you're the soldier. Your well-being is paramount. You need to trust me on that."

Annie nodded, even though Elena couldn't see her through the phone. She flopped onto a sofa—now that she was convinced her director hadn't orchestrated the attack, her night of fitful sleep was catching up to her. She laid back and closed her eyes, thinking a morning nap sounded wonderful.

"Besides," Elena added, her tone cocky once more, "you think I need verification of my theories before I can get funding? Darling, people are begging to give me money. Rest well, captain." She laughed and hung up.

Just before Annie drifted off to sleep, she wondered how Elena knew she was taking a nap.

Salvatore took notes as he leaned against the metal bleachers. Two small-town armies were duking it out in a field in front of him, but he'd honestly lost interest.

He was in Pondera County, Montana, searching for some rural soldiers looking to upgrade their careers, but so far, he hadn't seen a single soul worthy of being first-wave fodder.

He couldn't even remember the names of the two armies, but he did remember that the battle was sponsored by a local car dealership. That told him everything he needed to know about the caliber of the armies.

The soldiers wore patchwork uniforms that were stained with dirt, blood, and grease from dozens of previous battles. More than once, a man had been killed simply because his second-hand rifle had misfired. The deaths enlivened the battle, to be sure, but there was no storytelling payoff to accidental fatalities like those.

Plus, the director clearly had no vision. The battlefield was just that...a field. No foxholes, no obstacles, no surprises for the audience whatsoever.

He put his notepad in his pocket—something he'd never once done before. But there was simply nothing remarkable.

As he tromped away from the bleachers, he felt a rock in his chest. Was he too good at his job? Had he already snatched up all the viable candidates in the nation, or were his standards simply too high? He had spent years scheming soldiers into Valkyrie's army, but could it be that he'd worked himself out of a job?

He'd scoured prisons, homeless shelters, barrooms, and suburban malls for years. No one excited him anymore. He hadn't found a truly thrilling candidate in as long as he could remember. No one was noteworthy anymore—it was all common.

He climbed into his electric-blue Lamborghini and dismissed the thought. What he needed was a week off, enjoying all the luxuries his home on Coronado Island had to offer. He'd relax and soak in the fruits of his labor for a while.

The phrase "week off" tasted sour on his tongue.

Even as he drove away, he knew there was no way that would happen.

Many weeks had passed since Jasmine had arrived in America. In that time, a new military superstar had taken center stage—one Captain Annie Kennedy. Almost immediately, Jasmine had known who the new focus of her show would be. People talked about Kennedy like she was a pregnant Joan of Arc with a machine gun. The public couldn't get enough of her, so Jasmine was confident CinemaStream would love a show devoted to her.

She checked her watch for the eightieth time as she sat at an outdoor café in Nashville. She had shelled out nearly all of her savings to a contact in Valkyrie Productions, who had told her that Annie Kennedy would be in Nashville on this date, doing some sort of impromptu battle. Details were scarce, even within Valkyrie.

At this point, she could only pray the contact had been telling the truth. Otherwise, she'd be stranded in an American motel with very little cash, and even fewer chances at salvaging her partnership with CinemaStream.

Twangy country music seeped out of the café's speakers. She had started to like the sound, although maybe not at the constant rate that she'd heard it the past few hours, waiting for her cameraman to show up.

She checked her watch for the eighty-first time. He was late.

Passersby wandered in and out of the café, as well as the many surrounding stores. They laughed, chatted, ate, drank, and generally enjoyed the lovely afternoon. Part of Jasmine dreaded the nebulous battle, the reason Captain Kennedy was coming to this city. She hoped things wouldn't get too out of hand and disrupt the peaceful day.

A man with a bulky bag slung over his shoulder strode toward her table. He pointed at her and asked, "Creedy?"

Jasmine jumped up and stuck out her hand. This was presumably her cameraman, and he would be the first member of CinemaStream she'd have face-to-face contact with, so she slapped on her widest smile. "That's me! And you must be Ravi."

"Guilty." He shook her hand with equal vigor. "Ravi Stockett, at your service."

The left side of his mouth constantly twitched, as if a fishing hook was attached to it. His hair was disheveled, and he wore a puka shell necklace and flip-flops—he would look more at home at a beach party than in an open-air café in Nashville.

Then again, Jasmine supposed she wasn't quite a cultural chameleon either. When she'd ordered tea, the waitress had asked her how much extra sugar she'd wanted.

"You mentioned on the phone," Ravi leaned in, as if he was part of a conspiracy, "that Captain Kennedy is in town? And we'll be filming her or something?"

Jasmine responded, "Or something. I'm not positive what direction our series is going in yet, but I'm sure Kennedy will be the focus. All I know is that she's in Nashville, and some sort of impromptu battle is going to happen."

Ravi pumped his fist. "Sounds fun. So we just wait until we hear explosions, and we run toward them, camera rolling?"

"Pretty much." She laughed as she said it, realizing how ridiculous this all was.

Luckily, Ravi appeared to be game. He beamed, "Sounds even funner. You gonna finish that sweet tea?"

Annie strode down a Nashville sidewalk, wearing a black shirt, jeans, and flexible boots—the clothes had been selected by a team of statisticians who pieced together the perfect "action scene outfit."

She spoke to the hidden earpiece, "Approaching the hotel."

"I can see you, Annie," Elena's voice replied, "but thanks for the update."

Annie scanned the street around her. Lampposts, passing cars, garbage cans, countless buildings and pedestrians...It all looked like a regular city to her.

She recalled the briefing Elena had given her on the way to Nashville:

"My contact in the FBI has told me that Invisible Dagger will be assassinating a major celebrity in Nashville *tomorrow*."

Annie had internally rolled her eyes at the mention of the FBI contact. Anytime Elena needed something to happen, she would mutter something about her vague, unseen mole inside the FBI, and Annie was getting tired of it. She wanted to press Elena and find out more about this contact. She wanted to know why the FBI was allowing her to make such a spectacle of real-world danger. Was Elena bribing someone? Screwing someone?

But she'd decided it ultimately didn't matter. She was a soldier, and what mattered was the mission: preventing harm and stopping the terrorists. It didn't matter how Elena got the information, as long as it was put to good use.

She had asked, "Which celebrity is the target?"

Elena had replied, "A singer, an actor, a banjo player, I don't care. All that matters is *it's happening*, and you'll be there to take out the assassin. In front of a live, unsuspecting audience. *And* broadcast simultaneously around the world. We'll have cameras set up all over the city, corresponding with the battle plan we've constructed. You won't see them, but trust me, they'll be there."

The two of them had then gone over the battle plans in meticulous detail. As a nurse in the Great Plains Brigade, she had seen plenty of plans over the years, and as captain of the Army of Liberty, she was even privy to their formation sometimes. Yet she had never seen something like what Elena Winn had cooked up.

From the streets to the rooftops, inside and outside, up and down... Every single step and punch of Annie's fight with the would-be assassin had been mapped out in advance.

It was spectacular. An action movie sequence brought to life.

As she strode down the sidewalk, trying her best to look confident for the hidden cameras, two thoughts made Annie quake in her boots.

One: Would she be able to remember the battle plans and stick to them when it all went down? The Invisible Dagger assassin, obviously, was not aware of the plans. He would undoubtedly be armed and reluctant to go down without a fight. A real, life-or-death fight.

Two: The thousands of bystanders weren't aware of the plans either. Would they muck things up, be in the wrong place at the wrong time?

But it was too late to worry about all that. According to Elena, the assassination was moments away. The celebrity was due to step out of a five-star hotel and into his limo—at that point, the Invisible Dagger terrorist would strike. With a gun, knife, or otherwise, no one knew. It was Annie's job to save the day.

Her fingers shook, so she stuffed them in her jean pockets.

This wasn't her arena. She could run, lift, and shoot—as far as physical specimens went, she ranked near the top.

But she wasn't a fighter. She didn't know real hand-to-hand combat. She'd beaten the knifeman in the museum by sheer luck. If a man who knew what he was doing tried to kill her, she didn't know what would happen.

When her brow started to crease and she felt a fearful tear in her eye, she remembered her battle-hardened persona. She was Captain Kennedy—the maternal warrior. Hard. No-nonsense. Stoic and in control.

She banished her emotions to a far-flung recess in her mind. No fear. No empathy. Nothing. She had a job to do.

Lightfoot and Gambol sat in the dark room in the Front Porch Retirement Center. The only light sources were inklings of sun fighting around the drawn shades, and the episode of *Wheel of Fortune* on the hundred-inch TV.

Gambol called out, "Don Quixote, by Cervantes," trying to solve the puzzle. The category was *Fun & Games*, and Gambol's guess wasn't even close.

Lightfoot was half-asleep, but he nodded to his friend anyway. "Good guess."

A box appeared in the lower-right-hand corner of the screen. Lightfoot perked up—he'd never seen an icon like that before. The box read,

BREAKING: *Captain Kennedy encounters domestic terrorist. Select here to watch LIVE.*

Lightfoot fumbled with the remote to click the box.

Gambol watched with mild curiosity. "What are you doing, Rick?"

"Just switching the channel." He didn't bother correcting Gambol, even though his name was Richard, not Rick. He clicked the icon, and the screen changed to a live view of a city street. "It's something interesting. I think you'll like it."

Lightfoot leaned forward to watch what was about to happen, and Gambol, not knowing what to do otherwise, followed suit.

Zeke stood in line at a taco truck, ready to chow down. After living in the eastern U.S. for most of his life, the trucks in San Diego had opened his eyes to just how magnificent a mere taco could be. But he was still five or six people from the front of the line, so he had to rein in his taste buds a bit longer.

His phone buzzed in his pocket. He withdrew it, curious—he wasn't very popular, and someone texting him in the middle of the day was unusual.

Then he noticed everyone else in line looking at their phones at the exact same time.

His screen displayed an icon, telling him that Captain Kennedy was about to take on a real-life domestic terrorist. *LIVE*, it said. *CLICK HERE NOW*.

Everywhere Zeke looked, pedestrians had their phones out, eyes locked on the screens. They were enraptured. Cars pulled to the side of the road, cyclists and joggers stopped in their tracks, and even a few electronic billboards had pulled up the live feed. The world held its breath.

Zeke tapped his phone's screen and stepped out of line.

∽⧸⧹∼

The clock ticked as Jody lounged on a sofa, chugging a two-liter energy drink. It was almost time for Staten to turn that country music star into a shish kebab, and he couldn't wait. He had his spiel ready for Invisible Dagger's online fans. According to Roderick's calculations, today's assassination, combined with Jody's words and enthusiasm, might double their total subscribers.

Not bad for a day's killing.

All Jody had to do was wait to hear that Staten had sliced and diced the singer. Then, he'd start filming himself and tell the world that Invisible Dagger was responsible. Maybe finally, once they got some blood on their hands, people would start taking them seriously. Holland had told them that the Boston blackout and the Baltimore factory explosion had been impressive, to be sure...but no one cared unless lives had been lost.

A smile tugged at Jody's lips just thinking about it. Any minute now...

His pants vibrated. It was a nice feeling, and he took his time realizing it was his phone. He looked at the display...and he nearly choked on his own tongue.

"Crap crap crap." He clambered off the sofa and ran to find Holland. "Hey, something's happening in Nashville! I mean, something in Nashville is happening to *us!*"

∽⧸⧹∼

Staten waltzed in front of the hotel, dressed in a loose-fitting buttoned shirt and some sensible slacks. He hated it. He was used to wearing tanks that accentuated his python-like biceps, but his little act wouldn't last much longer. At the moment, he was blending in with the usual crowd that a five-star hotel would attract. But in just a few seconds, a superstar would walk out the front door, and Staten would ram his KA-BAR knife right down his pretty-boy throat.

The knife was hidden up his right sleeve, and he'd be lying if he said he hadn't nicked his forearm a couple times on accident—again, he wasn't used to dealing with sleeves.

He wasn't great at the legwork of being a domestic terrorist. Holland and Roderick were smart, and Jody was charming—he could talk to anyone and be their best friend in no time. Staten could rip a phone book in half, sure, but he was a lousy performer. He hoped he would make Jody proud.

When he stabs the superstar in a few minutes, there will be millions of eyes on him—that will be the closest he'll ever get to being as famous as his friend. Just today, on the streets of Nashville, he had seen a few people dressed as Jody, with shaved heads, hoodies, and athletic pants. Invisible Dagger was taking the world by storm, and Jody was its face.

Staten inwardly beamed with pride. Good for Jody.

People started to chirp around him, and he got the feeling that the target was approaching.

And the next thing he knew, the hotel's double-doors flew open without anyone touching them, and a tall, sleek, carefully groomed man sauntered out. Cameras clicked, fans squealed, and Staten's muscles tightened.

Staten had seen this guy's picture online and on TV a lot, but he'd never learned his name. Even after Invisible Dagger had decided to kill him, the name couldn't quite stick in his memory. Didn't matter. The celebrity was important to millions of people, meaning they'd be devastated when he was killed in broad daylight, meaning Invisible Dagger would get all the publicity they could ever want.

He wriggled the long, deadly knife out of its hiding spot and approached the superstar. Time to perform.

~ঙ৲ঙ৲~

Annie frantically scanned the crowd that had amassed in front of the hotel. The celebrity had emerged in all his handsome glory, which meant the assassin couldn't be far behind. The guy was in no hurry at all, waving to the multitudes as he strolled in the general direction of his limo. She wanted to yell at the guy to get in the car and *go*, but she didn't have time.

Because she saw the assassin.

She recognized him as Staten, the brawniest member of Invisible Dagger. He wore nondescript clothes to blend in with the crowd, with one huge difference: the gleaming seven-inch knife he held over his head as he lunged toward the celebrity.

Her arms pumped. Her legs ran. Her teeth gnashed. Time to perform.

"Drop it!" The words erupted from her throat with more authority than she knew she possessed.

Staten locked eyes with her, about twenty yards away. His face flickered, debating between stabbing the celebrity and running while he still had the chance.

In that beat of hesitation, the crowd noticed his knife. People shrieked. Someone yelled, "Look out, it's a crazy man!" The audience turned into a churning mob, and the celebrity wised up and dove for his limo. Tires squealed, and the limo was gone in a puff of gray smoke.

Staten had no choice. He spun and dashed away, Annie right on his heels.

Traffic around the hotel was high, barring Staten from easily crossing the street. An overturned dumpster blocked an alleyway, and there were no vehicles readily available to be swiped, so Staten took the only accessible route: down a flight of stairs, into a subway station.

Just according to Elena's plan.

Annie followed him down the stairs, her vision quickly adjusting to the garish fluorescent lights. The station wasn't too crowded at this time of day, which was purposeful. As Staten and Annie ran across a platform, Elena's hidden cameras got perfect shots of all the advertisements plastered to the walls. And just like that, the entire day had become profitable.

Staten took a turn up another set of stairs, trying to escape the underground tunnel and get out in the open. That's what Annie would do in his situation, and she followed.

As soon as he surfaced on the sidewalk, he found a motorcycle waiting for him, keys in the ignition. His adrenaline kept him from asking too many questions—he hopped on the bike, brought the engine roaring to life, and zoomed into traffic.

Annie dug a key of her own from her pocket, hopped into a nearby Audi (sponsored, of course), and took off after him.

She wrapped her fingers around the steering wheel in a death grip. Sweat dripped into her eyes as she careened through Nashville.

Staten was going faster than she was comfortable with. His bike could cut and weave between cars, and he clearly didn't care about hitting people—

"Hey, Annie," Elena's voice rang in her ear. "Loosen your grip on the wheel. You look tense. You need to look cool, in control."

Annie shot a glare at the speedometer, where a tiny camera was planted. She did her best to relax the tension in her arms, shoulders, and face...but she was also rocketing down a busy city street, and she didn't think that was possible.

Elena hissed one more comment. "Speed up, captain, you're losing him!"

Cars already whipped past her windows. At times, she only had inches of space between her car and the others. If she sped up any more, she'd run the risk of hurting innocent people—

"Don't lose him!"

Annie shoved her emotions into an even dustier corner of her mind.

Her foot smashed the gas pedal.

The Audi nosed other cars out of its way. Horns ripped through the air, and Annie tried to block them out.

She saw Staten's motorcycle just up ahead. He cut down a backstreet and vanished.

With a snarl she hoped looked good for the camera, she cranked the wheel to the side, aiming directly for the alley where Staten had gone. If anyone got in her way, that was their problem.

Metal crunched, rubber burned, and people yelped in confusion and shock. But she made it across the street, and she threaded her car into the alley.

She dug through her memory for one of the predetermined lines Elena had written. There were at least ten that Annie was supposed to sprinkle throughout the chase. Unfortunately, she couldn't remember a single one. So she set her jaw and glared forward.

Far down the alley, Staten's bike suddenly stopped running—that was by design, forcing the chase to evolve. According to Elena, an audience's attention span could only stretch so far. Staten cursed loudly and pounded the handlebars, but no amount of profane persuasion could make the engine start again.

He ditched the bike and ran to a metal ladder leading to the top of a building. His biceps pulled him to the roof quicker than Annie would have expected. Once he was at the top, he yanked the ladder halfway up. It clicked into place, and he turned to start running across the roof.

Annie screeched the Audi to a stop and bounded out. The ladder was too far up the side of the wall to reach, so she clambered on top of the car, squatted, then leapt with all her might. Her fingers snagged the bottom rung of the rusty ladder, and she barely held on.

"Captain, you're *crushing* this," Elena said in the earpiece. "Viewership is off the charts. Don't you *dare* fall."

Annie grunted and, using only her arms, climbed up the ladder until her feet could reach the rungs. She panted, but couldn't spare a moment to rest, and ascended to the roof—probably five stories, if she had to guess.

She reached the top of the concrete building, and the wind nearly knocked her back. She was higher up than she'd thought—the cars and people below looked like toys. A whining sound flew overhead, and she squinted against the sunlight to see a drone whiz past. Elena had eyes on her still.

Staten was running across the roof, headed for a neighboring building. Annie sprinted after him. She remembered to quickly pat her stomach— hopefully, the viewing audience all gasped at that moment, remembering in amazement that she was supposedly carrying a child even while chasing a terrorist.

"Nice," Elena said. Annie couldn't help but smile a little to herself. She was getting pretty good at this.

Staten let out a primal yell, sped up, and hurdled off the roof. For a long, breathless second, he traveled through the air, absolutely nothing between him and the long journey to the pavement. But then he landed on the next rooftop, stumbled, regained his balance, and kept running.

Annie had never jumped from rooftop to rooftop before, but she was plenty confident in her athleticism, and with the drone's camera pointed right at her, she couldn't afford to hesitate. So she too sped up, catapulted herself across the empty space, and stuck the landing on the next building.

She could practically hear the world going berserk. If her performance in the battle stadium was any indication, she had leagues of fans on every continent, screaming her name.

"Hah! Hoo! Annie's coming for you!"

Elena had been right. Fighting in stadiums was one thing—being a warrior in real life elevated her to an entirely new level. Annie felt like an Olympic hero. The stuff of legends.

Staten peeked over his shoulder and barked at Annie, "Let me go, or you'll be sorry!"

This was a perfect opportunity for a snappy comeback...but Annie didn't say anything. Instead, she sped up.

Elena whispered, "Perfect," in her ear. She had stopped trying to massage Annie's persona into a typical quippy action hero.

Staten leapt off the roof, aiming for the next building...however, this stretch of empty air was wider than the previous one, and he didn't make it. He slammed into the concrete wall, hanging on to the side for dear life.

His screams echoed throughout Nashville. He tried to pull himself up, but his sweaty and shaky hands couldn't quite get a good enough grip. His feet kicked helplessly in the air.

Annie made the jump easily, and she stood over the dangling terrorist. He stared up at her, his face blanched with fear. "Help...Help..." he hysterically sputtered between breaths.

Hordes of people had gathered on the sidewalks and streets below. They took photos and pointed excitedly, waiting to see what Captain Kennedy would do next.

Annie panted and wiped sweat from her forehead as she waited for direction from her earpiece. "Well?"

No response. Elena was leaving this up to her.

Annie sighed and bent down next to Staten. "Give me your hand." The terrorist was eager to comply, and she yanked him to safety. It had to be an embarrassing image for Invisible Dagger—their biggest, strongest man had been chased down by a pregnant woman, and now she was saving his life.

The muscular man steadied himself on his feet. His shirt and slacks had been scuffed and dirtied by the chase. He dusted himself off and eyed Annie warily. "Thanks, lady..." He dug for a good line, and, finding none, blurted out, "But no thanks!" He drew the wicked KA-BAR from his sleeve, its blade flashing in the sun.

But Annie had anticipated this. She threw a fist into his Adam's apple. Staten gagged and clutched his neck in agony, all while instinctively swinging the knife. Annie curved under the blade, reared up, and kicked him squarely in the chest.

He stumbled back, flailed his arms, and toppled off of the roof.

Annie turned and walked away without waiting to hear his body hit the pavement far below. It took a few seconds, but the wet, splintery sound reached her ears just as she found the stairs to begin her descent through the building's interior.

Danny sat in a bistro down the street from the Valkyrie building. A TV hung in the corner of the dining room, an older unit that typically played sports and was almost always ignored by patrons.

Not today, though. Today, every single eyeball, including those of the chefs and wait staff, was glued to Captain Kennedy's live, high-octane escapade. They gasped as Kennedy stopped the assassination, winced when she nearly crashed her car, and applauded when she leapt across rooftops.

Danny had to mentally persuade himself to look away from the TV to check his phone. From what his assistants and analysts were telling him, a record-setting number of people were watching all over the globe.

His heart felt like it was glowing. At first, he'd been ticked he hadn't thought of this angle. A tangible action movie seemed like the next logical step from live warfare, but it had taken Elena Winn to push Valkyrie in that direction.

The diners inhaled a collective gasp, and Danny's attention snapped back to the TV. Kennedy was lending a hand to the egg-for-brain terrorist, who was dangling off the side of a building. Danny wondered how that would play with the audience—would she seem merciful, or soft? She had killed without hesitation in battle stadiums—would the public think she's wishy-washy?

But then.

The guy drew his knife and attacked the woman who had saved his sorry butt.

Every person in the bistro booed and hissed.

Kennedy kicked the guy right in the sternum. He fell and fell and fell.

And the people cheered. They pounded the tables and held up their drinks in celebration. When the terrorist's body went *splat* and painted the pavement red, they cheered all the louder.

Danny cheered too. He cheered for Annie Kennedy, Elena Winn, and the future of spectatorship.

Screams intermingled in the air with applause. Nashville was in a tizzy—they'd witnessed something one witness had called "freakin' awesome."

Jasmine and Ravi the cameraman fought against the throng on the street surrounding the building Annie Kennedy was currently in. Police cruisers and an ambulance had screeched onto the scene to scoop the terrorist's body into a Ziploc bag, as well as to, presumably, get Captain Kennedy out of there without being mobbed by the fans.

She had interviewed as many witnesses as she could, as quickly as possible, while the emotions were still raw. They hooted and hollered, keen to be on camera. More than one person had flipped out at Jasmine's accent, which was far from her favorite thing, but if that made them excited to talk to her, so be it.

A few memorable soundbites: *"I've never been so stoked in my life."*

"Marry me, Captain Kennedy!"

"The sound of the guy hitting the ground was so gross, but I loved it!"

"This was very possibly one of the coolest days of my life. I never thought something like this would happen right in front of me."

Jasmine asked a few leading questions to try to coax out the witnesses' feelings, but for the most part, no questions were required—people bowled each other over for the chance to talk to a camera about how "awesome" what they just saw was.

Ravi had filmed every encounter, ever the professional. During a lull between interviewees, he smiled to Jasmine. "This is fun! Everyone's so happy!" His boyish enthusiasm was infectious, and the crowd cheered again—or maybe it was the other way around, and he had soaked up his enthusiasm from the crowd.

A car pulled away from the throng, and Jasmine realized with a wave of defeat that Captain Kennedy had left the building. She'd slipped away without a word, or even a wave. Jasmine respected that, but if she was going to make a series about Kennedy, she needed interviews with the actual woman. Jasmine stamped her foot, frustrated with herself for getting distracted by all these witnesses and letting Kennedy vanish.

Jasmine refocused. She tried to calm her spirit and regain the essence of her work. What had she been going for when she created that first episode, the one where she spoke with the veterans support group in the Enfield borough of London?

"What does spectatorship leave in its wake?"

"Follow me," she said to Ravi, and they scuttled away from the crowd, back through Nashville. Past the roofs Annie and the terrorist has run upon.

They stood on a street corner that had been previously bustling with pedestrians, families, and laughter. Now, the traffic had been cleared and there wasn't a smile in sight. Several cars had pulled to the side of the road, some with scratches and dents, others totaled. At least two cars had crashed: one into a lamppost, and the other into a kiosk selling sunglasses. Ambulances helped the injured, and bystanders comforted sobbing victims. Jasmine spotted a gurney blanketed by a white sheet, the shape of a lifeless body molding the topography of the sheet.

She muttered to herself, "What happens *after* the heroics?" That was it. She'd found an angle.

Ravi nodded in awe. "Boss, that's bloomin' brilliant," he said, adopting her accent. Then he flinched a bit. "Oh, I'm sorry, can I do that? Is that offensive?"

"It's fine, Ravi." Jasmine readied herself. "Ready to go talk to some people?"

New York City at night was a special kind of energetic, like a maniac strapped to a chair. Distant sirens wailed, cars revved, and millions of voices mingled in the air. Salvatore didn't love visiting the Big Apple—he preferred open spaces and public transportation that wouldn't give him Hep-C. But here he was, walking down a dark alley at two in the morning, all because he'd lost the thrill.

"You sure you want to do this?" The investigative journalist peered over his shoulder as he led Salvatore through the labyrinthine alleyways. He was a finicky little man with yellowed teeth. Not quite the intrepid reporter Salvatore had pictured.

"I paid you, right?" Salvatore wore his most powerful outfit—a tailored suit, emerald cuff links, and his platinum Rolex. He knew he was in no danger. No one would dare mug him tonight...because he was in control. He was too commanding to threaten.

The journalist buried his protests and led Salvatore past enough garbage and vermin to fill a thousand dumps. What a glamorous city. Salvatore scoffed and tread lightly, avoiding puddles of who-knows-what.

Finally, the journalist stopped before at a corner. "He should be just up ahead."

"*Should* be?" Salvatore glared, the moonlight flashing in his eyes.

"Look, I'm not a psychic. Judging by his patterns and a little detective work, he'll be here. But listen..." He cleared his throat. "I could get ripped apart if someone finds out I gave this information to you rather than the cops."

"Are *you* going to tell anyone?" So far, Salvatore had spoken with this guy exclusively in the form of questions. It was his favorite tactic when conducting conversations with little-minded people.

The journalist shuffled. "Well, no."

Without another word, Salvatore rounded the corner, leaving the small man behind.

There, in a dingy parking lot behind a dingier restaurant, was a medium-build male lugging a duffel bag across the asphalt. A big duffel bag. Large enough to hold a body, if one was creative with the packing arrangements.

Salvatore's voice rippled through the night. "Frank Walsh?"

The male jerked upright and froze—an insect about to be crushed, but too stunned to flee. His shirt was dappled with blood that didn't belong to him.

According to the journalist Salvatore had paid, Frank Walsh was a serial murderer who had been on a spree for the past few weeks. And it looked like he was right.

Frank grimaced, his eyes pinpricks of obsidian. "Who're you?" His baritone was intimidating—he'd make a fine soldier for Valkyrie. Maybe even an officer, given the fact that he was a good enough performer to evade police capture so far.

Salvatore withdrew a business card and held it out, intentionally making his cufflinks glimmer in the moonbeams. "You like to kill, Frank?"

~⁂~

Suzanne sat in Danny's top-floor office. The boss was out—to be honest, she wasn't sure where, but if she was asked, she would spit out an answer that made her sound omniscient. She was good at that.

The office's phone rang. She sat in Danny's plush chair, set her feet on the desk, and lifted the phone to her ear.

A gruff voice spoke to her in Arabic. It was the president of the State of Palestine.

She smiled and replied in the language: "Oh, hello, President Ahmar! Good to hear from you again. How was your niece's birthday? Did she get the gift we sent?"

Her kind words and tone took Ahmar off-guard. He thanked her personally for the Shetland pony they had given his niece.

"That's wonderful," Suzanne said, firmly controlling the conversation, even though Ahmar was the one who called. "I hear your Palestinian army is doing well for itself. There are usually some growing pains when a nation first wades into the world of spectatorship. That's normal, Mr. President. You're handling it all very well, I promise."

She didn't know for sure that Ahmar had doubts about his leadership abilities, but then he meekly thanked her and admitted things had been rough lately. She grinned and comforted him.

Several minutes passed. Once their impromptu therapy session had naturally wrapped up, Ahmar remembered the reason he'd called—he wanted the Army of Liberty to do battle with Palestine's newly formed army.

"Hmm, I'm afraid Captain Kennedy is all booked up for quite a while. Let me tell you, though, I just got off the phone with another Valkyrie army in Russia. They're looking to expand their relevance, and a war in the Middle East might do the trick. How does that sound?"

She then arranged a war between Palestine and a lower-tier Russian army. It was best for Palestine to start out slow and build its confidence.

When she hung up, she decided to rearrange everything in Danny's drawers. He needed to know that his "castle's drawbridge" wasn't impenetrable.

Jody stood in the center of the frame with his hood pulled over his bald scalp. His typically magnetic demeanor was dampened—unshaven stubble decorated his face, and his eyes were red and droopy.

"Hi, Daggsters," he spoke to the camera, addressing their fans. "I'm sure you've heard about the tragedy that occurred a few days ago. I bet a lot of you were even watching. In Nashville, one of our own was killed in battle. Staten, this goes out to you."

He pressed play on a radio, and a 1990s slow jam filled the air. He cracked open a bottle of beer and poured it onto the floor.

"They say you should pour one out for your homies. I say, pour out the whole thing for your *real* homies."

The camera held on him for several long, uncomfortable seconds as the beer *glug-glug-glugged* out of the bottle. Finally, he chucked the empty bottle off-camera and sniffed.

"Invisible Dagger will never be the same without you, Staten. And now, Daggsters, you can honor his memory." An evil smile coiled on his face. "We declare war on Captain Annie Kennedy, and we need your help. If you see her in public, give her hell. If you live near her, tell us where she is. She's our number one target."

He paused—usually, this would be because he'd forgotten his next line, but today, it was purposeful. He let his words soak in, then concluded.

"Like and subscribe. And tell your friends to jump on the bandwagon too. Cuz this ride is about to get crazy, and you don't want to miss it.

Keep sending us suggestions for where to attack next as we make our way across the country. Boston, Baltimore...Who's next?"

He started to walk away, but one last thought popped out of his mouth.

"We won't stop, Kennedy. Not until you're done for. Invisible Dagger, *out*."

And the video stopped streaming.

Annie's arms dropped. She had been doing pull-ups in her private room in the landing grounds of a stadium in Jackson City, just minutes before the start of a battle, when she'd seen the video on TV. Invisible Dagger's declaration of war. Against her.

She panted and leaned against the wall.

A terrorist cell. Gunning for her.

No plans. No directors. They were honestly and earnestly trying to kill her.

Her hands shook as she finished gearing up. Even with grenades on her belt and a rifle over her shoulder, she jumped at every sound. When the AC made the air ducts creak, she went for her gun.

"Crap," she muttered. There was no way she could let those half-wits get to her. She was Captain Annie Kennedy, after all. A few frat boys with pea shooters didn't stand a chance.

But what if they infiltrated the Army of Liberty? Or maybe they were on staff at the stadium, selling merch and hot dogs. All it took was one shot, and she'd be gone.

She couldn't remember what army she was about to fight, but maybe Invisible Dagger had paid someone to disregard the battle plans and go after her specifically. Just like what happened to Ranger Monroe.

Would there be a memorial built for her? It'd likely be in Wichita, her hometown. Would it be popular? She'd been captain for such a brief time. More than likely, her body would be carted off with no fanfare, and another woman would be brought in the replace her. A perky supermodel this time, with luscious hair and dazzling eyes.

Annie Kennedy would be a footnote. A trivia question. No one would remember her, not even her killers.

There was a knock on the door. Annie realized she was huddled in the corner of the room, knuckles white, sweat beading her forehead.

She barked, "What is it?"

A voice she vaguely recognized spoke from the other side of the door. "Captain?" It was the director of the battle. "It's time for you to line up with your army to enter the field."

Annie started to stand, but then she imagined herself among the hundreds of soldiers, filing into the stadium. So many bodies so close together. Any one of them could be an Invisible Dagger man—Holland, Roderick, or Jody—in disguise. Or any of them could be a traitor, ready to slip a knife between her ribs when she least expected it.

Her knees shook and she fell back to the floor. "No," she said, forcing her tenor to be steady. "No, I'll enter after them. Right before the battle starts."

A pause of confusion. "But captain—"

"No!" The syllable cracked, despite her best efforts. She wanted to take out her pistol and shoot the word full of holes, then stamp her boot heel on it until it vanished from existence. But that wasn't possible.

The director didn't respond, but Annie heard footsteps as the person left.

Then more footsteps. More rapid, more intimidating.

The door flew open, and Elena Winn invaded Annie's space.

"Get up and pull yourself together," she snapped. "That director thinks you're a sniveling little coward now. *No one* can ever see you like that."

Annie croaked, "What if Invisible Dagger is out there?"

Elena pursed her lips. "You're going into *battle*. You've done it before. Half of the people out there will be trying to kill you, and it's the jobs of the other half to make sure that doesn't happen. It's *my* job too."

Cheers emanated from the battlefield. The crowd wanted the fighting to begin. They wanted to see Captain Kennedy.

Elena grabbed Annie's forearm and dragged her to her feet. "Wipe that sweat off your face. Now. No one wants to see you like this."

Annie's feet moved without her permission, taking her toward the battlefield. The words rang in her mind—no one wanted to see her like what? Scared? Vulnerable? But that was how she felt. She couldn't help but feel what she felt. Did the people want an emotionless hero, a statue, a void they could project their own violent glee into?

She answered her own question:

Yes. That's exactly what the people wanted.

The Army of Liberty was already on the battlefield, waiting for her to join them. She scrubbed her sleeve across her face, trying to sponge off her emotions along with the sweat.

Zeke bounced on the heels of his feet. He still wasn't used to fighting in real battles, where there were actual stakes and kinetic crowds. But he was prepared to show his superiors that he was the real deal. He had thrown himself into his work, exercising his body and mind. He could fight, shoot, and explain the most effective tactical strategies, all while doing a hundred sit-ups.

Today's battle wasn't special in and of itself, but he was determined to make every single battle of his new career extraordinary. It wasn't enough to be a passable soldier—not after years of going through the motions in the Union Army. He was ready to show what he was made of to everyone: General Lightfoot, the audience, and Captain Kennedy.

He consciously kept his dad's name off the list of people he was hoping to impress.

As he stood in the stadium with the rest of the Army of Liberty, under the lights, in front of a jittery crowd, the announcer's voice rumbled from every direction.

"Ladies and gentlemen..."

The audience in the stands had already started going nuts. They knew who was coming.

"...welcome to the battlefield the pregnant protector, the mad matriarch, one bad mother-gunner—the new captain of the Army of Liberty, Annie Kennedy!"

He stood on his tiptoes to see over his peers. The captain entered the battlefield, her face frozen in a grimace. Her steps were jerky, as if she were forcing her muscles to make each movement.

Zeke felt for her. She likely wasn't comfortable performing for such large crowds under the scrutiny of lights and cameras. He definitely wasn't used to it yet, and he didn't think he ever would be.

He itched to be next to her, to speak words of encouragement. He had hardly said anything to her since Chicago. He began to shuffle through the army, making his way to her, wondering if he could make her smile—

And then, the lights dimmed. A horn blared, and bullets tore over his head. The battle began.

The air thrummed as people cheered and guns blazed, but Annie didn't pay any attention. She ran for cover, trying to get her bearings before her head was blown off her shoulders.

Fighters sprinted to and fro, yelling, shooting, and posing for the crowd. Her eyes scanned each and every face on the field. She still didn't personally know the soldiers that comprised the Army of

Liberty—Elena hadn't considered that a good use of time—so she didn't recognize anyone. They wore her uniform, yet she didn't know them. That fact put her even more on edge. She gripped the rifle harder to hide her tremoring hands.

The field had quickly transformed into a circle of hell. One minute ago, soldiers from opposing armies had been cordially chatting, joking about their friendly rivalries and pumping up the crowd. Now, they were all screaming like banshees and taking deadly aim at each other. It always shocked Annie how a battle could turn strangers and friends alike into sworn enemies.

Foxholes, boulders, barbed wire, and other miscellaneous cover spots dotted the field. It was fairly simple, prompting the audience to pay closer attention to the actual fighters. That usually meant the directors had a trick or two up their sleeves.

Annie dug through her memory for the battle plans and layout. She'd known it all backward and forward...but among the explosions and bullets, she couldn't remember a thing.

And it didn't help that every face she saw was a potential Invisible Dagger assassin, coming for her.

She cowered behind a rock, paralyzed by uncertainty and...dare she say it...fear. In the midst of the brutal warfare, she was afraid of being killed.

❧

Zeke bounded across the field. Electricity coursed through his veins, and a laugh even escaped his throat. He felt *amazing*. His legs were strong, his lungs full, his mind sharp—all his extra training was paying off.

Best of all, he felt the eyes of the audience settling on him. More than once, when he made a difficult shot or leapt over a piece of debris, he heard a collective cheer. He was making fans left and right!

The announcer's voice echoed in the stadium: "On the screens, you'll see Private Zeke Smith, a new recruit for the Army of Liberty this season. So far tonight, he's racked up an impressive seven kills...three of them headshots! If you have the Army's app, there's still time to place your bets on how many headshots he'll amass in tonight's battle."

Zeke smiled and screeched to a halt. He cocked a mischievous eyebrow to the crowd, lined up his rifle, and let a bullet fly.

Across the field, an enemy soldier fell. The crowd applauded.

"Make that eight kills, four headshots!" The announcer barked a laugh. "What a showing!"

Zeke took cover and reloaded. He felt the warmth of the people's affection. It swaddled him and gave him a big hug, as if he were in a sauna of self-esteem.

Storytelling. If he'd learned one thing from his time in war reenactments, he knew that it was all about storytelling.

He was a fresh-faced private. Very young—twenty years old (almost twenty-one)—but he'd had the courage to enter the big leagues. The other soldiers weren't performing nearly as well as he was—they must be complacent, lazy, and slothful due to their success. He was putting in the work, and it showed.

That was the story he pushed, and it seemed the people were accepting it. Actually, they were *loving* it.

He peeked out from behind his cover and fired. The bullet flew dozens of yards, burying itself into a grenade that dangled from an enemy soldier's belt.

The fireball lit up the stadium.

The director of the battle shouted in Annie's earpiece. "Kennedy! Get up and get moving! You may be Carr's new favorite action figure, and people walk on eggshells around you because you're knocked up, but I won't handle you with kiddie gloves. Get out from behind that rock, follow our battle plans, and put on a show, or you'll be *sorry!*"

Annie didn't move. She didn't even flinch—it was as if she honestly didn't hear the tirade.

Thoughts of assassins and traitors filled her head. But no one knew that.

What the cameras saw was a small, trembling, frightened woman woefully out of place on a battlefield.

A far cry from the stoic, unfeeling warrior they'd fallen in love with.

Across the country, viewers changed the channel. People stopped searching her name online. T-shirts, keychains, and posters were returned—not all of them, but enough to move the needle.

In a matter of seconds, public sentiment began to tilt away from Annie Kennedy.

~⁓~

Zeke surveyed the field, looking for his next target.

There—one of his fellow soldiers was on the ground, surrounded by enemies. He had his hands up, but it looked like the enemies weren't going to accept his surrender.

Zeke raised his rifle, but...*click*. While showing off for the crowd, he'd run out of ammo.

He rolled his shoulders and flexed for the cameras. No matter.

He charged straight at the soldiers, swinging his fists and bellowing like a diesel engine. His raw strength and the element of surprise gave him an edge, and the scuffle lasted mere seconds. He stood over the fallen enemies, panting and sweating. When he heard the applause, he knew the cameras were focused squarely on him. He helped his fellow soldier stand, and he said, "Doing all right?"

The other man scoffed and trotted away, rejoining the battle.

Zeke couldn't help but chuckle. His drive and solo training had put him on better footing than anyone else in the Army of Liberty—he'd be surprised if his peers weren't jealous or bitter toward him.

He grabbed some extra magazines of ammo from the fallen enemies' belts, reloaded his rifle, and leapt back into the fray.

Explosions and bullets clogged the air, and bodies littered the ground. Soldiers ran around, seemingly in circles, as if they were caught in a bloody cyclone. It was sheer chaos. Aimless ferocity.

Zeke was still new to the professional army scene, but he sensed that this battle was adrift. Directionless. The story felt nonexistent. The Army of Liberty wasn't pressing toward a clear, specific goal, so the audience didn't have a reason to care about all the action they were seeing. Currently, the arena was full of noise and flashing lights with no semblance of order.

He recalled the battle plans the army had been drilled on. This fight was supposed to end when Captain Kennedy wove her way past the enemy's defenses, defeated its captain, tossed a grenade into a bunker, and tore down the enemy's flag.

But...he didn't see Annie anywhere. No wonder the Army of Liberty was directionless—its captain was MIA.

A grenade arced through the air, toward him. He rolled away and took cover. As shrapnel and ashes tickled his exposed skin, he spotted her.

Annie was crouched behind a rock, clinging to her rifle like it was a raft in the middle of the sea. Her eyes were wide and shifty, fearful of every sound, each movement.

Zeke crawled toward her, keeping out of the line of fire. "Captain?" She didn't hear. "Annie, you okay?"

He settled next to her, and she stared right through him. One of her hands left her rifle and clamped onto his forearm. She muttered, "Zeke?

That's you, right, you're Zeke?" She sounded disoriented, as if she'd just woken up from a nightmare.

"Yeah," he nodded, "yeah, it's Zeke, remember?" His heartrate ticked up, dreading her answer. Had she forgotten him?

She exhaled in relief. "Zeke!" Her muscles relaxed ever so slightly. But then an explosion rocked the stadium and a severed arm flew over their heads. She readjusted herself and drew Zeke closer. "I trust you. Don't leave my side, okay?"

Zeke didn't know what she was talking about. Did she not trust anyone else? But he didn't argue. Her words almost made him burst with pride. Or was it more than pride? Even in the middle of the battle, his palms got sweaty and he felt butterflies in his stomach being so close to her. The red-and-orange explosions illumed her face, sweat dripped from her hair, and he couldn't help but want to kiss her right then and there.

But he didn't have time to indulge his feelings. She stood and ran, and he followed, providing cover fire.

Annie couldn't catch her breath, and her knees felt like they were going to buckle any second. She'd never had a panic attack before, but this had to be pretty close to one.

As she ran across the field, the heat of battle searing her skin, one thought pounded in her brain: She had to end this and get out of here. She needed to retreat into an enclosed space where Invisible Dagger's sights wouldn't be set on her.

Where to go? What to do?

The battle plans rattled around in her memory like loose Lego pieces in a box. She recalled she had to blow something up...And then there was something about the enemy's flag?

She wanted to slap herself. Even with Zeke, a trusted ally, by her side, she was still so flustered, she couldn't think straight. She couldn't even remember what army they were fighting. This was an unmitigated disaster. An embarrassment. A train wreck.

Zeke shouted, "Annie, look out!" He yanked her out of the way of an incoming mortar shell. The explosive flew past, missing them by inches.

Annie clutched her thudding heart. They were terrifyingly close to going the way of Ranger Monroe...all because of her.

A rival soldier popped out from behind a large, mounted gun. He must've been the one who fired the mortar shell right at them...which, now that Annie thought of it, was overkill for only two fighters.

The soldier then pulled out a sleek, wicked-looking, multi-barreled Gatling gun and leveled it at them.

At that moment, Annie recognized him, and she remembered which army they were fighting.

Tremaine Dodson, of the Sun Tsunamis. This was a rematch between the Army of Liberty and the Tsunamis. A grudge match, after Tremaine Dodson had gone off-script and killed Ranger Monroe. Tremaine was supposed to have been punished for disobeying the battle plans and allegedly accepting a bribe for killing Monroe. But there he was, on the field, gunning for Annie with a wide array of overly-deadly weapons.

She froze. This had to be Invisible Dagger's doing. They'd pulled some strings and implanted Tremaine in this battle, so that he could be the one to rip her to pieces. The man who'd killed two back-to-back captains of the Army of Liberty. What a story that would be.

Tremaine's finger curled around the trigger. The gun's barrels started to spin.

Annie collapsed in a fetal position, wondering what hundreds of bullets tearing through her flesh would feel like.

Someone flopped on top of her—Zeke, using his body to shield hers.

Then, explosions. Many, many blasts, bright and hot enough to singe Annie's closed eyes.

Silence. Motionless, deafening silence.

Annie and Zeke untangled themselves and surveyed the battlefield... or what was left of it. Tremaine Dodson and most of the Sun Tsunamis had been incinerated by mines concealed in the ground. Embers and ash flitted through the air, like scorched snowflakes in a nuclear winter.

The Army of Liberty's soldiers slowly got their bearings and realized they were suddenly victorious. They mumbled to each other, knowing this battle hadn't gone remotely to plan.

And the audience knew it too. They didn't cheer or yell. A smattering of applause was all they could muster. The explosions decimating the Sun Tsunamis were too random, too *deus ex machina* for their liking. Captain Kennedy had gotten out of a sticky situation too easily, through no action of her own—the story had a cheap ending.

Then, the most dreaded sound in all of spectatorship echoed through the stadium.

"*Boo!*"

One person jeered from the nosebleed section. Ten more joined in. Then fifty, then hundreds. Thousands.

Annie shakily got to her feet as insults were lobbed her direction.

"Trash!"

"Stupid!"

"Lazy!"

She knew what had happened behind the scenes: When Tremaine Dodson was seconds away from eviscerating her, Elena Winn had hit the emergency alarm and activated some sort of last resort. She couldn't afford to have a pregnant superstar die on a global stage, so she'd broken every rule of spectatorship and fudged the storytelling.

Surely, Millennium Enterprises, who owned the Sun Tsunamis, would be furious that its army was blown to bits, along with the battle plans.

Elena's head would be on the chopping block.

Scores of fans would turn against the Army of Liberty.

And it was all because Annie had been scared.

She hung her head and let the thousands of insults rain down on her.

The audience was escorted out of the stadium faster than Annie had ever seen. Medics and custodians took to the field to drag off the injured Sun Tsunami soldiers and sweep up the dead ones. The Army of Liberty shambled to their area of the landing grounds, stunned into silence. None of them made eye contact with her, except for Zeke, who walked with her until a director dragged him away for a debrief with the rest of the army.

He tried to keep her gaze but was quickly swept along with the confused crowd.

She weaved through the landing grounds, keeping to herself, until she was finally sequestered back in her private room.

The walls pulsed as Annie ripped off her uniform. Her guns clattered to the floor, and she almost stomped on them but stopped herself at the last second. A primal scream was lodged in her chest, vibrating like a pressure cooker about to blow.

What a catastrophe. She had made it to the top of the dogpile—after years of pushing her body and putting up with the monotonous system, she'd bucked all expectations and had become a real soldier. The hundreds of voices that had told her she was too shrill, unlikable, or boring had been definitively proven wrong.

And the moment she had let the pressure get to her, she'd frozen. When the possibility of assassination loomed over her like a guillotine, she had turned into a sniveling, worthless little girl.

Her time was over. She felt it in her bones.

She slumped against the wall, emotionally, spiritually, and physically exhausted.

Footsteps. Rapid, intimidating.

The door burst open, and Elena stormed in. Her pointed earrings looked dainty compared to her eyes.

"What..." She paused to collect the words swirling inside her mouth like laundry in a dryer. When she spoke again, it was ferocious. "What was *that*, Kennedy?!"

Annie didn't have the energy for this. She glowered and kept her mouth shut.

Elena threw her arms up. "Oh, *now* you decide to be stoic! Where was that on the battlefield?" She fished a sheet of paper from her pocket. "I usually don't give the numbers any credence, but I can't help it when they're screaming at me."

Annie was surprised that her audience approval numbers had already come in, but she still didn't say anything. She'd entered this conversation silent, and she had to stick with it...and if she opened her mouth, she didn't know if a shout or a sob would come out.

"Let me interpret these figures for you," Elena snapped as she skimmed the paper. "In a word: nosedive. In a matter of minutes, you went from a real-life action hero to trembling weakling." She balled up the sheet and lobbed it at Annie. "Battles that would usually be sold out are *not*. Polling has *plummeted*. Online fan clubs have *evaporated*. You know why?"

Silence blanketed the room for a beat as Elena caught her breath. They both knew Annie wasn't going to answer.

"Because that was the entire idea of this experiment! The audience would be attached to *you*, not battles. I'm *your* director, not the director of some large-scale pissing match. People latched onto *you*...and it all backfired. Your victories were great, but your defeats are devastating."

Annie stared at the floor, a blend of anger, shame, and sorrow churning in her gut where an unborn child was supposed to be. She was close to tears, but there was no way she could let them fall.

Elena had made her point, but she kept attacking. "They don't want to see *you*. They want the captain! Strong, heroic, unbreakable." Her bark had bite. "You need to be loved, or else this is all for *nothing!*"

She pivoted toward the door. As she left, she hissed over her shoulder, "Get good sleep tonight. In the morning, you're picking a name for your kid."

Elena stomped away, leaving Annie to pick through the debris her words had created.

Annie stood alone, with no allies, no friends, no hope whatsoever. The slightest breeze would reduce her to atoms, like a dandelion scattering its seeds.

More footsteps approached. Annie winced at each sound. She couldn't take anymore abuse tonight.

Zeke Smith rocketed into the room. "Annie! Are you okay?"

She stared at him. Zeke, the one person who'd shown her a shred of respect before she'd become captain. The person who'd used his own body to shield hers during the battle. An ally. Perhaps a friend? She didn't know—she'd only met him a few times.

Before she knew what she was doing, she launched herself at him. She kissed his mouth, his cheeks, anything to keep her screams and sobs contained.

Almost immediately, Zeke kissed her back. His strong, youthful hands cupped her head.

He pulled back to speak. "Annie, I—"

She put a finger on his lips to shush him, then leaned around his frame to close the door.

Zeke took in a shaky breath and smiled.

She wanted to feel good. For the first time in months...years...she closed her eyes and simply felt good.

The sun rose over San Diego like any other morning. Clouds decorated the sky. Waves tickled the beaches, and people bustled through the city with all the drive of the first guests at an amusement park. Just as they did every day.

But Danny's morning was far from typical. The previous night, during a battle in Jackson City, the heights Annie Kennedy had reached had quickly transformed into lows. This soldier-focused real-life-action-movie experiment, headed by Elena Winn and approved by himself, had turned out to be less than fool-proof.

He shook his head as he walked down the streets of the city's Gaslamp Quarter. He should've seen this coming, or at least anticipated it. As long as soldiers were human, there was always a chance that they could do something that ticked off an audience.

"Idea," he muttered into his phone. "Android enemies. They'd make perfect antagonists. Get R&D on that." He put his phone away and continued his daily stroll.

After getting coffee from a small local vendor, he crossed to Horton Plaza Park. Early-morning yoga groups and soccer games covered the lawn.

He wondered how many of them were ex-fans of Annie Kennedy.

In the past, when a prominent Valkyrie soldier wound up being a despicable person behind closed doors, it was easy enough to flip the situation on its head to benefit the enterprise. A few years back, a superstar sergeant was revealed to be a serial sexual harasser. Dozens of women came forward to accuse him, and Danny believed them all. As such, he recruited them into another Valkyrie army. He scheduled the two armies to duke it out, and when the moment came, all the fighters pulled back except for the sergeant and his accusers. Each of the women got a chance to shoot him—justice was served, and the crowd loved it.

Presently, however, Annie Kennedy's case didn't present such a clear solution. Kennedy's only offense was being scared. Human. Her humanity—the fact that she carried a life in her belly—was one of the big reasons the public loved her in the first place. Danny didn't want to punish Kennedy, but she was undeniably less popular than she had been two days ago.

Across the park, a dad and his small daughter started to run basketball drills. The girl wore a shirt with Kennedy's face on the back, and Danny loitered to watch.

When the dad noticed his daughter's attire, he scoffed. "Sweetie, I don't want you to wear that anymore."

The girl was more puzzled than heartbroken. She looked up at her father and asked, "Why?"

"Captain Kennedy's not strong or brave, like I want you to be. Who you look up to is important, you know."

She thought for a second, then nodded. "Okay, cool."

Danny tossed his coffee in a trash can. "Crap," he muttered as he quickly walked toward Valkyrie's building. He stuck his phone to his ear. "Suzanne, you know that space battle we have on the back burner? Make it a priority—we need good buzz for Valkyrie. And I have a new idea about androids. We'll talk more. I'll be at the office in ten minutes."

He passed a pizza parlor that wasn't set to open for a few hours. A memory flashed through his mind: him and his son Zechariah eating an extra-large pepperoni pie. They were stuffed and bloated by the time the platter was empty, but they still got gelato afterwards. The ensuing evening was largely spent in the bathroom, but it was still a wonderful memory.

Shortly after Zeke had graduated high school, Danny had woken up one morning and realized all his son's belongings were gone. Zeke had moved out. Danny had tried to convince himself this wasn't that big of a deal—he was a rich and powerful man, and he could keep an eye on his son through any means.

But it had stung all the same. His son didn't want anything to do with him. So Danny had moved out of the house too, buying a condo in midtown San Diego without a second thought. A few months later, he bought a luxury cottage on the beach. A year later, a penthouse. Then a mansion. Then more condos and mansions...and so on. He kept buying new homes, each one grander than the last.

He hadn't thought about that first home in years. The modest little house he had shared with Zeke and his mother.

He wondered if he still owned it. He honestly had no idea.

He hoped so.

He impulsively wanted to call Zeke, just to check in and see how his experience in the Army of Liberty was going. But he'd called Zeke countless times over the years, and his son had never answered. So this time, he didn't bother calling.

The café in Jackson City was busy this morning. The battle the night before had ignited opinions from coast to coast. No one was indifferent on the subject of Annie Kennedy—people either adored her or hated her rotten guts. Servers, patrons, and chefs all buzzed with conversation as they went about their breakfast.

Jasmine sat across from a small, middle-aged woman with unwashed hair and bags under her eyes. Jasmine had figured this woman would be the most sought-after interview in the world, but much to her surprise,

Margie Dodson's schedule was completely empty...especially now that her son and only living relative was no longer alive.

Ever since Nashville, Jasmine and Ravi had been wandering the southeastern quadrant of the U.S., waiting for sightings of either Annie Kennedy or Invisible Dagger. The terrorist cell was making its way across the country in a westerly fashion, so it stood to reason that their next target after Nashville would be in that radius.

As soon as Tremaine Dodson and most of the Sun Tsunamis had been wiped out during the previous night's battle in Jackson City, Jasmine had sprung into action. Following her notion of what happens after the heroics, she had tracked down Tremaine's mother, called her up, and asked to speak with her. Between trembling sobs, Margie had agreed.

"Tremaine and I live in Pensacola, Florida," Margie meekly explained. "The battle last night was here in Jackson City, and I needed to get up for work at the hospital this morning. So I couldn't drive out to watch the battle."

Jasmine, who was still getting the hang of local geography, nodded along.

Margie continued. "I watched on TV as my son and his comrades were blown up."

Her voice was hoarse and unsteady. Jasmine hoped her audio recorder on the café table was strong enough to catch all her words. Ravi was waiting outside—Jasmine hadn't wanted to shove a camera in Margie's face mere hours after her son's death.

Margie coughed out a laugh. "But I didn't go to work this morning anyway. I drove up here to identify his remains. So I should've been at the stadium last night. I should've been in the audience for his last moments."

Jasmine asked, "Are you a nurse? A doctor?"

"I clean the sinks. They won't miss me. I'd rather be here, talking to you." She leaned in to speak directly into the recorder. "I want everyone to know that Tremaine was good. He killed that Monroe man, yes, but he was literally in the heat of battle. No one gets angry at the thousands of soldiers who kill thousands of others every day. Tremaine just did what the war wanted him to."

Jasmine kept her emotions in check. She wanted to empathize with Margie, sob alongside her and offer to buy her breakfast. Instead, she stayed detached and tried to draw out the sort of soundbites that she needed for her show. "Are you angry at anyone, Mrs. Dodson?"

"Ms.," Margie corrected. "And you'd best believe I'm angry." Her voice rumbled, as if a sleeping dragon had been roused. "I'm angry at Millennium Enterprises, but mainly at Valkyrie. They're the ones who set off those mines. That's what the internet's saying! Danny Carr, General Lightfoot, Leigh Gambol...And to tell the truth, I'm not too happy with Annie Kennedy either!"

A gruff-looking man perked up across the café. "Kennedy? That blubbering excuse for a soldier. Don't get me started on her."

"Hey!" A woman in her twenties joined in. "You don't get to have an opinion on her. She's a strong woman in a man's world. A hero!"

"Strong? Bah!" The man spat on the floor, riling up those around him. "She's strong as a snail. I could be a better captain than her."

Someone else yelled, "I'd like to see you try, jackwad!"

Another angry voice: "I hate Kennedy too, but you're no captain."

"I could kill a whole army by myself! Soldiers today are so soft."

"No kidding. Did you see how scared Kennedy was last night? No backbone."

"You wanna see backbone?!" SMASH.

The once-quaint café quickly devolved into a battlefield of its own. Strangers screamed at each other. Food and cutlery flew through the air. Glass shattered. A punch or two were thrown. Annie Kennedy's name had divided the crowd and turned everyday people into sworn enemies.

Jasmine pocketed her recorder and steered Margie out to the sidewalk, where Ravi was waiting. With his flip-flops, shell necklace, and camera bag, he stuck out like a hitchhiker's thumb. He peered through the window. "What's going on in there?"

Margie sighed, deflated. "Nothing. A whole lotta nothing." She shuffled away without asking Jasmine if the interview was done.

The alarm clock blared in Annie's ear, and it took every ounce of self-control she had to not crush it into a million pieces. She slowly readjusted herself to the land of the living, taking in her hotel room.

She groaned, remembering she was still in Jackson City. The disastrous battle. Her tanking poll numbers. Her docket for today: naming the baby in front of a bunch of cameras. It all came rushing back, and she wanted to stay in the cocoon of blankets. But she knew Elena would personally drag her out of the hotel by her big toes if she was late.

It took a few tries to get out of bed, thanks to her aching muscles. She staggered to the shower and let hot water run down her body.

Then, more memories bubbled to the surface, and she shivered with delight. Her night with Zeke in her private room at the stadium. Well, it wasn't so much a night—more like an hour.

As soon as they were done making each other feel good, she'd led him out of the stadium to the parking lot. He had looked self-conscious as he called for a taxi, while her ride was a chauffeured stretch Humvee. She wasn't used to people being embarrassed around her or hoping to impress her, and she thought it was cute.

She wanted to see him again. Soon. He made her heart pound...and not in the same way warfare did. He was a good deal younger than she, but he had a kind way about him, a caring spirit, and boundless energy. Lots of energy, for sure.

A giggle rustled her throat. She hadn't giggled in a long time.

Someone pounded on her hotel door, but no words followed. Annie shut off the shower and prepared herself for a public appearance. With military efficiency, she groomed and dressed in less than five minutes, then tramped down the stairs to the lobby.

Like a tireless wraith, Elena Winn waited for her by the stairway. She wore the same clothes and sour expression as she had last night, but her hair was only slightly ruffled. No doubt, she had been up all night, combating the fires of Annie's poor performance, but she didn't look fatigued in the least.

She eyed Annie and cocked a single brow. It was as if...

Annie dismissed the notion.

But then Elena chuckled silently to herself.

Did she know about Annie and Zeke?

Surely not. How could she?

"Right this way," Elena said. "Your public awaits." She gestured to the exit, where reporters and bloggers must be lingering outside.

They walked toward the door together. Annie quietly asked, "What am I naming the baby?"

Elena mockingly responded, "I thought *you* wanted to be the one to name it?"

Annie swallowed. "Clearly, my instincts aren't driving us in a good direction. I defer to your direction, ma'am."

"Oh," Elena chortled, "I'm back to *ma'am*, am I?" She sighed dramatically and handed Annie two sealed envelopes, one pink and the other blue. "Read them both on the air. You're waiting for the birth to know its sex, so one name is for if it's a boy, one is for if it's a girl."

They stepped out to greet the ocean of reporters...but the ocean was more of a puddle. Previously, the press had been glued to Annie. This morning, only a handful of correspondents were present to hear the name of Annie's unborn child, information that would've been headline news a few days ago.

Annie waved at the people and cleared her throat, signaling she was about to begin. One of the reporters hoisted a camera onto his shoulder and aimed its black eye at her.

A thought pricked Annie's mind.

Cameras. Elena had access to microscopic, easily hidden cameras, like the ones that had filmed Annie during her chase through Nashville.

Is that how Elena knew about Annie's tryst with Zeke? Had she watched the whole thing? Elena was devious and sly, but would she do something like *that*?

She honestly didn't want to answer that question, even in her own mind.

"Thank you for coming out today." She tried to put some bounce in her voice to mask her anxiety. Her heart was still pumping at the thought of Invisible Dagger gunning for her, but she didn't dare show that vulnerability. Not after last night's performance.

With all the charisma of a caged bear, she continued, "It means the world to me that you would come hear this special announcement..."

It was no use. The reporters and bloggers were zoning out. They could clearly tell that she wasn't being sincere, and she had never been a good actress.

The words "lacking," "shrill," and "unlikable" flashed before her eyes.

She changed tactics. "So here we go," she muttered as she opened the pink envelope. Her stoic persona was a better bet than trying to come across as earnest or bubbly, two things she definitely wasn't.

She read her prospective baby girl's name, and she almost groaned. The name Monroe stared back at her in bold letters.

If the girl's name was Monroe, she had a good guess as to what was written in the blue envelope.

The journalists and cameras waited for her to speak again, but with less-than-bated breath. Most tapped their phones, and one was even eating a messy breakfast burrito.

An ember of resistance burned in Annie's chest. *She* was the one to come up with her strong-and-silent persona in the first place. Elena had wanted her to read cheesy lines and preen for the audience. Why should she follow Elena's every direction?

Before she could talk herself out of it, Annie squared her shoulders and said, "If my child is a girl, I'll name her Junior. If it's a boy...Junior. Or I might change my mind. I'm open to suggestions, but it's ultimately my kid."

Much to her shock, a few reporters laughed at her candor. Others nodded along.

She crumpled the envelopes in her fist. "That's all I have to say about that. Any questions?"

With the smaller number of reporters, they felt closer to Annie. The overall vibe was more personal. They asked her lower-stakes questions about her childhood, where she grew up, how many miles she could run... fluffy interview questions like that.

Annie gave short but honest answers, and she could feel the trust forming between her and the journalists. It was refreshing, after the literal and figurative battle she had gone through the night before.

As she spoke with the reporters, she ignored the chilly breeze emanating from Elena Winn.

Jody paced back and forth in the grass behind the dingy motel. Back and forth, back and forth. Rod was off making a food run into town, but he was taking forever. How long did it take to pick up a Happy Meal and a McFlurry?

Invisible Dagger had been laying low since Jody declared war on Annie Kennedy. Rod managed their public image, and he'd thought it was best to strike as soon as possible, but Holland was their leader, and his decision was to spend a week or two underground.

Metaphorically underground. Jody had been disappointed when Holland explained to him that they weren't going to stay in a literal bunker.

As they laid low, Jody needed to stay inside. His face was too recognizable, thanks to Invisible Dagger's online presence. In the past week, their subscribers had skyrocketed, news outlets talked about them nearly constantly, and a Funko Pop figure of Jody had hit the shelves. As much as he wanted to buy one, Holland told him to wait a bit—the FBI might be using the Funko as a means of drawing him out and capturing him.

Invisible Dagger was as successful as ever, but that very success meant Jody couldn't go out in public and draw attention. Hence, he waited as Rod fetched their dinner.

Not a day went by that he didn't miss Staten. Heck, not even a minute. He'd been the best friend Jody had ever had.

Jody rubbed his bald head and paced faster. He had a ton of pent-up energy coursing through his body. He needed to get back in the action. Moreover, he wanted to strike back at Kennedy.

Speak of the devil...

Tires approached the motel. Their red van rolled into the parking lot, with Holland behind the wheel.

Jody knew what this meant. Each time before an attack, Holland disappeared for a few days, driving off in their van and returning with the supplies they needed to complete their mission. Jody didn't know where he went, but he trusted his leader.

Holland, the brains. They would be dead in the water without him.

Jody waved, but as usual, Holland was all business.

"Come back to the room." The thick scar bisecting his face wriggled as he spoke. "It's time to start planning our next move."

Jody pumped his fist. "'Bout time. Where're we headed?"

Holland smirked. "How do the Great Lakes sound?"

"Great!" Jody cackled at his own joke, but Holland merely sighed. Jody tromped back to the motel room, deflated. Staten would've loved that joke.

Two weeks later, Annie was back in San Diego, being driven downtown. She was satisfied with the smaller, close-knit interviews she had given over the past few days.

She had an appointment at the headquarters of the Army of Liberty. Twice a year, the general and captain met together at HQ to discuss strategies, tactics, and other military matters. This was Annie's first summit with the army's longtime general Richard Lightfoot, other than meeting him briefly on the field.

As soon as she saw the blinking lights and gaudy signage, she knew she was in the right place.

A massive, kaleidoscopic billboard screamed at her, "*Welcome to the Army of Liberty Headquarters, Resort, and Casino!*" Hundreds of cars clogged the parking lot, even at the afternoon hour. She could hear the stock music thrumming from inside.

Her car pulled up to the entrance. She donned wide sunglasses and a floppy hat, hoping to avoid any public attention, be it adulation or disgust. She hopped out and was greeted by a cocktail of smells: sunblock, barbeque, Lemon Pledge, deodorant, cigarettes...

She felt like she was committing a federal crime when she stepped into the lobby, because the tile floor was designed like a sprawling American flag. Live eagles were perched above, costumed Uncle Sams took pictures with families, and lights simulating fireworks flashed in every direction.

Beyond the lobby, the bustling casino beckoned to her with the sounds of winning—bells, whistles, kazoos, and sirens. People of all ages (the legal gambling age had recently been lowered to twelve) were hunched over slot machines and gathered around craps tables. Despite the festive atmosphere, most everyone looked browbeaten, like they'd just lost more money than they'd intended.

She headed for an elevator toward the back of the large room. General Lightfoot's office was on a higher floor, and she assumed that was where the meeting would take place—Lightfoot's communications with his underlings were notoriously scant.

An overhead voice reminded everyone to visit the all-you-can-eat buffet before checking out one of the resort's ten swimming pools. Many people followed that cue and shuffled out of the casino, opening up plenty of slot machines and poker tables for a new batch of guests.

Annie passed a line of slots, and in the corner of her eye, she recognized someone.

General Lightfoot lounged in front of a colorful machine, lazily inserting coins, yanking the lever, gathering his winnings, and repeating the process. Even among this crowd, Lightfoot was far older than most, his uniform nearly swallowing his frail body.

"Sir?" She approached him.

His yellowed eyes flicked to her. "Oh, hey. Kimmy—no, Kendell—wait, I got it. Kennedy, right? Pleasure to see you, hope you're doing well, and all that."

He'd seen through her sunglasses and hat faster than Annie had anticipated. Everyone knew of the old man, but few had ever spoken with him directly. The talk around Valkyrie was unanimous: Richard Lightfoot was a ninety-eight-year-old fossil. Senile. Practically worthless. A wet sandcastle ready to be knocked down.

But she saw something behind those yellow eyes. A stubborn spark, unwilling to be stomped out.

She nodded once. "Are you ready to talk strategy, sir?"

Lightfoot exhaled, then continued playing with the slot machine. "Strategy...Sure thing, skipper. Let's chat down here."

"Down here?" She looked around at the gambling tourists, flashing lights, and overall Chuck E. Cheese ambiance. "Sir, wouldn't it be better to discuss military matters upstairs?"

"Meh, I don't think so." He hit a button on the machine, which illuminated a light above him, signaling that he wanted a drink. Then he shrugged to Annie. "I'm the general, you're the captain. We do what we want, right?"

A server appeared out of nowhere with a tray. She gave Lightfoot a glass of white-and-brown liquid, along with a pill, then vanished just as quickly.

Lightfoot rolled his eyes and grumbled, "My usual." He downed the pill with the drink before anyone could see him taking it. He stabbed a knobby finger at Annie. "Don't tell anyone."

Annie deduced that the drink was a White Russian, and the pill was a Lactaid. She innocently replied, "Tell anyone what, sir?"

"Yeah, yeah." Lightfoot chuckled dryly and stuck another coin in the slot machine. "How about this?" He set his hands on his knees and hoisted himself into a standing position—no easy feat. "We head to a poker table. You beat me, we can go talk upstairs. But if I beat you, we stay right down here." He gazed at the casino floor with wide eyes, as if it were Shambhala.

She slid the sunglasses off her nose and tilted a brow at him. "Sounds good, sir."

He waved his hands in the air as he shuffled away from the slots. "Sir, sir, sir. Blah, blah, blah. I get enough of that everywhere else. Call me Rich. Or nothing. I'm fine with that too."

As they walked, a few patrons noticed Annie without her large sunglasses, and a wave of whispers spread across the casino floor. A few photos were snapped, a boo here, a cheer there. Not as bad as Annie had feared. She shed her floppy hat as well, letting her hair breathe.

Another thought landed in her gut...She was captain of the Army of Liberty *in* the Army of Liberty's headquarters. Of all places, this is where her most vocal fans and opponents should be. And yet, she was walking through without being swarmed.

Had apathy already taken root among the Army of Liberty's followers? Could that be worse than being derided?

She shook her head to evict those thoughts. She had a poker game to play.

Lightfoot approached a full table. He snarled at two players, "Hey, lowlifes. Buzz off." They scrambled out of his way, and he casually said to Annie, "Oh look, two seats just opened up. Our lucky day."

They sat.

Despite her better judgment, Annie was starting to like the old general.

When the dealer prepared to start a new game, Lightfoot told him, "Don't mind us, Barry. We won't be placing down any chips, but take some cash out of my account to make it up to the other fine players at this table. Oh, and one more thing...Make it a seven-card stud, will you?" He leaned back in his chair and smirked at Annie.

She settled in too. Seven-card stud was a variant of Texas hold 'em she wasn't too familiar with, but it wasn't a hurdle she couldn't surmount.

After the other players placed their wagered chips on the table, the dealer gave each player two cards facedown. And so the game began.

Players folded left and right until Annie and Lightfoot were the lone survivors. A small crowd had amassed around the table, watching the two military giants duke it out over cards.

The final round arrived. Annie and Lightfoot received their blind cards, and Barry dealt three more cards face-up.

Lightfoot peeked at his cards, then sighed. He glanced at Annie and, apropos of nothing, asked, "How many bullets are inside you right now?"

Annie paused, taken aback by the question. "None. Why?"

"The way you scowl and glower, I would've wagered you had some steel pushed up between your cheeks." The crowd around them burst into churlish laughter, but Lightfoot only smirked, never taking his eyes off her.

Barry dealt the final card, face-down.

Annie kept her face stony. Blank. Unfeeling. "Well, how many bullets are in *you*, general?"

"Six," Lightfoot answered naturally, as if commenting on the weather. "And I'll leave their locations to your imagination."

Again, Annie was surprised, but she didn't let it on. She then remembered that Richard Lightfoot was a remnant from the era before spectatorship. He had participated in real wars, without directors or battle plans. The fear Annie had felt while being targeted by Invisible Dagger had been constant for Lightfoot while he was on those battlefields.

"And so," Lightfoot revealed his cards, "it comes to this." He had a full house. A good hand. The crowd clapped for him, and he waggled his white eyebrows at her.

"And so it does." Annie released a breath and uncovered her own hand... four of a kind. A better hand, but only just.

Cheers erupted from the audience, and for a moment, Annie felt like she was back in a stadium, and she soaked in all the applause she could.

Lightfoot laughed as the crowd dissipated. "Not many people can beat me. How'd you do that?"

"I was a nurse in the Great Plains Brigade for ten years. A lot of night shifts, a lot of card games."

"Well, I'm true to my word. Care to move upstairs and chat?"

Annie wanted to smile, but she kept her stony mask in place. "I wouldn't say no to one more bout."

"I'll drink to that!" He waved a finger again, and another White Russian came swooping in. "What's your poison, captain?"

She patted her stomach. "Can't."

"What, are you full? You can always fit in one more drink. I know that from experience."

"No, Rich, I'm pregnant. Remember, the maternal warrior, and all that?"

"Hmm." Lightfoot swallowed another pill along with half of his drink. "Must've missed that. But I have to say, you don't look very knocked up."

She gulped and deftly avoided the implication. "I'll take that as a compliment. Ready to play?"

Lightfoot eyed her warily but dropped the subject. "Alright, Barry. Deal us up."

"Suzanne! Where are you?"

The walls of Danny's office on the top floor of the Valkyrie building were covered with photos and blueprints. Suzanne strolled in and nearly tripped over a model of an Orion rocket. She refrained from rolling her eyes, as much as she desperately wanted to.

She liked and respected Danny Carr a lot. His mind was sharp, and his personality could...Well, could win over both the prime minister of Israel and the president of Palestine. She believed he was the sole person in the world who could've done that.

Yet, he was prone to obsession. He wasn't accustomed to failing, so when Annie Kennedy's numbers had plunged a couple weeks ago, Danny had followed them into a tailspin of his own. He'd thrown himself into orchestrating an epic battle in outer space, the first of its kind.

It was going predictably poorly. Not even the great Danny Carr could get gravity and orbits to obey him.

She readied herself before speaking. There was no telling what sort of mood he would be in. "Yes, Danny, I'm here."

Danny emerged from behind his desk. Judging by his unkempt hair and rumpled suit, he had stayed in the office overnight. Again.

His voice jittered from being overly caffeinated. "Let me know as soon as a call from Oleum Corp comes in. If I can sway their CEO just right, we could have enough fuel to launch..." He checked a spreadsheet taped to a window. "...a hundred soldiers and rifles, ten camera operators and their gear, ammo, explosives, uniforms..." He tapped his chin as he thought.

She offered, "What about food?"

Danny spun to look at her. "Huh?"

"You know, eating? All those people have to eat and drink. Space travel isn't a half-day trip. They'll be up there for a whole orbital cycle, and they'll need enough food."

He hung his head. "Food is heavy."

She stepped away to let him wallow with his spreadsheet. Before she walked away, she said, "Don't count out Annie Kennedy yet. She's strong."

Danny ruffled his hair as if trying to jump-start his brain. He gazed at Suzanne desperately. "You think so?"

She nodded.

"How do you know?"

"Call me a believer." She turned to leave. "Let me know if you need anything else."

Salvatore checked his plane ticket one more time to make sure he was at the right gate. Yes, he was. Plenty early.

When given the choice between sitting and standing, Salvatore always chose to be on his feet. It kept him from feeling idle, and it allowed him to keep his head on a swivel, always surveying his surroundings. As he stood, he feasted on a Cinnabon, which was probably his favorite thing about airports.

He was headed to West Texas without an exact plan. He imagined he could pick any town on a map at random, and he would find a few restless teens who dreamed of excitement and were enthusiastic about firearms. It shouldn't be too hard to rope a few of them into joining a Valkyrie army.

If they threatened or shot at him, he wouldn't complain. Quite the contrary—he was looking for prospective soldiers with a little spunk.

A TV fixed to the wall caught his attention. On it, Annie Kennedy was being interviewed by some blogger.

Salvatore admired Kennedy. After her disastrous showing at a battle a few weeks prior, she had bounced back, inch by inch.

The interviewer asked, "Captain, what do you consider to be your greatest asset to your army?"

Kennedy stared right back at the interviewer with eyes made of flint. Most people would try to build a rapport, laugh a little, or at least smile. Instead, Annie Kennedy was as impassive as one of those Easter Island heads.

She answered, "I'm fast, I'm strong, and I lead." Short and to the point.

Another question: "And how would you summarize your strategy for leading?"

"I win battles."

All her answers were clipped and matter-of-fact. Just as one would expect from a powerful warrior.

Salvatore chuckled. It was clear to him that Kennedy was leaning hard into her stoic persona. He thought it was a brilliant move—after freezing in the middle of a battle, that was her best response.

Over the years, he had seen military superstars rise and fall. If Kennedy could cement her identity as a cold, calculating, unfeeling soldier, she had a shot at being one of the greats.

Even though she couldn't hear him, he gave a piece of advice to the image of Annie Kennedy on the TV. "If you want anyone to care about you, you can't care about anyone."

The airline announced that his flight was boarding. Salvatore finished his Cinnabon in one huge bite, wished Kennedy luck, and got in line to board.

～✦～

Annie fidgeted at a table in a back corner of the restaurant. Stringy music flitted through the air. More pieces of silverware than she had seen in her entire life sat in front of her. She desperately craved a hearty gulp of wine to calm her nerves, but she had to maintain her image as a mom-to-be. Thus, her nerves had nowhere to go, and she resorted to fiddling with the condensation on her water glass.

Why was she so nervous?

She obviously knew the answer to that question, so she tried to ignore it with more fiddling. She rubbed the tablecloth between her fingers, absently wondering if she could buy bedsheets as soft.

So far, no one had recognized her. At least, no one had made it obvious that they had recognized her. Hopefully, the class of people in this restaurant wouldn't hiss and throw food at her if they were so inclined.

A large window displaying the street outside briefly lit up as a stretch Humvee rolled into view.

Annie breathed in...then out. In...then out.

The rear passenger door opened, and Zeke Smith stepped out. Annie was no expert, but the suit he wore looked to be on the expensive side. He was the son of an executive producer at Valkyrie Productions, after all. He surely had some cash to toss around.

She glanced at her own attire. She wore a modest red dress she had bought for a wedding years and years ago. It was plain and low-cost—the opposite of ritzy. She'd never had a reason nor the means to purchase fancy apparel or glittering jewelry. And to be honest, she'd never much wanted to. Clothes weren't her number one priority.

But now she was a woman of means. She had money and influence. And...she had someone she wanted to impress. She made a mental note to beef up her wardrobe very soon.

Zeke entered the restaurant, and a tuxedoed manager pointed him toward Annie's table. He sauntered between the tables.

When he locked eyes with her, all she could hear was her own heartbeat. Something about his presence simultaneously made her nervous and put her at ease. Around him, she felt recklessly safe.

He sat across from her and smiled. "Hey, Annie. How're you doing?"

She nodded her greeting. How did people chitchat on dates? This was light years outside her areas of expertise. "Good. I'm good."

An internal heckler bashed her for that incredibly ineloquent reply. She wanted to say something witty or smart, but that wasn't her thing. Being unemotional had won her fans—some soldiers were quippy and sassy, some were violent brutes, others waxed poetic and were members of Mensa...but she had built her newfound reputation on stoicism. Even before then, she hadn't exactly been a prom queen. She didn't know how to make friends, much less go on dates.

Despite all her private worries, Zeke smiled. He nodded in response, too. "Good. That's good."

She let out a breath, and tension fled from her muscles. She remembered how pleasant it had been hanging out with him in the waiting room in Chicago. Neither of them were chatty, but they were both fine with that. It had been a relief then. She hoped this night would be the same.

The waiter approached and asked for their orders. She had googled the menu beforehand, and so she ordered a simple dish without too many fancy toppings that she would have to discreetly pick off.

Zeke then told the waiter, "Same."

Annie sputtered for a moment as the tuxedoed waiter scuttled away. "Oh, Zeke, I, uh...Sorry, I ordered something easy. Not very fancy."

He shrugged. "Good. Fancy food isn't all it's cracked up to be."

The orchestral music filled the silence between them, along with clinking forks and murmured conversations. But it wasn't an uncomfortable silence. They smiled and allowed themselves to simply enjoy each other's company.

She remembered and asked, "Oh, how was the car that picked you up? Everything okay? Do I need to beat up the driver?" The last sentence had meant to be a joke, but she wasn't accustomed to being funny, and it sounded like a genuine question.

"It was nice." He sipped his water. "Really nice. Thanks for sending it to pick me up." He moved on from the topic. "What'd you do today?"

"Well…" She thought as she twiddled with her polished silverware. "I talked with Elena Winn, my director, for a bit. We're still doing interviews to recover from my performance a few weeks ago." He gazed at her sympathetically. She hated it, so she kept talking. "Umm, then I confirmed this reservation, and I scheduled that car to pick you up. Should I call the driver again to take you home after dinner?" She reached for her phone, hoping to impress Zeke with her ability to have such a luxurious vehicle at her beck and call.

He held up his hands. "I, uh…No thanks. Fancy cars and fancy food, the high-end executive kind of life…That's not my scene."

Annie gulped. Had she offended him by arranging for the car to drive him here?

She kept her face impassive. "So what'd you do today?"

He rocked his head side to side. "Not much. Worked out, mostly."

"All day?"

He chuckled. "Does it not look like it?"

If she was honest, it absolutely looked like it. His broad shoulders and strong arms filled his suit well. Memories of their night together flashed in her mind. But she didn't want to sound crude, so she calmly said, "No, it does. What's your fastest mile?"

"I'm not much of a runner. You?"

"In my prime, seven minutes, forty-nine seconds." She sighed inwardly and trailed off. "That was about ten years ago."

Zeke blinked a few times, as if he'd just realized their age difference. It was true, he was only twenty, and she was long past thirty, but she didn't see it as an insurmountable hurdle. She enjoyed his company. He made her feel comfortable.

And the way he was beaming at her, she hoped the feeling was at least a little mutual. It took every ounce of willpower in her body to keep her face stoic, to suppress a giddy smile.

Their food arrived, and they ate, content to listen to the music and not fill every second with conversation.

All in all, Annie thought their first date was going very well. The warmth in her chest and the glint in his eyes told her there would be many more to come.

Jody and Roderick stared in awe at what lay on the ground before them.

A dozen cylinders, each about the size of a piece of carry-on luggage, sat in a pile in the middle of the living room at Holland's feet. Invisible Dagger had several safe houses established throughout the country...with safe house being defined as the residence of a willing fan. Currently, Jody, Holland, and Rod were staying with Darnell, a forty-something divorcee who, as such, had several empty rooms available for his favorite domestic terrorist cell to crash in.

Jody leaned in for a closer look at the cylinders. "What are they, Holland?"

Holland leered with wicked pride. "These are..." He prattled off their technical/scientific/artsy-fartsy name, which flew right over Jody's head.

When Holland saw the glaze that had instantly formed over Jody's eyes, he clarified. "Militaries have nicknamed these beauties Needle Drops."

That told Jody everything he needed to know. He exhaled and rubbed his hands together with glee.

Bombs. The twelve luggage-sized cylinders were bombs.

Jody gaped. "Where do you get these things?"

Holland patted the air as if dismissing an inquisitive child. "I have my ways. Let's pack them up and get moving."

Rod asked, "What will we do once we get to Milwaukee?"

This question, Holland answered with relish. "We'll rain down hell from the sky—"

"Cupcakes!" Their host Darnell barreled into the living room, stepping on Holland's big evil moment. He held a tray of garishly colored sweets.

Holland stewed silently at being interrupted, but Jody stampeded toward Darnell and stuffed as many cupcakes into his mouth at once as he could.

Darnell flashed an expectant smile. "Well? How are they?"

Through a full mouth, Jody mumbled, "Pretty dry." Then he ate five more.

❧

Nothing put Annie in a great mood like a five a.m. run. She set out from her home and started a lap around the neighborhood, dressed in whatever clothing she wanted, because there would be no cameras around to catch her. Who cared if she wore a top that clashed with her shoes? Not her, that's for sure.

As she jogged away, she peeked over her shoulder at the home that she still didn't think of as hers. She didn't sleep much in the primary bedroom, preferring the living room couch or one of the plush recliners. Rest didn't come easily to her when she was nestled in the same bed that the late Ranger Monroe had used.

The sky was a soothing shade of dark blue. Almost no one else was out and about. And if she listened carefully, she could almost hear the ocean in the distance. That was likely just her imagination, but the sound of waves kept her heartrate steady, so she went with it.

Crash...Hiss...Whoosh...Hiss...

She loved the sound of the ocean. So relentless and wild, yet constant and rhythmic. That's how she wanted to come across when on the battle-field: strong, unremitting, impassive, unpredictable.

The maternal warrior. As beautiful and harsh as the sea.

She nodded to herself. That was a good angle for marketing—she should call Elena today and tell her.

Her sneakered feet took her around a corner, and there, leaning against a stranger's mailbox, was the devil herself.

Elena saw Annie approaching and waved cordially, as if they were meeting in a café for brunch. She looked as if she'd been awake for hours, complete with makeup, jewelry, and a dossier tucked under her arm.

Annie slowed to a stop, her lungs trembling with a pleasure that only a runner could know. But her pulse ratcheted up a gear at the sight of her director, waiting for her on a random route around her neighborhood at five in the morning. It was just like the day they had first met—Elena had somehow found Annie casually strolling on a beach.

"Morning," Elena said, her voice rupturing the early-morning silence. "How was your dinner with Private Carr last night?"

Annie eyed her director warily. She didn't like Elena's sharp tone when calling Zeke "Private Carr"—for one, she seemed to be shaming Annie for going out with such a low-ranking soldier. Also, Zeke had purposefully tried to obfuscate his relationship with Danny Carr. Elena touting his real name was the opposite of what Zeke wanted.

Annie stood up straight. "It was very nice, ma'am."

"Good to hear." Elena flipped open the dossier and read something to herself. "Get back to your house and pack. We're flying to Milwaukee in a couple hours."

"Milwaukee?" Annie wiped sweat from her forehead. "What's there?"

"My contact tells me Invisible Dagger is gonna bomb it. You're going to stop them and get your numbers back up." Elena closed the dossier and spun on her heel. She walked to a car idling down the street and said, "See you at the airport, captain."

Rays of sunrise began to dye the horizon. Annie took a breath—it was going to be a long day.

BANG. THWICK. POP.

Zeke took his eye away from his rifle's sight, and he smiled. He'd blown the head right off a dummy. He turned on the safety, set down his gun, and turned away from the shooting range. He sauntered to his backpack, which was waiting on a bench away from the practicing soldiers.

The Army of Liberty's private shooting range was right on the border of Mexico, with targets affixed on the massive stone wall that separated the two countries. Mexican armies had the same deal arranged, with targets on their side of the wall too. As such, the wall was peppered with more bullets than could be counted, and gunfire filled the air twenty-four hours a day.

There were more soldiers practicing here than there had been a month ago. Zeke smirked to himself—he couldn't help but attribute that fact to his excellent performance in recent battles. He was rising in popularity due to his drive and persistence. It seemed his fellow soldiers were finally willing to rise to the occasion and put in the extra work to become as good as he was.

Yes. He was on the rise. A director had told him his polling numbers were great. A few online fan clubs had cropped up. People were starting to cheer for him specifically. If he kept pushing and excelling, he knew there was no ceiling on his success.

And being seen going on dates with Captain Kennedy surely couldn't hurt.

He shook his head to dismiss that Machiavellian thought. He cared for Annie—he truly did. He liked being around her and spending time with her. The night of passion they had shared was just as enjoyable as their friendly dinner date. He smiled at the memories.

He fished his phone from his backpack. No missed calls, no texts. A thought niggled its way forward: Why wasn't Annie calling him?

Again, he didn't give himself time for that question to take root. Annie was the captain of the army—she was likely busy, off saving the world or something. He was confident they'd had a great time at dinner and that she would reach out when she could.

But it was strange that his dad hadn't called either. Zeke wouldn't have answered or called back...but it was strange. He usually called every day or so.

For the first time that he could remember, loneliness prodded his heart. He couldn't stop the avalanche of negative thoughts that were piling on top of him one by one: His fellow soldiers didn't like him very much, he didn't have any real friends, Annie didn't care enough to reach out to him, and his dad wasn't calling anymore.

Zeke didn't even like his dad, but every time his old man called, he felt a little important. Sought out. Wanted. He got more than a little kick out of rejecting his dad's calls each time, as if he finally held the upper hand in the relationship. *"No, no, Dad, I'm busy at the moment. Busy being successful and popular. You'll have to wait. I'll get back to you. Never."*

But now, his dad had taken that away from him.

Zeke stuffed his phone back in his bag and returned to his rifle, ready to rip more dummies to shreds.

⁓⟞⟞⁓

Jody rubbed his eyes. He hated driving overnight—he could never get good sleep on the road, and, for some reason unknown to even him, being stuck in a seat for hours on end played havoc with his bowels. But now they were on the streets of Milwaukee, ready to do some damage.

They had driven their red van, the twelve bombs packed snugly in the back, all of the way from the eastern part of the country to the outskirts of Milwaukee. Holland had parked outside a breakfast joint, where they were going to eat before starting their mission, and he was now leading Jody and Roderick somewhere on foot.

The apartments and stores were a bit older, but far from run-down. A crisp breeze from Lake Michigan mellowed everything out, as if the whole world had taken a chill pill. It was nice. Nestled. Quiet and contented. Jody felt a tuft of melancholy at the idea of bombing this place. Just a tuft.

He pulled his phone from his pocket and started livestreaming as he walked down the sidewalk. It was still early enough in the day that there were no pedestrians around to recognize them and swarm them for autographs and selfies.

"What's up, Daggsters? It's your main man Jody. We're here in..." He caught himself at the last second. "...an undisclosed city, and we're about to make a scene. So tell your friends, like and subscribe, and keep an eye out. Once we get started, you'll get a front-row seat to watch the action!" He turned the phone to show Holland and Rod walking beside him. "Guys, say hi to everyone!"

Rod's face lit up. He wasn't accustomed to being on-camera, and he took a second to compose himself. He cleared his throat and opened his mouth, clearly elated at the prospect of the world hearing his voice for the very first time—

But Holland shoved his palm over the camera's lens. "Jody, turn that off!" He wrestled the phone out of Jody's grip and cut off the livestream.

Jody simmered. "Dude, *never* do that again." He machine-gunned his words. "Our connection with our fans is what keeps us alive. If it looks like you're hiding something from them, you could undo everything!"

Holland glared at Jody, but Jody didn't back down. Jody knew without a doubt that he was in the right—he was the one who communicated with their fans. One word from Jody, and their millions of followers would turn on Holland without hesitation.

And Holland knew all this too. So he didn't retort. He simply gestured ahead. "We're here."

A huge warehouse loomed at the end of the street. The rising sun peeked out from behind it, casting massive shadows across the street. Across the entire city, it seemed.

Holland unlocked the warehouse's door and slid it open. "All right," he huffed, "get the bombs loaded. I don't want to be in this city longer than necessary."

Jody saw what was being kept in the warehouse, and his gut churned. It was a tall, wide, monstrous helicopter. It looked military, but Jody was no expert.

"Ugh, I hate flying..." he muttered.

Holland bustled away to swing the van around, so they could pack the bombs onboard. Jody bristled and shot Rod a side-glance. In that moment, they made a silent agreement.

They would stall as much as they could. They didn't want to get out of Milwaukee quickly. They wanted to give Annie Kennedy plenty of time to show up and try to save the day.

And then, they would show her what happened when she messed with Invisible Dagger.

❦

Annie adjusted her leather jacket, making sure it covered the pistol tucked into her waistband. She strolled through downtown Milwaukee, headed in the general direction of McKinley Park, which was on the shore of Lake Michigan. The city's geography was foreign to her for the most part, but Elena had told her to stay in the metro vicinity.

Invisible Dagger would want to cause as much damage as possible in front of a large crowd, and downtown fit the bill.

After hours of traveling and getting situated, it was now mid-afternoon. Almost evening. Annie suppressed a yawn. It had been a tiring day full of nothing, and it didn't help that violence loomed just out of sight. Strangely, the impending action drained her of energy, made her preemptively exhausted.

The city was lively. Families and couples bustled all over the place. Riding bikes, walking dogs, getting food, enjoying the day...Annie's heart panged briefly. A flicker of jealousy passed through her. Why couldn't she have a relaxing evening with people she cared about?

She refocused and pulled the baseball cap further over her face. This was another of Elena's directives—they couldn't afford to have passersby recognize Annie and interfere with the action, whether they were haters or admirers. Also, a tiny camera was sewn into the front of her hat, so the viewing audience would have a first-person view of Annie Kennedy's latest clash with Invisible Dagger.

A kiosk on the sidewalk called to her. Ice cream. In a cake cone. Drizzled with caramel.

"Why not?" she muttered to no one in particular.

"Because," Elena's tinny voice buzzed in her ear, "you need to stay on your toes."

"Ice cream is mobile," Annie rebutted.

"These morons could start dropping bombs at any second, and you want to get dessert?"

Annie ignored her director's derision and bought a cone for herself. She also ignored the drone hovering across the street, keeping an eye on her. She was confident the camera wasn't broadcasting her to the world, since the action hadn't yet started, but she kept her face impassive all the same.

Clamping down on her emotions and maintaining a stoic persona had become intuitive. Not even second nature—it was her first instinct. Annie the regular person had slowly morphed into Captain Kennedy. The thought shook her a little, but if that was what it took to not be ravaged by the public, then that was what she would do.

Even as she licked her ice cream, she didn't crack a smile.

Then, a breeze tickled her exposed ears. She craned her neck to breathe in the Lake Michigan air. It reminded her of the beach in San Diego, but earthier, less salty. The air filled her lungs, and she could almost taste the murky water. It was nice—she liked the ocean breezes better, but both were vastly superior to the scratchy winds of Wichita, her hometown.

As she breathed, she saw something in the sky. Something bulky and black, weaving between the buildings. Getting closer. Thrumming and pulsing in the air.

"You see that, Annie?" Elena verbally nudged her. "Up above, twelve o'clock."

Annie's muscles locked up, and she dropped her cone onto the sidewalk.

A huge, beastly helicopter descended upon downtown. Its blades spun like gnashing teeth, preparing to attack with vigor.

It had to be Invisible Dagger. They were seconds away from unleashing turmoil and destruction upon countless innocent civilians.

The chopper soaring among the skyscrapers didn't look real. It all felt like a scene from a movie. Even after fighting in staged battles and killing people who were more like actors than real soldiers, Annie had never imagined something of this scale could happen in real life. Her knees almost gave out—she'd never seen anything like it.

"Elena," she said, struggling to keep her voice level, "how am I supposed to beat that? How am I even supposed to get up there?"

"Adapt. Fight. Win."

Annie tried to keep her tongue in check, but the words burst out: "A little FBI backup would be appreciated. Call up the agent you're screwing and get them here now."

"I'm going to pretend I didn't hear that." Elena paused as she yipped a few words to someone, then came back to Annie. "Get ready, captain. We're going live to the world in three...two...one."

Annie felt the air shift. All at once, she was hyper-aware of the fact that several invisible, microscopic cameras were pointed at her, transmitting her every movement to millions of viewers.

Her inner-ears popped—something else had changed too.

She looked up, and she stared in horror.

A metal cylinder fell from the helicopter. It dropped like a razor-sharp knife carving through flesh—smooth, unimpeded, and deadly.

The city was silent for a half-second as everyone braced for impact.

The bomb disappeared behind a line of buildings, out of Annie's sightline. But the camera affixed to her ballcap got a perfect view of the explosive black-and-orange plume.

A concussive blast of air hit Annie before the noise did. She rocked back on her heels and covered her eyes against flecks of tiny shrapnel.

Following the explosion, chaos set in. Pedestrians began screaming and trampling each other, running around in circles like cornered livestock. Cars on the street blared their horns and screeched as they peeled away.

Annie bared her teeth and sprinted toward the helicopter. If she had to guess, it was about a half-mile away...and hundreds of feet in the air.

She still had no idea how she was going to get up there, but she couldn't stand by the ice cream kiosk as downtown Milwaukee was bombed to hell.

As she ran, she said to her earpiece, "Do we know how many bombs they have?"

"Hold on," was Elena's reply, followed by rapid keyboard clicks.

Annie wanted to spit back, "*I'm holding*," but that wouldn't fit her character, so she merely grunted and pumped her legs harder.

The street rocked back and forth, and Annie nearly bit the pavement. She regained her balance, but not after waving her arms around like a windmill.

Another bomb had dropped.

People coursed past her in the opposite direction, away from the helicopter and explosions—she felt like a salmon racing upstream. Common sense would say that she was going the wrong way, but she had a city to save and poll numbers to boost.

Elena's voice piped up again. "Turn your head and give us a nice POV shot of the chaos in the streets."

Annie obeyed.

Smoke. Broken glass. Frantic, running people. Tears and screams. Stalled and abandoned cars.

Annie imagined it was a great shot. The number of viewers had to be record-breaking.

For a moment, she wondered if Zeke was watching. She slapped her wandering mind into shape and glued her focus to the helicopter.

Only a few blocks away.

She yelled to the panicking civilians, "Take cover! Everyone, get inside! Inside!"

Was this actually good advice? She had no idea, but it felt like the right thing to say.

The city rumbled as another bomb hit the concrete...but the rumble turned into a quake that lasted far longer than it should have. A wall of gray dust enveloped the street. Annie tried to cover her mouth, but the dust coated the inside of her throat, and she nearly choked. Somewhere, a building had collapsed.

Maybe her advice of taking shelter inside wasn't very good after all.

She turned a corner, and a shred of hope made her heart flutter. A handful of police officers were among the crowd...but they looked as frazzled and terrified as everyone else. She called out, "Officer, can you help—"

But the cop didn't listen. He screamed, "Every man for himself!" He sputtered and cowered away from the explosions—all natural reactions to a terrorist attack, to be sure, but she had hoped the cops would show a little more backbone.

As she ran by, she snarled, "At least direct these people to safety!"

The cop drew his sidearm and held it with two trembling hands. He yelled at the crowd, "If any of you get close to me, I'll shoot!"

Annie scowled, glad that she'd gotten his cowardly response on video, and kept running. Hopefully the world would hold him accountable once the dust settled.

Not likely. But hopefully.

Jody stood in the middle of the helicopter, holding on to a pole for dear life. He hated flying, he hated heights, he hated Milwaukee, and at that moment, he wasn't a huge fan of Holland either. Couldn't his boss have come up with a plan that didn't involve zipping through the downtown skyline like the freakin' Blue Angels?

Roderick was piloting the chopper like a pro. (Jody added that to the ongoing list of things Rod was surprisingly good at.) Holland stood by the chopper's trapdoor that released the bombs.

Still, even Jody had to admit—watching the cylinders fall through the hatch, waiting for a second or two, and then hearing the massive BOOMs was pretty satisfying. There was a reason the militaries called these things Needle Drops. He supposed he wouldn't get that feeling on the ground.

But all the same, he was ready for the mission to be over. If it went on much longer, he'd be taking a second look at what he had for breakfast

Holland barked, "Jody! Ready the next cartridge!"

Jody inched away from his pole on his hands and knees, placing another metal cylinder on the chopper's trapdoor. They had deployed half of their dozen bombs, and the city was in an absolute panic. From their bird's-eye view, they could see the people scrambling and the smoke rising. Fires dotted downtown, and cars zipped all over the place, looking for a safe haven. Of course, a safe haven didn't exist.

"Guys!" Rod yelled over the noise of the chopper's rotors. As he was piloting, he was also keeping an eye on social media. He held up his phone. "Annie Kennedy is here! I'm watching her run through the streets below us right now. Just like in Nashville, they're broadcasting her live as she's trying to beat us!"

Holland grimaced. He hadn't wanted to get involved with Captain Kennedy today.

Jody, on the other hand, smirked. He wanted a shot at Kennedy, and he was going to make sure he got one.

Holland snapped at Rod, "Gain some altitude. I don't want her getting too close to us."

Jody traded a pointed glance with Rod...and Jody knew that, somehow, Captain Kennedy would get on this helicopter.

❧

Annie picked a building—a tall one—ran inside, and found the stairs leading up. Her years of running hadn't prepared her for dozens of flights of stairs, but she didn't have time to wallow. She lunged up the steps two at a time.

Around the fifth floor, Elena droned in her ear, "Getting your steps in for the day doesn't exactly make for compelling television."

Annie wanted to bite back, *The city is being bombed, and elevators can collapse, genius.* But instead, she kept her mouth shut, furrowed her brow, and picked up the pace. Her thighs burned, and an iron band wrapped itself around her chest, but she couldn't stop. Every few minutes, she felt the world tremble as another bomb hit the city.

Surely, people had died. Those explosions were haphazard and devastating. Invisible Dagger wasn't smart enough to carefully target certain marks—it seemed they had simply loaded their bombs on a chopper and dropped them where they pleased. Buildings crumbled around them and entire streets were destroyed.

If Annie remembered correctly, this would be the first time Invisible Dagger had taken lives. They'd tried to assassinate the singer in Nashville but failed.

They had elevated themselves from destructive nuisances to full-blown terrorists. Warfare had leapt out of stadiums and back into the real world.

Annie's heart thudded in her rib cage like a prisoner trying to break free. Her vision swam, but she was almost to the top of the building. She had to be.

There. The door to the roof. She exhaled in relief, wiped sweat from her face, and rocketed through the door.

What was a pleasant breeze on the ground was a strong wind this high up. Annie was tempted to rip off her ballcap and toss it away rather than be concerned about it blowing off, but that wasn't an option. If she got rid of her POV camera, Elena would slit her throat in her sleep.

She scanned the Milwaukee skyline, finding smoke, broken glass, and sheer panic. As below, so above.

A deafening gust buffeted her from behind, nearly knocking her to her knees.

WHACKA-WHACKA-WHACKA.

She drew her handgun from under her jacket and made sure a bullet was in the chamber, ready to go. Then she squared her shoulders and turned to face the hulking helicopter.

It was right in front of her, hovering in the air like a mutated wasp about to strike. Its sides were open, so she could see right in. Three men—all of Invisible Dagger—were in her sight.

She had a clean shot.

The man with a scar across his face, Holland, shrieked at the pilot, "Turn, turn, turn! She's right there! Get us out of here!"

The pilot, Roderick, heaved his weight against the chopper's controls, and the airborne machine began to drift away from her.

The third man in the chopper locked eyes with Annie—he was bald and wearing a hoodie. This was Jody, the spokesman of the group, the most affable and easygoing. His pleasant onscreen persona was responsible for most of Invisible Dagger's popularity. But in that moment, his eyes dripped with hatred. He glared at Annie with all the venom of an angered rattlesnake.

She quickly scanned what she could see of the rest of the chopper's interior. A single trunk-sized cylinder say at Jody's feet.

They had one bomb left.

Her fingers tightened around the handle of her gun, and she aimed its barrel at the center of Jody's forehead.

But the chopper turned to make a hasty getaway.

Hot anger flared in her stomach and nearly spewed from her mouth like a dragon's wrathful fire. There was no way she could let these men get away. After all the death they had rained from the sky, she wouldn't be able to call herself a soldier if she didn't feel their bones break beneath her fists.

And so, without a moment's hesitation, she dashed across the rooftop and leapt into the air.

Never mind the hundred-foot plummet beneath her. Never mind the probably-armed terrorists she was leaping toward. Never mind the fact that she had no exit strategy in mind.

She arced through the air, feeling very much like a mythical Valkyrie, and she wondered if Ranger Monroe ever felt half as heroic as she did in that moment.

And for a nano-second, she thought about how her polling numbers were doing. Surely jumping off a building and into a helicopter should score her some points.

But then, her feet landed inside the chopper, she rolled to slow her velocity, and she planted herself in the center of the triangle of men. She had all three terrorists in sight, and she held her gun out.

"Don't move!"

She wanted to snarl and gnash her teeth at these lowlifes for all the damage they had caused over the past few months. It took every ounce of self-control she had to not bash their brains in that very second. But these were dangerous men, and she couldn't let herself underestimate them—and she had a stoic persona to uphold.

So she steadily repeated herself. "Don't move...you swine." She tossed in an insult, like letting a little bit of steam out of a boiling kettle.

Holland shot a glare at Jody, then set his eyes on Annie and slowly raised his hands, palms out, the thick scar on his face trembling with fury. Or was it fear?

Annie almost smirked—she liked to think it was fear.

The helicopter pitched lazily to one side, and she had to take a couple half-steps to keep her balance. She peeked out the open sides and saw the gray concrete of the city had been replaced with a light blue carpet—they had flown over Lake Michigan. Every second, the water colored darker and darker as they flew further from land, over deeper water. Invisible Dagger was trying to make its escape.

Annie swung her gun toward the pilot's seat and placed the back of Roderick's head squarely in her sights. "Listen up. You're going to turn this vulture around and take us back to the city, or so help me—"

A voice from behind sneered at her, "So help you what?"

Her military instincts screamed, and she spun around—and metal crashed into her nose. Stars exploded in her eyes, and the next thing she knew, she was sprawled on the floor. Her gun clattered out of the helicopter, dropping a hundred feet only to be swallowed by the lake.

Jody loomed over her, clutching the last remaining bomb in both hands. He tossed it aside and drew a knife from his hoodie's pocket.

She gasped and tried to tumble away. He lunged on top of her, driving his knife down toward her chest. She kicked her foot at his wrist, but the blow from the metal cylinder had warped her vision, and she ended up striking his knee. It did the trick and forced him to back up, but her head whirled in blinding agony. She was seconds away from blacking out.

Something dripped down her chin. Blood. A lot of it.

Holland bellowed, "She's useful to us alive!"

But Jody didn't listen.

Annie dragged herself across the floor, trying desperately to get away from her attacker. Every semblance of strategy or tactical prowess had evaporated from her mind. Fear clogged her veins and clouded her judgment.

This was nothing like being in a stadium. There were no cheering spectators, no battle plans, no lights or microphones or directors. There was only a knife, wielded by a bald man with furious eyes.

Annie realized with sick certainty that she was going to die.

She kicked at Jody again, but her body betrayed her—tendrils of unconsciousness began to wrap around her mind.

Jody stomped on her ankle, and she let out a yelp.

Holland scoffed, but he didn't try to stop Jody.

Annie panted and clawed toward the side of the chopper. If she could only reach the open door, she could tumble out and fall into the lake. The height of the fall might do some damage, but it was a better option than staying put.

But Jody grabbed Annie's jacket and flipped her over, so that she stared at the ceiling. Jody planted his feet on either side of her torso and towered over her. He snarled and brandished his knife. "You don't get any last words, lady." His voice was low and sinister, spoken only to her.

He didn't know about the camera sewn into the ballcap she was wearing. His menacing threat had been aired live to the whole world. Everyone would know how Annie Kennedy had failed and was murdered...if Elena hadn't already pulled the plug on the broadcast, that is.

Then, she felt something. A click. A shift. A split-second vibration beneath her, as if gears were grinding together. She almost dismissed the feeling as her brain firing off random neurons before death. But something mechanical was happening underneath the floor she lay on.

Her instincts hadn't abandoned her entirely.

Using the last of her strength, she lashed out and kicked Jody right in the sack between his spread legs. He howled like a neutered wolf and staggered to one side.

WHOOSH.

She was laying on the helicopter's trapdoor, which was designed to drop bombs. Now, it dropped her.

The chopper grew smaller and smaller as she plummeted. Her stomach clenched while her arms and legs flailed helplessly.

Mere minutes ago, she had leapt through the air like a fabled Valkyrie. Now, she fell like Icarus.

The drop only lasted a few seconds, but it felt like an hour.

She was unconscious when her limp body crashed into Lake Michigan.

Salvatore watched the whole thing on TV in a dingy Midwest bar. When Annie was strolling the streets of downtown Milwaukee, he ordered a beer. When she saw the first bomb drop, he had just finished a bowl of peanuts. And while she scaled the building's staircase, jumped into the moving helicopter, fought the terrorists, and nearly died while tumbling into the lake, he had vacuumed up a plate of garlic chicken wings, a chili dog, and an appletini.

It was riveting television. He couldn't take his eyes off of it, even as he was eating.

The other patrons in the bar were enthralled too, but the emotions ran the gamut. Some rooted for her, others hated her stinking guts. A few drunkenly cocky men tried to backseat-drive Annie's actions, saying she was doing everything wrong and that they would handle the situation much better. A contingent of women applauded Annie for doing her best, even if she ended up getting her face bashed in.

Ultimately, the bar was split right down the middle between Captain Kennedy's admirers and haters. That seemed to be the trend for the entire world.

Salvatore liked Captain Kennedy. He really did—he admired her stoic-hero shtick. The witty wisecracking soldier angle was too played out. He'd seen it a million times, and he liked that she was trying something new. And the baby too. He liked that she had the guts to stick with that narrative.

He was a fan. No doubt about it.

Yet as he watched the attack in Milwaukee, he couldn't help but notice the three men of Invisible Dagger. An idea lodged in his brain like a fishhook, and he couldn't shake it, as much as he desperately wanted to.

That evening, as he left the bar, he started making plans. Plans that would solidify him as the greatest military recruiter in history. Plans that would allow him to truly retire in luxury. Plans that would, most importantly, put some thrill back in the hunt for him.

If he could recruit the terrorists of Invisible Dagger into an army, he could hang up his hat, content that he had done something remarkable in his field. So that was what he set out to do.

The city smelled of embers, dirt, and sorrow. Every square inch of downtown Milwaukee seemed to be blanketed by ash.

Where, mere hours ago, families and pedestrians had bustled back and forth, only craters and burnt-out shells of cars remained. Not a soul was in sight, and the only noise came from a weak breeze sliding between damaged buildings.

Jasmine and her cameraman Ravi tiptoed through the carnage, unconsciously making as little sound as possible, as if they were in a church. He held the camera on his shoulder, getting footage of the aftermath from a boots-on-the-ground perspective. Jasmine had noticed that, as usual, the press had vanished as soon as the bombings had stopped. Media attention followed Captain Kennedy as her body was scooped out of the lake, and television talking heads speculated about what would happen next. No one cared about what was still happening—the ugly aftermath didn't make for must-see TV.

Downtown Milwaukee looked like a still painting. Nothing moved. No one was around. Jasmine felt trapped in a violent video game left on *pause*.

After the attack, the National Guard and emergency services had swept through the scene, quickly gathering up corpses, and those who were injured were slowly moved to nearby hospitals. Everything had been done quickly and, as a result, messily. Trails of blood smeared the sidewalk where bodies had been dragged onto trucks. Dirty clothes and shoes were left behind in heaps. Here and there, dead bodies had been left behind under chunks of concrete or huddled in smashed cars.

Despite her job as a professor of history in London focusing on warfare, Jasmine had never seen a corpse. Not with her own two eyes. Not even in a battle-stadium—for all her talk, war spectatorship wasn't her cup of tea. Today, in the wake of such a severe terrorist attack, it took a few minutes for her to become numb to the sight.

"Boss," Ravi whispered to her, "which way?" He gestured to the cross-street at which they had arrived.

"This way." She spoke in a regular volume, and her words bounced through the air like a stone across a pond. She walked confidently eastward, not because she had any real sense of direction, but because she wanted to give the appearance for the camera that she did.

This street was covered in debris and twisted metal. Cars were overturned, windows were gone, and entire buildings seemed angled in the same askew direction. A huge, jagged crater sat where a bank used to be, and scorched dollar bills now floated in the sewage-filled hole.

A bomb had dropped right here.

"Whoa, boss," Ravi said, following her lead by talking a bit too loudly. "Look at this!" He pointed his camera at a column, which was all that was left of a building across the street from the ex-bank.

Jasmine took a closer look at what Ravi had found. A metal shard had buried itself into the concrete column. It was blackened by soot, but she could see raised markings on its surface.

A serial number.

It took a few powerful yanks, but she eventually pried the metal out of the column, and she ran her fingers over the grimy numbers. "If this is from one of the bombs," she said, "we could find out where they came from."

"And if we find out where they came from," Ravi continued her thoughts, "then we might be able to find out who exactly took them."

"And maybe we can find out where they'll be next." Jasmine took off her jacket and started bundling the metal shard in it. "And when we do that, we can give that information to Captain Kennedy."

Ravi scratched his head. "Will that help? Kennedy knew Invisible Dagger would be in Nashville and Milwaukee before they struck. I bet she already knows where they'll be next."

A chill raced down Jasmine's skin, and not just because she had just shed her jacket. She hadn't thought of that.

She sighed. "First thing's first. Do you think tracking serial numbers from a bomb shard will make for compelling TV?"

Ravi patted his camera. "It's all in the edit."

She smiled. "Then let's get to it."

～❦～

Zeke bounded off the city bus and ran into the hospital. It had been three days since Annie fell from that helicopter on live TV, and no one had spoken a word about her condition. Not her director Elena Winn, not even a Valkyrie spokesperson—no one. The world was left to wonder if Annie Kennedy was horribly injured, or even alive.

Not to mention the baby in her womb. The unborn child who had captivated a global audience and propelled Annie into the spotlight in the first place. Was the baby okay?

Zeke had been calling Annie's cell phone nonstop for the past seventy-two hours, but there was no answer. He was in the dark, unable to sleep or eat without knowing if the woman he cared about was all right.

But then, just forty-five minutes ago, Zeke had heard a rumor at the Army of Liberty's gym. A couple of guys said that Captain Kennedy was at Valkyrie's private hospital in downtown San Diego. Without a moment's hesitation, Zeke had sprinted out of there, headed to the hospital to see for himself.

He burst through the front doors, and the offputtingly clean smell of sanitizer and latex made him squint. He saw a sign for the VIP patients' wing and marched in that direction.

A stodgy old doctor stepped in his way. "Young man, you can't go—"

Zeke reared up and spat his words. "My name is Zechariah Carr. Danny Carr is my father. He runs this place and pays your salary. I am going to see Annie Kennedy. Try and stop me."

The doc's jaw hung open as Zeke barreled past him.

Each hallway looked identical. Every door was a clone of the one next to it. Zeke felt like he was having a panic attack—sweat pebbled on his forehead, and his fingers were numb. "Where is she...?"

In that moment, the extent of his feelings for Annie came into sharp focus. The fact that he wasn't with her in her hour of need was taking a physical toll on him.

He took a breath to calm his nerves—if he kept charging around like a bull, someone was sure to call security on him. He spotted an info desk and made a beeline for it.

"Hi," he said to the woman behind the desk. "Where can I find Captain Kennedy?"

She eyed him. "Are you family?"

He pulled his military ID from his wallet. "Closer than that. I serve with her."

The woman nodded pensively, then checked her clipboard. "Captain Kennedy is in with her doctor right now, Mr. Smith. Take a seat, and I'll take you to visit her as soon as possible."

Zeke swallowed his thudding heart and, with legs made of rusted tin, walked to a plastic chair against the wall. It felt wrong to wait and do nothing, but he had done all that he could do. He would be there for Annie when she was up for it. So he sat.

Everything hurt. Even as she lay in a padded hospital bed with more blankets and pillows than she could count, every inch of Annie's body throbbed. She had hoped that the pain would ease as time went on, but over the last three days—after a Valkyrie boat had fished her out of Lake Michigan, she was flown home to San Diego for treatment, and a throng of military doctors had examined her like a lab experiment—the aches had only gotten worse.

The good news was that nothing was too serious. She was going to live. The bad news was everything else. Her nose had been broken, which turned breathing into a chore and sneezing into a nightmare. She subsequently had two nasty black eyes, and her head felt stuffed with steel wool. The fall into Lake Michigan had shattered her right wrist and dislocated both arms—they were now back in place and functioning well enough, but they radiated pain. She could barely move a finger on her good hand.

Worst of all was the rock in her stomach. It wasn't a medical issue or a physical injury. It was the knowledge of her failure.

She had flopped in front of a live audience. Again. The world had had a front-row seat to her gravest defeat.

She wanted to pull the blankets over her head and never come out again.

Her doctor had just left the room to go get the results of one test or another. Annie had lost track of all the procedures, scans, and assessments. Her head hurt enough without trying to remember everything that was wrong with her.

The door creaked open, and Annie closed her eyes. She didn't want to see the expression on the doctor's face when he told her about another sprain or fracture in her bruised body.

But it wasn't the doctor. Instead, she heard a familiar voice.

"You don't look very heroic, I gotta say."

Her eyes snapped open, and she couldn't contain the warm smile that crept across her face. She tried to sit up straight in her bed, but her muscles simply didn't obey. She winced in pain.

General Lightfoot held out a hand. "No, don't get up. I'd say you have a good enough excuse." He hobbled across the room and sat in a chair next to her bed. "Whew," he exhaled when he got a closer look at her battered face. "Hope you don't have any photoshoots scheduled."

"What," Annie murmured, trying not to move her face too much, "did I overdo my eyeshadow again?"

Lightfoot laughed. "Ah! Is that a joke? Not very in-character, missy."

Annie caught herself, clenched, and felt her cheeks flush.

"You think I care about that crap?" Lightfoot gently patted her hand. "I..." He seemed to search for the right words, but the crusty old man came up short. He settled on, "I'm glad you're okay."

She nodded her thanks, not ready to drop her stoic demeanor entirely. It was like a corset—she desperately wanted to take it off, but she also didn't want to put it back on again later, so she dealt with it.

After a pause, she asked, "Why are you in the hospital? Are you okay?"

"Yeah, yeah, I'm fine. I'm here with Leigh. I dropped him off at his room, then I went to use the pisser. When I was walking back, I saw your name on the door and dropped in to say hi."

Annie tried to raise an eyebrow, but her facial muscles weren't cooperating. She asked, "Who's Leigh?"

"Gambol. My friend."

"Leigh Gambol..." Annie's foggy mind put the pieces together. "The president of Valkyrie Productions? *That* Leigh Gambol?"

"Mhmm. He took a tumble in his room at Front Porch Retirement Center—the old people farm. I found him there, sprawled out on the carpet. Probably broke his hip." He pinched the bridge of his nose. "He said he thought he was fighting in a war. Being a big hero again."

"He was in war, right? I mean, long ago. Before Valkyrie. Before spectatorship."

Lightfoot chuckled to himself. "Believe it or not, yeah, he was. That old marshmallow was a colonel in one of the last real wars in human history."

Annie felt sorry for the man. "He thought he was back in the war he fought in?"

"Oh, no!" Lightfoot's chuckle was promoted to a belly laugh. "Leigh's old, but he's not *that* old. He fought in the Pacific Wars. Today, he thought he was fighting in frickin' Saratoga. In the Revolutionary War, under General Washington."

Lightfoot rocked back and forth, wiping tears from his eyes. Annie wanted to join in, she really did, but her weary, beaten body didn't allow it.

She smirked. "Please don't tell Mr. Gambol I suggested he was old enough to fight in the 1770s."

"I make no promises, captain." Lightfoot's laugh faded, and an air of melancholy cloaked him. "He wouldn't remember if I told him anyway." He shook his head. "He climbed on his couch and jumped off, waving an umbrella around like a saber. That old coot. He'll kill himself someday." He sniffed back another tear, but not from laughter this time.

His tired, yellowed eyes moved around Annie's room, taking in every detail—the fluorescent lights, the medical machinery, the plasticky flooring—before finally landing on Annie's prone, helpless form.

He growled under his breath, "I hate hospitals."

As if on cue, the door opened and the doctor strolled in, carrying Annie's chart. He was a cheery-looking guy, with a bright face and bouncy steps. His white coat had the Army of Liberty's emblem sewn on the shoulders.

Lightfoot hoisted himself to his feet. "I'm outta here." He nodded to Annie, then walked out, giving the doctor the same wide berth he would give a plague victim.

The doctor gave the general a small wave as he exited, then beamed to Annie. "Well, Captain Kennedy, I have good news this time! The latest scan we took came back thumbs-up all around. Don't worry, ma'am, the baby is fine!"

Annie blinked. A thousand thoughts careened through her mind at once.

She didn't recognize this doctor. Was he with Elena? Was he in on the secret that she wasn't really pregnant? If so, why was he acting so happy? Was he joking? No, he seemed truly relieved that the "baby" wasn't hurt. But there was no baby. It was all a story to make Annie stand out from the crowd of other celebrity soldiers.

Or...

What if...

Her body went numb. All her pain was replaced with a cold bath of realization.

Zeke. The night they'd shared together several weeks ago.

The doctor stared at her with naked enthusiasm, waiting for her response. There wasn't an ounce of dishonesty on his face—he had just told her she was pregnant...and he was telling the truth.

She managed to muster a word: "G-Good."

The doctor flipped through his chart as he prattled on and on. "I must say, Captain Kennedy, if I may...I know this may not be appropriate, with professionalism and everything, but I'm a *huge* fan. I've been following your career for the past few months, ever since your very first battle. You're my favorite soldier in the world, and I *adore* your choice for the baby's name. Junior! How clever! Anyway, when I saw you fall out of that helicopter, I was worried about you, of course, but my thoughts immediately went to little Junior in your tummy! I couldn't sleep! I was so scared the baby would be hurt. And I just have to say, now that I know you and Junior are both okay, I'll get a good night's rest." He sighed happily and looked up at Annie. "You must be so relieved!"

She could barely move, the weight of reality pinning her to the bed. "Yes. Yes, I'm relieved."

The doc's eyebrows furrowed slightly. "Now, I am a teensy-weensy bit concerned about one thing. The baby is much smaller than it should be at this point in its development—"

Thankfully, the door opened again, interrupting the one-sided conversation. Elena rushed in, her gaze fixed on the bruised captain. Her eyes flashed like lighthouses sending Annie a message—what the message was, Annie couldn't tell.

"Doctor," Elena said as she set a hand on the man's white-coated arm, "I'd like a moment to speak with my captain in private."

Annie wanted to bristle at the phrase *"my captain,"* but she didn't have the energy.

"Oh, by all means!" The doctor nearly tripped over his own shoes trying to accommodate Elena. As he scampered out of the room, he shot Annie one last fawning glance and waved. Elena shut the door in his sunshiny face.

The room was silent for a second. The lights buzzed in the ceiling, and Annie tried to focus on the sound. Or the stiff agony in her arms. Or the beeping machine right next to her head. Anything to keep her from thinking about the news the doctor had inadvertently sprung on her. The news that was supposed to be true, but had been a lie, but was now true.

Annie Kennedy. The maternal warrior. For real.

Elena crossed the room and sat in the chair next to Annie's bed. She slowly inhaled and held it for a while. Finally, she said, "I saw the test results." She spoke quietly, slowly, as if talking with the bereaved at a funeral.

Annie didn't know how to respond, so she kept her mouth shut, eyes fixed on her director. She let her stoic persona work in her favor for once—if she took off the mask of impassiveness, she didn't know what emotions would overtake her. Sorrow? Regret? Anger? Maybe joy? She had no idea how a pregnancy would make her feel, so she kept her wall up, choosing to feel nothing rather than facing an unknown situation.

Elena continued. "Don't worry. I'll assure the doctor that if he breathes a word about the baby being a few weeks along rather than months, he'll spend the rest of his career popping pimples in a strip mall."

Annie asked, "Can you follow through with that threat?"

Elena didn't answer, but her sharp earrings glinted in the artificial lighting.

"Right now," Elena said, "I want you to rest. We'll talk strategy later."

Annie was surprised—she never would have imagined the cunning and shrewd Elena Winn to speak with such warmth, much less compassion.

It put her on edge. Something was coming. An ulterior motive had to be under Elena's kind words.

Elena stood and smiled. "Get well soon, eh, Ace?"

With that, she glided out of the room, leaving the door open a crack. Annie could see a sliver of the hallway, and she locked eyes with Zeke.

Zeke. Sweet, kind Zeke. It looked like he had been waiting to see her.

He practically left skid marks on the floor as he dashed into her room. "Annie! I'm so glad to see you!" He didn't sit in the chair—instead, he slid to his knees next to her. He started to wrap her in an awkward hug, but he jerked back, not wanting to hurt her. "I-I-I saw the attack three days ago. It was horrible! A-And..." He caught his breath. "And you fell from such a height. No one could confirm if you were okay. Officials are being weirdly tight-lipped. I'm just...Annie, I'm so glad you're alive."

He stared at her with wide eyes. Eyes that screamed soliloquies and radiated warmth. Eyes the likes of which had never been directed at Annie Kennedy. Eyes that almost made her heart soar.

Almost.

Her internal wall kept any and all emotions clamped down tight, including what very well might have been love, if it had any room to blossom. As much as she wanted to reciprocate Zeke's feelings, her face remained blank.

She had to. She didn't know what she would feel if she set her heart free.

"Zeke," she said. She was shocked, pleased, and alarmed all at once when she realized it was very easy to keep her voice impassive. "I have news to tell you. Big news. You have to promise to not talk about it with anyone else."

He nodded, his own face betraying a hurricane of emotions within him. He was clearly confused, nervous, happy to see her, and more than a little hurt that she hadn't expressed any affection for him. Instead, he simply said, "Okay."

She pressed, "*Swear.*"

"Yeah, yes. I swear." He touched her hand, but when she winced, he drew back. "I swear, Annie. What is it?"

And so she told him about her false pregnancy, which had started as a way for her to stand out among the male celebrity soldiers.

She told him about how she had used the character of the maternal warrior to launch herself to stardom in mere months.

She told him that, now, she was actually expecting. With child. Pregnant.

And he was the dad.

She said every word without a hint of emotion, as if she were reporting the weather. Even when Zeke started gently sobbing and smiling at the same time, her mask didn't crack.

❧

Danny sat behind his desk, massaging his temples. He just couldn't catch a break lately. Ever since Ranger Monroe had gotten his head blown off, things had gone downhill. First, Monroe's replacement had seemed like a smash success, which made her subsequent collapse all the more painful.

Kennedy had been a media darling and the public's new favorite action figure. The gravid gunner was on a meteoric rise.

Gravid Gunner...Danny jotted that name on a notepad, just in case Kennedy ever regained her status and needed another snappy moniker.

Then, Danny had taken a risk on Kennedy and Winn by giving the green light to their real-life action movie scheme. It had been great in Nashville when Kennedy kicked that terrorist off a roof, but it was only a matter of time before Valkyrie's prospects followed his lead—*splat*.

Kennedy had frozen in battle, and Winn had crossed the line by tampering with the arena. She had detonated explosives under the feet of the man about to shoot Kennedy.

Even after all this time, Danny fumed at the thought. The cardinal rule of spectatorship was *never break the illusion*. Obviously, the soldiers and generals didn't actually believe they were fighting real battles, and no one in the audience actually believed they were watching real wars.

There was an unspoken agreement between creator and consumer that everyone involved would pretend these battles were *real*. Or, at least, real enough. Danny had been in the business of war spectatorship long enough to know that this silent covenant was the key to the entire industry. If directors exhibited too much influence and shattered the illusion of reality, the jig was up. The Wizard of Oz would be revealed as a fraud. And Elena Winn had done exactly that.

Danny had wanted to can Winn right then and there, but he'd held out for a bit longer...only for Kennedy to crash and burn in Milwaukee. She had failed spectacularly in front of a live global audience. Civilians had died, much of downtown had been destroyed, and Kennedy had *lost*. That was unacceptable.

He snorted and stared out of his office's panoramic window. The Pacific stretched beyond the human eye's grasp, like an endless quilt. Some patches were deep sapphire, others light as a shard of aquamarine. He couldn't help but visualize Kennedy plummeting from the sky, splashing down, and flailing around in the middle of the lake.

And as a rotten cherry on top of everything, Danny had gotten a memo last night that a young Army of Liberty soldier was among those killed in the attack on Milwaukee. Marlon Diggs was on leave, visiting family in his hometown on the day Invisible Dagger had blown the place to hell. His body was nearly unrecognizable after being crushed by a skyscraper, but Valkyrie had an open-casket-funeral policy for all its soldiers—dead men and women seem more heroic when mourners can see their faces.

Nothing was going well for Valkyrie. Tickets sales were down, merchandising had evaporated, public opinion was fickle at best and hostile at worst, and his space project couldn't get off the ground—literally and figuratively.

He wanted to buy another house. That would make him feel better. Not just any house, though—the biggest, grandest, most nauseatingly wealthy mansion he could find.

Rumor had it that Salvatore Caracas owned a ridiculously nice house. Maybe Danny could persuade him to put it on the market.

And maybe Zeke would want to come visit...

"You ready for more?" Suzanne's voice came from behind him, interrupting his aspirations.

Danny spun from the window and sagged in his chair. He moaned to his assistant, "What? What now? Did Australia declare war on Peru? Did one of our armies go rogue and take over the U.S. Capitol? Did someone take a dump in front of Monroe's memorial, spray paint boobs on it, and burn it down?"

"All of that. And a meteor is headed right for your favorite seafood place." She shot him a pointed look. "You done?"

Danny sniffed and clenched a fist under the desk. Typically, Suzanne's headstrong attitude was a breath of fresh air, but he wasn't in the mood today. He stood and adjusted his overly expensive business suit, hoping to remind her who was in charge. "What happened?"

She set her jaw against his peacocking. "Leigh Gambol is in Valkyrie's private hospital. He needs a hip replacement."

Danny clenched the bridge of his nose. "So the one-hundred-and-two-year-old head of this war enterprise needs invasive surgery?"

"That about sums it up."

"Crap." He knew what was around the corner: power struggles among the board members, never-ending streams of paperwork, a funeral he would have to cry at, interviews, eulogies, and a lot of delivered bouquets. He had a migraine already.

"Valkyrie could use a boost." Suzanne sauntered to his desk, leaned against it, and crossed her arms.

"I'm aware." A timpani pounded in his head. Banter with Suzanne was the last thing he wanted at the moment.

"You know what would spruce things up?" She smirked. "A sneak attack."

"What do you mean?"

"Our Palestinian army is currently at war with a Russian army. A small-potatoes Russian army, mind you, not anything like the Red Square

Ruskis. When the Palestinians travel to Russia for a battle, we could arrange a few...extracurricular activities for them. They could storm in and actually overthrow a Russian city!" She beamed proudly.

"That would spark a war, Suzanne. A real war." Danny shuddered at the thought.

She retorted, "If Russia declared real war on *one* of our armies, it would declare real war on *all* of Valkyrie, Earth's premier military superpower. I've crunched the numbers—it's a fact. Valkyrie Productions could take on the world singlehandedly."

That took Danny aback. "Is that true?"

"You better believe it. And that fact should boost our public image a bit." She strolled around Danny's desk and stood beside him. "But you know what they say: Show, don't tell. If we simply put out a press release or something, spouting numbers about our military might, that'll fly right over people's heads. So..." She splayed her hands matter-of-factly. "We need to demonstrate it. A sneak attack. The world's only Palestinian army, formed and controlled by Valkyrie, marching into a Russian city and *taking* it. And no one will be able to stop them."

Danny beheld Suzanne with wide eyes. He grinned and pulled out his chair for her. "Have a seat, ma'am. Can I make you a pot of coffee?"

She returned the impish smile, settled behind the desk, and picked up the phone. "I have a few calls to make, Mr. Carr. Calls that have to do with discreet, international subterfuge."

Danny nodded. "I'll make sure you're not interrupted, ma'am."

Jasmine burst into Ravi's motel room, her phone clutched triumphantly over her head. "I got it!"

Ravi jerked awake from a seated position on his bed. His laptop sat open in front of him—the poor guy must have fallen asleep waiting for her instruction. "I-I'm up. I mean, I wasn't sleeping."

It was either very late at night or very early in the morning. Crickets filled the Midwestern air with their orchestral songs, but Jasmine didn't pay any attention.

This motel was cheap, just like all the others they had stayed at while chasing Captain Kennedy's exploits around the country. Even then, CinemaStream was hesitant to keep paying for two separate rooms for a prospective docu-filmmaker and her cameraman, but Jasmine had ramped up her accent, and Martin, the CS exec, had begrudgingly allowed her to keep charging the company.

The bomb shard they had found in Milwaukee was safely tucked away in Jasmine's room across the hall. She had taken photos of it at every conceivable angle, and then she started digging through her list of contacts. Hopefully, someone she knew in the intellectual community would be able to steer them in the right direction as they tried to hunt down the bomb's origins.

Finally, after twenty straight hours of dialing, being on hold, asking questions, and being met with shrugs and I-don't-knows, she had hit pay dirt.

She waved off Ravi's excuse as she sat in a chair across from him. "It's okay!" Her spirits were high...or maybe that was adrenaline. The thrill of the hunt had seeped into her bloodstream. "Listen, I just got off the line with a colleague of mine at the University of London. A brilliant man, an expert in modern military artillery. He recognized the type of metal of the shard and the pattern of the serial number, and he knew what type of bomb it'd come from." She checked her notes on her phone. "An ND-85 Incendiary Device. They're colloquially referred to as Needle Drops."

Ravi rubbed his eyes and mumbled, "Wow." He shook his head like a wet dog and snapped to attention. "Okay..." He started plinking on his laptop's keyboard. "Now we just need to find where in the world someone can get some of those Needles."

"Already did." Jasmine smiled. "I called around a few war enterprises and asked. You'd be surprised how much someone will tell you when they want to show off their knowledge of things that blow up." She scrolled through her notes. "ND-85s are built and stored in the U.S. exclusively. And as a matter of fact, Valkyrie Productions is the only enterprise that uses them. A few other enterprises are trying to buy them and get in the game, but right now, Valkyrie owns them all."

The motel's heating unit kicked in, blasting them with sauna-like air. Ravi ignored the temperature change and kept working on his laptop. "Nice job, boss. That'll narrow things down for me."

"What are you doing?" She moved from her chair to sit next to him on the bed. She gaped at Ravi's screen—it was covered in an ocean of numbers and letters.

"Just a little hobby I enjoy sometimes." His fingers flew across the keys like Liberace playing a sonata.

She nearly yelled, "Are you hacking into Valkyrie?"

Ravi shot her a guilty glance. "...Maybe."

A smile bloomed across her face. "Fantastic! We'll crack this case *tout suite*."

A minute passed. Then five. Then fifteen. Ravi's fingers never slowed down.

Her adrenaline started to ebb, and that, combined with the clicking keyboard, lulled Jasmine into a sleepy daze.

The next thing she knew, Ravi clapped and whooped. "Got it! Toot sweet!"

Sleep rushed out of Jasmine's body as she jolted upright. She must've fallen asleep on the bed, sitting next to Ravi. She wasn't sure how long she had been out...but the stale taste in her mouth and the tendrils of dawn seeping through the windows told her it had been a while.

She mussed her hair and stifled a yawn.

"Oh, uh, sorry I woke you," Ravi said, once again guiltily.

"Not a worry." She widened her eyes to try to convince them it was time to start functioning. "What've you got?"

"Well..." He jittered where he sat, pride evident on his face. "It was a basically a game of connect-the-dots. I got into Valkyrie's records and found out where they keep their Needle Drops. There are only fifteen facilities in the United States where those bombs are stored. So next, I checked their inventories."

"Geez, Ravi, you're good at this."

He puffed out his chest a little. "I do what I can. Anyway, I checked the inventories, and last week, twelve Needle Drops were checked out from a facility in North Dakota. I also checked the records for all Valkyrie battles that have taken place in the past week—no Needle Drops were used."

Jasmine thought back. "Eleven bombs were dropped on Milwaukee."

Ravi nodded. "They must've not used the last one. Or they got an extra, just in case?"

"Yes, regardless of the number, no other Needle Drops were reportedly used in the entire world in the past week. This has to be what we're looking for."

"That's what I thought. So then, I hacked into the North Dakota facility's security cameras." He said it all very casually, which made Jasmine chuckle. "The weapons' inventories are only updated once a day, so I wasn't sure what exact time those twelve bombs were taken. So I sped through the footage of the day the bombs were checked out."

On his laptop, he pulled up security camera footage of a dusty road that led away from a gray warehouse.

Jasmine asked, "That's the North Dakota weapons facility?"

"Yep yep." He pressed a key, and the footage sped up. Dozens of trucks, tanks, and armored vehicles entered and exited the facility throughout the day.

Jasmine was crestfallen at first. Any of those vehicles could have taken the bombs. It was a needle in a haystack.

She tapped her chin and thought aloud, "The members of Invisible Dagger have presented themselves as men of the people. Commoners. Non-military. Do you think a civilian vehicle could have taken the bombs?"

Ravi beamed. "Again, that's just what I thought. Only one non-military vehicle rolled into and out of that facility on the day the Needle Drops were checked out. A red minivan."

He hit a few keys, and an image filled the screen—a blocky crimson car drove down the dusty road, leaving the weapons facility. It was covered in dents and dings, and its bumper sagged more than it should. At least they were smart enough to have the windows tinted.

Jasmine almost burst out cackling. "This terrorist organization gets around via minivan?"

"Hey, it's a cool minivan," Ravi rebutted, a little offended. "But not so fast. I grabbed that red van's license plate, then went back to traffic cameras in Boston, Nashville, and Milwaukee on the days leading up to Invisible Dagger's attacks."

"Let me guess? That big red monstrosity was there every time?"

"Well, that's a strong word..." Ravi seemed ready to fight for the minivan's honor, but he tabled the discussion for the time being. "But yeah, this same car can be linked to all the attacks. I think we found Invisible Dagger's wheels."

"Success!" Jasmine sprang to her feet and clapped...and she immediately felt light-headed and flopped back down. That's what she got for standing up too fast.

"You good, boss?"

"I have an idea," Jasmine said. Already, she felt the adrenaline returning. The thrill of the hunt had reached the next stage. "It's fairly technologically advanced. Think you're capable?"

Ravi popped his knuckles. "Call me Captain Capable. What's your idea?"

"Can you set up a system that monitors every traffic cam in the country, scanning for that minivan's license plate?"

Ravi was already typing. He continued her thought. "And every time that license plate pops up, we get a ping on their location."

She finished. "Thus, creating a trail we can follow."

"Boss, I've said it before, I'll say it again..." He donned his fake English accent. "You're bloomin' brilliant." He paused for a second, smiling at her. "You've sure come a long way."

Jasmine tilted her head. "What do you mean?"

"I googled you when I was first assigned to be your camera operator. I saw your little interview where you went through the history of spectatorship."

She laughed a little. "You saw that?"

"Oh yeah. You sounded crazy smart. And don't get me wrong, you still do...But you're a teacher, right?"

"A professor of history at the University of London, thank you very much."

"Cool, that's cool." He leaned back and gazed at her, as if she were a painting he was trying to understand. "But you don't seem like a teacher anymore. You're out in the field, getting your hands dirty, tracking down the truth."

"Heh." Jasmine sarcastically struck a pose like a superhero. "I'm making my own heroics, eh?"

She started laughing at the absurdity of it, but Ravi cut her off.

"Yeah, exactly! People will have to start studying *you* instead of the other way around." With that, he got to work on his laptop.

Jasmine basked in his words. It was true that, as of late, she had gone quite beyond her job description as a professor. She didn't really feel like one anymore.

Once this was all over, would she even want to go back to the university? What if CinemaStream wanted more docs from her, looking into the effects of warfare all around the world? She realized she liked the sound of that. After seeing the aftermath of Milwaukee firsthand, talking with Margie Dodson face-to-face, tracking down these terrorists and uncovering the truth...

She might have found a new calling.

The highway was, for the most part, empty. Since the attack on Milwaukee, travel had petered out. Concerts, festivals, and other large gatherings had been quietly postponed, and few believed they would ever be rescheduled. The nation was at a standstill, wondering what Invisible Dagger would do next.

The red minivan puttered into a rest stop, and Jody unfolded himself from the backseat. The van was roomy enough, but after several days of covert travel, the interior had gotten clogged with trash and man stench.

And he needed the bathroom.

And he wanted to get away from Holland.

Speaking of which, Holland got out of the driver's seat and carped, "We're moving out in five minutes."

Jody rolled his eyes. *Moving out.* Did he think he was a general now?

Nothing got under Jody's skin like cowardice. And coconut—he wasn't a big fan of coconut. But cowardice really got on his nerves.

When Annie Kennedy had been at their mercy, Holland had wanted to spare her. Not for some high-minded anti-killing ideal. Jody would think that was stupid, but at least he'd understand it.

No, Holland hadn't wanted to kill Kennedy simply because he'd been scared and wanted to flee. They weren't likely to get another clear shot at Kennedy, and Holland had hesitated.

Never mind the fact that Jody had been standing right over her, and she'd slipped away. Never mind that. He conveniently overlooked that little detail.

He stewed as he stomped across the parking lot. It struck him that he wasn't sure what state they were in...Nebraska? It felt like Nebraska.

There was only one other car in the rest stop: a sleek, high-end, strikingly blue Lamborghini. Jody gazed at it as he passed, and its sheer beauty lifted his spirits a smidge. Compared to their rustbucket minivan, the sports car was the Ark of the freakin' Covenant.

The blue door popped open, and the driver stepped out. He was a paunchy guy with one bushy eyebrow, wearing thick glasses and a tailored suit. He smiled at Jody. "Do you like my car?"

Jody rubbed his shaved head and shrugged. He knew he shouldn't engage with the stranger—Holland wouldn't like that. Still, he said, "Yeah, it's nice."

"Nice..." The guy chortled. "It's more than nice. It's a work of art. I should know—I have an eye for beautiful things." He extended his hand. "Good to meet you, Jody."

Jody stopped before the stranger. He waited for the guy to introduce himself, but he just kept smiling cordially at him. Eventually, Jody took the man's hand.

The stranger said, "I'm Salvatore Caracas. I'm a recruiter for Valkyrie Productions. And you're the infamous Jody, the mouthpiece of Invisible Dagger."

Jody scrunched his brows. "Valkyrie, huh? Just like Kennedy. I take it you're not one of our subscribers."

"Believe it or not, I'm a huge fan."

"Jody!" Holland's voice boomed from across the lot. "What are you doing? Get back here!"

Salvatore snickered. "He's a lot more shrill in person, isn't he?"

"You have no idea." Jody cocked his mouth over his shoulder and yelled back, "Coming! Just a second, *Mom*."

"I'd suggest hearing me out." Salvatore withdrew a microwaved burrito from his suit jacket and started snacking. "Excuse me, I had a long drive out here, and I'm famished."

"How'd you find us?"

Footsteps started clomping behind Jody. He turned slightly and saw Holland and Roderick walking toward him.

"Anything is possible with enough cash…and I have more than enough." Salvatore took a big, sloppy bite. "You might want to ditch that minivan. I was able to track you pretty easily. As you can see, I even predicted where you would stop for a potty break."

"All I'm hearing is a lot of jabber." Jody's fingers started twitching. A freight train was loose inside his skull, bleating and chugging and bouncing all over the place. He felt like he was about to explode into a thousand pieces.

Salvatore cleared his throat. "Well, I have a life-changing proposition for you and your team."

"Life-changing?" He took out his phone and muttered, "One second, Sally." He held the phone out so that its camera captured both himself and Salvatore behind him.

Salvatore stammered, seemingly caught off-guard for the first time in his life. "Wh-What're you doing?" He dropped his burrito.

Jody started streaming to Invisible Dagger's millions of subscribers. "What's up, Daggsters? It's Jody." He didn't put on his loud, expressive persona. The pounding in his head made it impossible to be upbeat and charming at the moment. He gestured to Salvatore. "Hey buddy, can you introduce yourself?"

The pudgy man adjusted his cufflinks and shifted from foot to foot. "Er…I'm Salvatore Caracas, a recruiter for Valkyrie Productions—"

Jody cut him off and roared at the camera, "Hear that, Kennedy? One of yours!" In a single motion, Jody reached into his hoodie pocket, drew his knife, and slashed it across Salvatore's neck.

Salvatore Caracas fell to his knees and gaped like a fish on dry land. He shoved his hands against his throat, but he couldn't staunch the gushing wound. With every heartbeat, he was closer to the end. He collapsed in a heap on the asphalt and stopped moving.

Jody stooped down with his phone to get a close-up. He hissed, "Like and subscribe, douchewads."

Holland and Rod ran the rest of the way across the parking lot as Jody wiped his knife clean on Salvatore's suit jacket.

"What was that about?!" Holland's scar contorted into a question mark as he screamed.

Jody answered, "I just got us a thousand more subscribers, I'll betcha." He also noticed that the pounding in his skull had subsided. He riffled through the dead man's pockets, pulling out breath mints, business cards, and—aha!—car keys.

Holland shoved a finger in Jody's face. "You had *no* right to go rogue like that. As if we needed to tick off Valkyrie any more than we already have!"

"I was playing to our base." Jody looked to Rod for verification. "Our subscribers would like what I just did, right, marketing man? Reliability will lead to loyalty, and all that crap."

Roderick's shaky eyes flicked between Jody and Holland, until he finally exhaled. "Yeah, Jody's right. Our current base of fans will go nuts for a random killing like this."

Jody clapped once and thrust the air. "Take that!"

Holland rolled his eyes. "Fine. What's done is done, anyway." He checked the time. "We need to keep moving. Everyone back to the van. I'll drop you two off at the motel, then I'll go and get the materials we need for the next attack."

"You go on ahead." Jody jingled the Lamborghini's keys. "Rod and I will head to the motel ourselves. Easy peasy."

The leader of Invisible Dagger sized up Jody, and the air sizzled between them. Finally, he scoffed. "Okay then. Both of you go straight to the motel. You have the address. No funny business. If anything goes wrong, I'll know about it." He glowered at each of them for a moment longer—probably hoping to look intimidating, but he ended up looking constipated—then headed back across the parking lot. He climbed into the red van, started its asthmatic engine, and got back on the highway.

Rod nudged Salvatore's body with his toe. "What do you think we should do with this?"

But Jody only had eyes for the sports car. "Drive it like we stole it." He giggled at his own joke.

The red minivan was already a speck on the horizon. Jody smiled as he watched the vehicle—which, according to the dearly departed Salvatore, was easy to track—vanish in the distance.

Annie hobbled down the stairs of her home, cursing the architect who put the bedroom on the second floor. She had only been released from the hospital the day before, and her legs were still as weak as a scarecrow's. Due to her shattered right wrist, her arm was in a cast from her elbow to her fingertips—if she slipped down the stairs, she wouldn't be able to catch herself. So she moved slowly. Carefully, as if her life depended on it. Which it sort of did.

The doctors had ordered her to wear a clear plastic mask over her broken nose. Combined with her bruised eyes, it made her look like a villain from a cheap superhero movie.

It was a good thing no one had seen her leave the hospital or slip into the house. Her pathetic visage would run nonstop on cable news for a week, and jerks online would have a field day.

She reached the ground floor and paused to collect herself. Without even thinking, she set a hand on her belly.

Her occupied belly.

She still didn't know how she felt about her newfound pregnancy... nor did she want to. If she opened the floodgates of emotion, she knew she would drown. She kept all her fear, joy, anxiety, and distress in a steel safe, shoved into the attic of her mind.

Clink. A sound echoed from the living room, like a mug being set down on a counter. Annie flinched, but she didn't feel anything. Her heart didn't pound, and there was no sickly feeling in her gut that typically preceded danger.

Did that mean there was no danger, or had she put her instincts in timeout along with her emotions?

Regardless, she made her way to the living room.

Elena sat on the sofa, waiting for her. Sure enough, a mug of coffee sat on the end-table next to her. She smiled softly. "Hey, Ace." Her demeanor held the same tone it had at the hospital: that of a child psychologist working with a new patient.

Annie watched her warily. The fact that Elena was in her house didn't shock her too much, even though she wasn't thrilled about it. But the gentle lilt to her voice was cause for concern.

She wanted to keep standing—simply to show that she could—but her body was already exhausted. Her bones were made of straw, and all it would take to blow her down was a huff and a puff from the big bad wolf.

With a grunt, she sat on the sofa across from her director. She let out a pained breath and waited.

Elena took her time before speaking. She sipped her coffee again, pushed her hair out of her eyes, and stared back.

Somewhere in the house, the AC came rumbling to life. A clock ticked. The world tried to make noise to fill the silence.

Finally, Elena spoke. "Annie, I think you would agree that this isn't working well."

That wasn't what Annie had expected. Her crooked nose and black eyes throbbed. She wanted to press her palms against the bruises to try and stem the pain, but she knew that would make it so much worse.

"It would be best and easiest for you," Elena continued, "if you quietly retired from your role as captain of the Army of Liberty."

Annie croaked, "Because I lost?" She hadn't spoken in a while, and her throat was dry.

Elena shook her head in defeat. "I don't know. I didn't make this decision."

"I've only been captain for a few months. People will be...suspicious." Annie didn't believe that even as she said it.

"The people who hate you won't care. As for your fans, you'll need to sell it. Put out a statement that you're looking for a peaceful life for your child."

Despite herself, Annie nodded. Elena was right about that—her haters would cheer that Annie Kennedy had had such a short tenure, and her admirers would be overjoyed that her baby would be safe.

"Do they have a replacement lined up?"

"I don't think so."

Annie sighed. Great—it wasn't that Valkyrie liked someone better than her. They just didn't like her in general.

"What about you?" Annie wasn't used to being the one asking questions all of the time.

"Well..." Elena waggled her shoulders. "Not sure. I'm *your* director, so I'll probably be tossed back in the pool they draw from whenever they need someone to direct battles."

She stood and closed the space between them. Annie thought she was walking over to hug her or comfort her in some way, but she was actually headed for the exit.

"I know this is hard news, Annie. But listen—it's for the best."

Annie realized she hadn't agreed to step down as captain...but she simultaneously realized she had no choice. She was a bruised, broken, lame, pregnant, incapacitated woman with a losing track-record and very little negotiating power.

The unseen clock chimed. Elena had left hours ago, and Annie had sat on the couch, unmoving, unthinking, unfeeling.

Just like that, Captain Kennedy was no more.

Jody had never seen so much corn in his life. This part of the country was flatter than a Frisbee, so there was nothing obstructing his view from seeing more corn. The scenery occasionally offered him fields of wheat for a change of pace, but for the most part, it was corn all the way down.

He and Roderick rode in the radiantly blue Lamborghini, and he almost regretted killing a guy who owned such a loud car. But then he remembered how sleek the Lamb was, and he decided he could forgive its noisy engine. Just to be safe, he stayed about a hundred yards back from Holland's van—an advantage of the horizontal landscape was that they could feasibly be miles away from the van and still be able to see it.

Jody flexed his fingers on the wheel. He wanted to gun the Lamb, run Holland off the road, and demand answers. He wanted to know how Holland got the weapons and gadgets they used in their attacks—those materials were how Holland flexed his superiority, and Jody intended to take that power away from him.

A headache waited in the wings of his skull. The freight train was in the depot, ready to make him miserable. He grabbed a stick of jerky from the glove compartment and chowed down, hoping the aggressive chewing would stave off the headache. (The Valkyrie recruiter had a huge stash of snacks in his car—no wonder he was so tubby.)

They had been following the red van for a few hours now. They passed through small towns, tiny towns, and collections of fast food restaurants that technically qualified as towns. Farms filled their rearview mirror, along with curious cows, rusty silos, and, of course, corn.

Afternoon turned to evening, then night. The sky was full of stars, like a metal sheet riddled with bullet holes. Eventually, they left behind any semblance of civilization and drove through isolated farmland. Holland's van and Jody's new sports car were the only vehicles on the dusty road, which forced Jody to hang back even more.

At long last, Holland pulled off the road and navigated the van through a field of corn stalks. Jody switched off the Lamb's headlights and similarly idled on the side of the road, about a hundred yards back from the van, keeping Holland barely in sight.

Jody pulled a small device from his hoodie pocket and flicked it on. Immediately, he could hear the '80s power ballad Holland had blaring in the van. Jody had left the device's companion in the van's glove compartment so that he could eavesdrop. The listening device was one of the gadgets Holland had acquired on his field trips, and Jody relished using it against him.

For the eight millionth time, Rod asked from the passenger's seat, "Are you sure we should be doing this?"

"For the eight millionth time," Jody groaned, "it's our right to know. Where does he go and what does he do when he gets our supplies, huh? How does he get these gadgets, or that helicopter, or those bombs? Don't you wonder a little?"

At that moment, Holland switched off his music, and Jody hissed "*Shh!*"

In the distance, the red van rolled through a cornfield, but it didn't bend any stalks—there must be a sneaky road cutting through it. The only possible destination was a silver silo that towered over the shoots like a rusty old scarecrow.

Jody craned his neck to try and get a better view. What could his leader be doing?

The van shuddered to a halt right next to the silo. Jody cranked up the volume on his listening device and smacked it against his ear.

A garbled, mechanical voice Jody didn't recognize spoke: "Present identification."

Jody gasped. There was something weird going on with that silo.

Holland responded: "Valkyrie 8-2-7 O-Q-T."

"Confirm purpose and payload," the voice said.

"I'm here to pick up two heads."

Jody furrowed his brow. What was a "head," and why did Holland need two of them?

"I don't believe it..." Rod set his head in his hands. To be honest, Jody had forgotten he was there. "Holland is in league with Valkyrie Productions? That doesn't make any sense!"

Jody put the Lamb in reverse and started making as quiet a getaway as possible. He got back on the dirt road and hightailed it away from there.

"Maybe," Rod scratched his head as he thought things through, "maybe he's stealing from Valkyrie. Like, he got someone's code and is using it to get bombs and helicopters and things like that. He's using their equipment for *our* purposes?" Even Rod didn't sound too confident in his theory.

Jody kept his eyes fixed ahead. "Then why wouldn't he tell us? Why does he always go on these supply runs by himself? Also, you'd think Valkyrie would notice a few missing Needle Drops and helicopters by now. No..." He gripped the wheel until his knuckles turned white. "This stinks. And it's not just the truck-stop taquito I ate today."

Rod ran a hand across his face. "What now?"

"We should head to the motel, since we know he'll go there once he has the supplies, and wait for him. We can confront him there and...demand answers."

That appeased Rod. But Jody didn't want answers. The freight train had started up in his skull again, and he'd learned there was only one way to quell it.

Zeke hated the music they played in grocery stores. It was always so boring and plain—the musical equivalent of beige.

He bagged some fruits and veggies for himself and headed to the check-out line. As he walked, he occasionally brushed against someone or accidentally elbowed another shopper's cart. The place was pretty crowded, and he was still getting used to his new bulk. He'd come a long way from the kid in a dead-end army, reenacting Gettysburg year after year.

The lens through which he saw the world had changed forever. He wasn't a lone soldier trying to become famous anymore—now, he was a dad.

A smile exploded across his face.

He was going to be a dad!

As much as he already strove to be the best fighter in his army, he was determined to increase that effort by tenfold. He needed to achieve greatness...not just for himself anymore. But for his child. And for Annie. For his family.

Plus, being a star soldier in one of the world's foremost armies would surely provide a nice lifestyle for them. They would never go to sleep hungry. A life of bliss, free from hardship, was just around the corner.

Despite his enthusiasm, even Zeke knew those expectations were impractical. Things weren't going to be perfect...but as long as he had Annie and their kid by his side, things were going to be pretty close.

He jostled against a middle-aged man who was dragging his small daughter behind him. Zeke nodded and said, "Sorry, sir—my bad."

The man ground his teeth. "Watch where you're going!" He yanked his daughter's arm, and the girl started to whine as they careened down a different aisle.

Zeke sighed, doing his best not to take the encounter to heart. His prove-himself mentality was hard to shut off, even when making a quick grocery run.

Everything was tense. The moment those bombs fell on Milwaukee, and Annie Kennedy had failed to stop them on live TV, the country had been pushed to the edge. People were scared their city might be next. After the impromptu clash in Nashville, everyone had been excited at the prospect of the unknown—maybe Captain Kennedy would show up in *their* town, run across *their* rooftop, and save *their* day in spectacular action-movie fashion.

But now that failure was an option, no one was excited. No one except for...

Even in a San Diego grocery store, Zeke saw a few of them: fans of Invisible Dagger. There was one guy with a shaved head, wearing a baggy hoodie and athletic pants. Then there was a lady wearing a t-shirt that told the world she was the *future Mrs. Holland Dagger*. And by the dairy section, there was a whole family sporting *RIP Staten* hats.

These fans weren't scared or anxious—they were jazzed. Electric. Energetic. They bounced on their heels and laughed at seemingly nothing. The guy dressed in the hoodie approached the family and high-fived the kids.

Invisible Dagger had admirers all over the world. In the dark corners of the internet, to be sure...but also out in the open. The domestic terrorist cell had become a beacon for those who used to be ashamed of their blood-lust. The lowlifes and degenerates had come out of their hiding places, convinced that it was okay to cheer for death and destruction.

It made Zeke sick. How could a person wear a t-shirt celebrating mass killers?

He ignored the "Daggsters" and got in the check-out line. Part of him was surprised no one recognized him. He was in San Diego, after all—the capital of war spectatorship—and he was making a name for himself in the Army of Liberty. His killstreak in his previous battle had made the record books: twenty kills, eleven of them headshots. That ratio was unheard of in the sharpshooting community. Even though he liked Valkyrie and the Army of Liberty, he was excited to get some under-the-table offers from other war enterprises.

He continued his daydream as a cashier scanned his produce.

Action figures. Public appearances and autograph lines. His own exhibit in the National Museum of Combat and Carnage. Soon enough, if he kept it up, maybe he would see people at the grocery store wearing t-shirts with *his* face on them...

His legs locked in place, and a knot formed in his chest. A single question ricocheted through his mind: *What's the difference between them and me?*

The Army of Liberty and Invisible Dagger...two groups of killers with massive fan bases.

Bile began to churn at the base of his throat.

He had never thought of the Army of Liberty in those terms. In fact, those terms could apply to all of war spectatorship.

He felt dizzy and needed to sit down. He needed to get out of the crowded store. He needed to get away from the fans of domestic terrorists and the fans of armies that killed for sport...mainly because he was afraid that he wouldn't be able to tell the difference.

He set his sights on the store's exit. A man in a suit stood there, holding an empty basket, surveying the scene. Zeke almost collapsed—his father had just walked in.

The last thing he needed at that moment—or at any moment—was to chitchat with his dad. Danny Carr was way too rich to shop at this grocery store...He must've come here hoping to bump into Zeke.

There was no way Zeke was going to let that happen. He dropped his bagged produce where he stood and disappeared into the crowd. His head still spun, but his dad's appearance forced him to focus. He meandered toward the back of the store, hiding among the crowd until he could slip away without drawing his dad's attention.

Danny thought he caught a flash of his son's figure among the mass of people in the store, but as he roamed the aisles, he couldn't find him anywhere.

When he saw a family wearing hats that mourned the Invisible Dagger member whom Kennedy had kicked off a building, his lip curled. He muttered, "Trash." No wonder he had his groceries delivered to his door every other day.

He finagled his way through the crowd so that he could "casually" walk past the family. When he was right beside them, he smiled and said, "I like your hats. Rest in *pieces* indeed. I heard it took them days to scrape ole Staten off the pavement."

When they started gnashing their teeth and screaming at him, Danny decided it was time to go. He didn't want to get any of their backwater spittle on him.

❧

Jody and Rod sat in their motel room in the mid-Midwest, watching *Wheel of Fortune* on the dingy old TV. The game had entered a speed round, and the category for the current puzzle was *Item*. Eight blank spaces flashed on the screen, two four-letter words. An "*S*" and an *H* ended the first word, and an *L* began the second word.

Jody was confident in the answer and shouted, "Fish love!"

Rod also offered a guess: "Wish list."

The contestant finished the puzzle using Rod's answer.

Jody stood and waddled toward the bathroom. "Hey, I was close."

"Um...yeah, buddy. You almost had that one." Rod leaned back on his bed and cracked open another soda.

As Jody headed for the toilet, he had to vault over piles of crumpled aluminum cans, empty chip bags, and Chinese take-out boxes. The motel room had accumulated quite an odor, since they hadn't opened the door to leave for three days straight.

They had been waiting for Holland for a long while. After having heard him using a Valkyrie ID at the silo, they had sped to the motel, ready to confront him. They had bounced around the room, bursting with energy—Jody had thought this was just like one of those *interventions* he saw on sitcoms all the time. They were prepared to lay into Holland and demand he come clean with everything he'd been keeping from them.

They waited all night. Then the next day. Then two more days.

Now, their righteous anger had ebbed. They were still ticked at Holland, but they were also in a perpetual sugar-crash and bloated from all the Doritos they'd eaten.

Jody saw himself in the bathroom mirror and jolted—his facial fair was unruly, which complimented his junk-food-encrusted fingers. He shook his head and jumped in the shower.

When Holland showed up, Jody knew he had to be ready for anything.

But that begged the question...where the hell was Holland, and what the hell was taking him so long?

The house smelled. Annie realized she hadn't washed dishes, done laundry, or cracked open a window in...

Annie also realized she had no idea what day it was. All she really knew was that she wasn't captain anymore. Her phone had died long ago. The TV was firmly locked on game shows and cooking competitions—she hadn't gotten a whiff of current events in a few days. No one had knocked on her door.

Her thoughts darted briefly to Zeke. Did he wonder where she was and if she was okay? How was he taking the news that he was going to be a father?

She dismissed those thoughts. If she started wondering how Zeke was feeling about being a parent, then she might start wondering how *she* felt about being a parent, and she couldn't have that. She just couldn't.

Her stomach rumbled. She didn't know if she was hungry, or if the baby was reacting to the house's stench. She decided she was hungry and migrated from the couch to the pantry.

The shelves were a wasteland, except for some cumin and granulated sugar. The fridge was similarly useless, unless she wanted to eat a double-A battery.

One option remained: delivery. She grabbed her dead cell phone, dug out its charger, and plugged it into an outlet.

She leaned against the wall and exhaled—those few moments of physical activity had worn her out. Her broken wrist pulsed within its cast as if it were trying to break free, and she was breathing so hard, her plastic face-guard fogged up.

She tried to distract herself by contemplating what food she would order. Pizza, noodles, salad...But she couldn't muster enough energy to care. She would eat anything it took to subdue her stomach so that she could go back to sitting on the couch and feeling nothing. Even the battery and sugar were starting to look good.

Then, the phone buzzed in her hand. It nearly leapt to the ground, as if it had been holding back for too long and was now getting all its jitters out of its system.

Annie checked the screen—she was getting a call from a number she didn't recognize. Before she had given it any thought, she answered. "Hello?" Her voice was deep. Hollow. Distant.

"Oh!" The voice on the other end of the line sounded taken aback, as if it hadn't expected to actually speak with someone. "Yes, hello! Is this Annie Kennedy?" It was a female. British. She sounded tired too.

Annie responded, "What do you want?"

"Captain, I'm Jasmine Creedy. I'm a—I'm an aspiring filmmaker, well, a journalist, I suppose. But that's beyond the point. Listen, captain..."

Annie didn't bother correcting the woman. She would find out soon enough that she wasn't captain anymore.

Jasmine continued. "I have vital information that I need to give to you specifically. My partner thinks it's pointless, frankly, but I think you can do something about this."

"You should listen to your partner." The words surprised Annie. The removal of all filters and emotions from her brain had revealed a person she never knew. Someone hollow. Distant.

"I'm going to say my piece!" Jasmine pressed onward, her voice rising a few octaves. "We did a lot of detective work to get this info, not to mention your bloody phone number, so you're going to hear it!"

Neither of them spoke. Maybe Jasmine was waiting for Annie to chew her out. Instead, Annie kept her mouth shut and waited. She couldn't help but want to hear what the journalist had to say—at the very least, this conversation was more interesting than the cooking channel.

Jasmine tossed out the next words as if they were burning her: "Nukes, captain. Invisible Dagger has taken two suitcase nuclear bombs from a Valkyrie cache."

Annie stiffened. She must have misheard what Jasmine said—there's no way Invisible Dagger had upgraded to nuclear warfare...Was there? Jasmine was still talking, so Annie leaned in and listened closer.

"The terrorist group has been traveling across the country in the same van for the past few months, and that van just recently picked up two portable bombs from a silo in Nebraska. From there, the van drove all the way out to San Diego—"

"San Diego?" Annie resisted the urge to peer out her house's window. Was Invisible Dagger on her doorstep, ready to nuke the West Coast?

"Listen, listen." Jasmine took a harried breath—she sounded simultaneously exhausted and frantic, as if powered by sheer caffeine. "I don't know why, but the van drove to San Diego, then just a few minutes later, turned around and headed back into the middle of the country. It's still on the move, but it looks like it's boomeranging back to where it came from."

"Strange." Annie felt an inkling of fear and shoved it away. "Have you told anyone about this?"

"I...I..." Jasmine sputtered and cleared her throat. "I'm telling *you*. You're Captain Kennedy, the maternal warrior. I figured you'd spring into action or something."

"That's not what I do anymore." Annie's shoulders sagged as the truth of her words seeped into her bones. "I'm not a captain. I'm not even sure if I'm still in an army. Nuclear attacks are above my paygrade."

"But..." Jasmine paused, and Annie thought the connection had been lost. When she spoke again, her voice was laced with bewilderment and more than a little anger. "Are you serious? I just told you these eejits have hijacked two nuclear bombs, and your response is 'That's not what I do anymore'?! I highly doubt they stole those bombs to put on their mantle! People are in mortal danger! What are you going to bloody-well do about it?"

People. The people who hissed and turned against her when she got scared. The people who loved her only when she was performing to their expectations. The people who crammed into areas and cheered for violence and destruction. Maybe a little violence and destruction was what they needed. What they deserved.

Jasmine panted, out of breath from her tirade. When Annie didn't respond, she meekly asked, "...Hello?"

Annie answered with a question of her own. "Where did the van go in San Diego?"

"Um...One moment, I'm not sure." Her voice became muffled as she presumably put her hand over the phone's receiver and spoke to someone next to her. The words "Ravi," "van," and "stopped" bled through. True to her word, she returned only a moment later. "Looks like some sort of retirement home. It's called Front Porch."

That name stuck itself into Annie's brain and wiggled around. It was so familiar, but she couldn't place its origin. Where had she heard it before?

Jasmine muttered to herself. "Hmm, that's odd. Why would they obtain two suitcase nukes, swing by an elderly persons' home, then drive back toward the Midwest?"

That phrase triggered Annie's memory. *Elderly persons' home...Old people farm.*

Front Porch—the center where Leigh Gambol lived, and where General Lightfoot visited him.

Invisible Dagger had taken Gambol, and possibly Lightfoot too.

Her heartbeat ticked upward as she marched through the house. She said to Jasmine, "Can you give me that van's trajectory and keep me apprised of its location? I'll be on the move in five minutes."

"Oh!" Jasmine was, once again, taken aback, but she quickly recovered. "Yes ma'am, captain."

Annie hung up. As she strapped on boots, combed her hair, and dug out her personal handgun from under the bed, she tried to convince herself that she was acting out of duty. Lightfoot and Gambol were her superiors, after all—rescuing them was something the captain of the Army of Liberty should do. Nothing more.

When she left her home, she had no idea where she was headed. "The Midwest" was her only direction. She set out to rent a car and hit the road, all the while forcing her heartrate to tap a steady, staccato rhythm.

No matter what, she couldn't allow her emotions to surface. Especially not as she headed into battle with no strategy, no battle plans, and no back-up. Especially not with nukes in play and Lightfoot's life on the line.

And especially not now that she had knowledge of a child in her belly.

It had been days and days since Jody had seen Holland at that silo in the middle of the cornfield. For days and days, he'd been sitting in their motel room, waiting to confront his leader and former mentor, formulating the perfect speech in his mind. He wasn't sure how, but he wanted to work the phrase "I said *good day*, sir" in there somewhere—he'd heard it on TV, and he'd always wanted to say it.

But as the days wore on, he got more and more lethargic. He stopped pacing back and forth and started watching the cooking channel. Instead of planning what he was going to say to Holland, he continually ordered pizzas to be delivered.

After so many hours of self-imposed isolation, he was practically comatose, a mummy in a sarcophagus made of take-out boxes. Rod tried to keep him active and awake, but Jody always waved him off. When Rod would pester him further, Jody would remind him of the knife in his hoodie pocket. Rod would then leave him alone for a few hours, and the cycle would start over.

Jody had entirely lost track of what day it was when the motel door swung open. The noonday sun blinded him, and he winced like a vampire. "Gah! Shut the door, Rod!"

The door closed, but it wasn't Rod. Holland stood in the threshold, his nose twitching as he took in the mountains of trash. "It smells like a monkey's diaper in here."

Rod shuffled out of the bathroom, frantically buckling his pants and tossing away the magazine he'd been reading on the john. His wide eyes asked Jody what the game plan was— Holland's sudden arrival had clearly caught him off guard.

Jody tried to lurch to his feet, but the sunken mattress had him trapped. It took a few attempts before he was on his feet, stepping over empty Mountain Dew bottles to stand in front of Holland. "What've you been up to?"

Holland scoffed and shook his head. "Getting supplies for the next target city, like usual. Check your attitude."

He tried to slide past Jody, but Jody mirrored his movements. "For this long?"

"Some of these supplies were far away," Holland growled, losing what little patience he had. "Our van isn't exactly a slick blue Lamborghini. It took time to drive there and back to your sorry mugs. Any more questions, or can I take a shower?"

Jody crossed his arms, subtly putting a hand near his pocket's opening. "Were any of those supplies from...Valkyrie Productions?"

The room froze. Rod held his breath, and Holland's scar quivered as he glared. But Jody didn't back down. In fact, he straightened up to his full height.

"You little putz..." Holland sneered, then snapped at Rod. "Did you two follow me? You saw me get those two nukes?!"

Rod opened and closed his mouth as he shrugged. He wasn't one for confrontation.

Jody, on the other hand, thrived on hostility. He also learned that the term "heads" was code for nuclear bombs, and that fired him up even more. "Yeah, we did follow you. And we didn't like what we saw, did we, Rod?"

Apparently, Rod had decided his role in the situation would be to stand at the back of the room and act like a malfunctioning animatronic.

Holland fixed his sights on Jody. "You think it matters what you like?"

"Why are you working with the enemy? Are you on their payroll? Is this all one big scheme to boost Valkyrie's popularity?" He gasped as his train of thought led him to a final conclusion. "You're in league with *Kennedy*, aren'cha?"

"Shut your trap! I'm only in league with who I need to be in league with!" Holland bellowed, then brought his volume back down. He turned and peeked through the window blinds, making sure no one had heard their argument. As he scanned the outside of the motel, he snarled, "You ought to know better than to—"

While Holland had his back turned, Jody thrust his blade deep into the nape of his neck. Holland flinched once, then tumbled to the floor, never to move again.

Jody knelt next to the body and fished the van keys from his pocket. He stood and faced Rod—the last two remaining members of Invisible Dagger. Rod stared at the corpse, but he didn't run, scream, or faint, which was a good sign to Jody. He asked, "What're you thinking, Rod?"

Again, Rod shrugged. "I'm mainly shocked you didn't livestream that. We would've gotten massive numbers. Season finale type numbers."

"Nah." Jody jingled the van keys. "If Holland got the supplies like he said he did, the season finale is next."

Jody and Rod rushed to the window. As they stepped around Holland's bleeding body, they craned their necks to look through the blinds.

There in the parking lot was the red van. Jody couldn't help but bounce on his heels as he pictured what was inside: two portable nukes.

"I have an idea for a tweak to the plan." Rod shot Jody an impish glance.

Jody didn't usually care for ideas that didn't belong to himself or his late buddy Staten, but the evil glint in Rod's eye was promising. "What're you thinking?"

Rod scratched his chin as he connected the final dots in his mind. Eventually, he said, "Well, we have *two* bombs, don't we? That's overkill for *one* city."

A wicked smile spread across Jody's face. "I think you're right. We oughta spread the love."

～～

Annie drove and drove. It was an odd sensation to travel without a clear-cut destination, but she kept moving all the same. She speared through Arizona and New Mexico, the sun and moon seemingly on a merry-go-round in the sky. She barely noticed time passing, and she only stopped to get gas when needed.

Whenever fatigue started to get the best of her, an image of General Lightfoot would fill her mind, and she'd snap awake.

She was somewhere near Texas's border, and she merged onto a northbound highway. Since Invisible Dagger had last struck in Milwaukee, it was geographically logical that they would attack somewhere in the mid-Midwest next. She flexed her fingers on the wheel and adjusted her seat—her buttocks were falling asleep for the eightieth time. She ignored the discomfort and stared straight out of the windshield.

Part of her wanted to ditch this human-driven car she'd rented and get a fancy automated one. That way, she could rest up for her looming confrontation with Invisible Dagger. But automated cars were too expensive, and she needed to save her money—that's what she told herself, anyway.

It had taken a while for her to adjust to driving entirely with one hand. Her bandaged right arm sat uselessly in her lap—she occasionally glared at it, as if shaming it would somehow make it heal faster.

Her phone sat in the car's cup holder. Every now and then, Jasmine Creedy would call to give Annie an update. So far, it seemed that Invisible Dagger's red van was at a motel in Nebraska, but they could leave and go elsewhere at any moment.

Speak of the devil—the phone whirred to life. Annie braced the steering wheel with her knees, snatched up the phone, and nearly answered, but then she saw who the incoming call was from. It was Zeke. Again.

He had called countless times as she drove the past couple of days. Annie wanted to talk to him, but she couldn't. If she was on the line with him, she might miss an update from Jasmine—that's what she told herself, anyway.

She dismissed Zeke's call, and almost immediately, the phone buzzed again. This time, it was Jasmine. She accepted the call and slammed the phone against her face, completely forgetting about her bruised eyes and the plastic face-guard. She hit the side of the guard, which jostled her head and made her vision swim. She ignored the pain, focused on the phone call, and got right to the point. "Are they moving?"

"Indeed." Jasmine had been awake the past couple days along with Annie. Her voice was made of dandelion fuzz, susceptible to disintegration at the slightest breeze. "We have a destination for you."

Annie was surprised. "Are you sure? How can you know exactly where they're headed?"

"Their van has been on the road for several hours now. We've been tracking their path—"

Annie cut her off. "They've been on the move, and you didn't tell me?" Anger peppered her words, which, compared to her usually emotionless tone, had the impact of a hurricane.

Jasmine pushed back. "If we told you they were moving, you would have gotten all in a tizzy over nothing. Now, we've been keeping an eye on their trajectory, and after a few hours, we're fairly certain where they're taking the bombs and hostages."

"Okay then, where?"

Jasmine hesitated. "Captain—"

"Just tell me so I can go there instead of driving around like an idiot!"

"It looks like Wichita, captain."

Annie sighed. She knew that she should have felt a pit in her stomach, or sweat should be lining her hairline, or she should cry out in anguish... but she just sighed. "Okay, keep me posted."

She hung up and gunned the rental car's engine, charting a course for her hometown.

Mere hours after Salvatore Caracas's death, his massive home on Coronado Island had been put on the market. Now, a week later, after dozens of multi-million-dollar bids, a new owner was about to get the keys. Things move fast in the world of ultra-rich real estate.

Danny strolled away from his chauffeured car and took in the sight of the mansion. Even his penthouse wasn't this opulent. The place had an underground garage, multiple swimming pools, crystal chandeliers, a private gym, and enough bedrooms to house a professional basketball team.

Just the sight of it boosted his spirits. Yes, it would make a fine addition to his collection of homes.

Part of him felt bad for swooping in like a vulture after Salvatore's death. But someone was going to buy the house one way or another, and Danny wanted it to be himself more than some other millionaire schlub. That was just the way of the world.

He withdrew his checkbook and waved at the realtor standing by the front door. "Hey there..." He'd forgotten the man's name. He knew he should've sent Suzanne to close on the house, but Danny couldn't help it—he wanted to purchase his new home in-person.

The realtor smiled painfully, as if he were holding in a burp. "Hello, Mr. Carr. I tried to reach you, but I must have the wrong number..."

A sixth sense rumbled in Danny's gut. He knew when a business deal was about to flop, and the realtor's tone of voice wasn't comforting. "What's wrong?"

"Well, another buyer appeared at the last moment and offered a higher bid on this property."

"No no no no, that's not how this works." Danny ripped a pen from his suit pocket and started forcefully filling out a check. "I have the highest bid, and you accepted."

"I'm sorry, Mr. Carr, but this new buyer offered a bid triple the amount of yours." He winced. "Very sorry."

Danny grimaced. He knew this loafer in human form wasn't sorry *for* Danny—he was merely sorry he had to break the news *to* Danny.

He stuffed his checkbook deep into his pocket. Money was all realtors cared about, so there was no way Danny could dissuade him without shelling out way more cash than he wanted to. "Thanks for nothing, blockhead."

He slumped away from the mansion, back toward his car—then he shoved his shoulders back and forced himself to stand erect. There was no way he could let anyone know how crestfallen he was to not buy Salvatore's house.

As he sat in traffic on the way to the Valkyrie offices, he couldn't stop wondering who this filthy rich buyer was. When he found out, he would make their life a living hell. No one outflanked Danny Carr.

❧

Jasmine paced in her motel room and checked the clock for the hundredth time. Ravi had left hours ago to get them lunch and hadn't called since. Either he was in trouble, unconscious in a ditch, or up to something.

She didn't want to come across as panicky or bossy...but screw it, she *was* panicky at this point, and she *was* his boss. She punched his number in her phone.

He picked up on the second ring. "Hey, boss!"

"Ravi?" She was surprised he had answered so jovially. "You sound like you're in the car still. You okay?"

"Umm..."

That wasn't the response Jasmine wanted. "Ravi, what the devil are you doing?"

"Okay, listen." His words spilled out. "I'm following Annie Kennedy to Wichita. If that's where the bad guys are, and that's where she's going, there'll be a big fight! And no one else knows about it! We'll have the exclusive, up-close-and-personal footage."

"No no," Jasmine said with her best stern tone, "Ravi, that's far too dangerous. We focus on the aftermath of the heroics, remember? *After* the fighting is done!"

"Sorry, boss," Ravi said, as chipper as ever. "Can't pass this up. You'll thank me when we have the top-watched show on CinemaStream!" With that, he hung up.

Jasmine clutched her phone in an iron grip. "Reckless bugger..." More than anything, she felt a hot pit of shame in her gut that, even if Ravi hadn't taken their car, she would never do what he had done. She would never get within a hundred miles of a live gunfight.

Martin, the executive at CinemaStream, had told her to up the ante. Instead, she had merely wallowed around in the aftermaths of real battles.

Was Ravi doing what was needed to succeed in their business, leaving her in the dust?

⁂

The house was pretty nice—not mind-blowing or anything, but nice. Definitely nicer than the house Jody had grown up in as a kid.

Popcorn ceilings, shaggy carpet, well-used couches, water rings on the coffee table…It wasn't a mansion, but it was clearly a place where happy people had once lived.

Jody still didn't know how Holland had found out where Annie Kennedy's childhood home was, but at that point, he didn't care. Holland had crafted a nice plan, and now that he was dead, Jody would carry it through. Easy peasy.

He and Rod had been more than slightly surprised to find two old geezers tied up in Holland's red van. The older of the two kept muttering random nonsense about his grocery list and old girlfriends from a century ago. The other guy was friskier, and he lashed out while bellowing curse words Jody had never heard before. Just to be safe, while they were driving to Wichita, Jody kept them knocked out with an occasional thwack with the butt of his knife.

Now, the two old men sat in dining room chairs, back to back in the middle of the family room. Jody had dragged them inside while they were unconscious, but they were starting to stir. "Hey," he called over his shoulder, "you got duct tape anywhere?"

He heard Rod rustling through drawers in the kitchen, and a minute later, Rod emerged with a thick roll of silver tape. "Where are the people who live here?"

Jody took the tape, unfurled some with a satisfying *riipppp*, and began binding the two men to their chairs. "Don't know. Don't care."

As Jody circled around and around and around the two geezers, he kept stealing peeps at the nondescript briefcase sitting on the fireplace mantle. Small, boxy, and relatively lightweight—the sort of thing you'd see thousands of at any given airport. Jody hadn't thought "suitcase nuke" would be literal.

And there it sat, just a few feet away. A weapon with the capability to level the city, send noxious gas across the entire region, and snuff out every trace of life in the blink of an eye.

Jody finished taping the two men, took a swig from a soda can, and set it on the suitcase.

Just then, the older of the gasbags jerked awake. He shrieked as if his feet were on fire: "GAH! Where am I? Who're you?!" His big watery eyes flicked from Jody to Rod and back again.

Rod leaned over to whisper to Jody. "Who are these guys again?"

Jody let out a carbonated burp and spoke at a louder-than-necessary volume. "Don't know. Don't care." He slapped Rod's forearm. "I think I'm good here, man. Get going. I'll see you in a few days." He handed Rod the keys to the Lamborghini, which was parked elsewhere in the neighborhood so as not to attract nosy stares.

Rod took the keys and smiled. "Season finale." He gestured to their elderly hostages. "Before I go, you want me to film your video for you, so you don't have to do it from a selfie-angle?"

"I'm not making a video."

Rod shook his head in shock. "What's with you? First you didn't livestream killing Holland, and now you don't want to advertise that we have captives? *And* you don't want to flaunt our new firepower either? I don't get it. You usually tell our subscribers when you're drinking a smoothie or taking a dump. This is huge! I figured you'd want to tell the world."

"You're right, Rod—this *is* huge. So we can't tell anyone until it's happened. We can't risk Valkyrie or the cops sending someone to stop us. This will be our biggest hit yet. We can't let anyone muck it up."

Rod opened his mouth to keep arguing, probably ready to gab all about data and public image and social media stats.

But the freight train in Jody's skull was running amuck. He shot Rod a glare that said *I have a knife in my pocket that's still stained with our leader's blood.*

"Okay…" Rod slowly backed out of the family room. "I'll just…be on my way."

Jody *riipppp*'d another piece of tape off the roll as Rod left the Kennedy home.

The hundred-year-old dinosaur struggled weakly in his seat. "Someone tell me what's happening!" His veins bulged against his papery skin, and Jody was briefly worried that he would keel over from a heart attack before the nuke went off.

The other old man began to rouse from unconsciousness too. "…Leigh? Where are we? Are we in somebody's house?" He glanced around the room before realizing he was strapped to a chair. "Aw hell, this is some bull—"

Jody fixed the tape over the old man's mouth. He set his hands on his knees and looked him in the eye. The geezer snorted like a bull and glowered with all his might, but behind the bravado, Jody could see glimmers of terror. Real fear. Knowledge that death was a very real possibility today.

"Hi, old man. I'm Jody, the head of Invisible Dagger. Nice to meet you."

Annie drove all through the day. No pit stops, no breaks, no food or water. She pushed the speedometer as far as she could without getting pulled over.

A fog of numbness shrouded her mind. Scenery and entire states flew past the car's windows without her even realizing. When she blinked and refocused, she found herself crossing Wichita's city limits.

The place hadn't changed since she left several months ago to go audition in Chicago. Homes and businesses, offices and fast food joints, lampposts and traffic lights...The whole place looked like a stock image she would find online by googling the word *city*.

She directed the car through town, knowing right where she was headed. If Invisible Dagger wanted to make a splash in Wichita, they would do it in the house where she grew up. Her childhood home.

For the first time in years—a decade, even—her thoughts drifted to her parents. She had no idea who or where her father was. For all she knew, he could be president of the United States, but she knew exactly where her mom was: sleeping in the dirt of a cemetery on the south side of town. If Invisible Dagger was indeed housing nuclear bombs in her home, Annie was strangely glad her mom wasn't there to see it.

The traffic light ahead of her changed from green to yellow to red, and she brought the rental car to a shuddering halt. After a few frantic days of driving, the vehicle felt like it was on its last leg.

Annie felt a pinprick in the soles of her feet—an instinctive prelude of what was just around the corner. She had barely registered the sensation when a tidal wave of pain washed over her body.

"Argh!" She doubled over in the front seat and clutched her torso as if holding herself together. Deep, profound agony burst from her gut, and she felt like a porcelain vase sitting on a hot stove, about to explode into a thousand shards.

"What on Earth..." she grunted through clenched teeth. This was a discomfort she'd never experienced before, and—with her two black eyes, flattened nose, and shattered wrist—she considered herself quite the expert.

And just like that, it was over. The pain passed as if it had never existed.

A horn honked behind her. She raised her head—the light had turned green. She reached behind her face-guard to wipe sweat off her forehead and drove on.

That was new. In all her years of working out and participating in battles, she had never felt pain like that in every cell, nerve, and bone.

She glanced down at her stomach, which had only recently taken in an occupant. "Great," she sighed and hoped this wasn't a precursor of things to come.

Without thinking, her muscle memory took over, and she headed for her old home. The place she walked to after school, the setting of a dozen birthday parties and sleepovers, the house where she had felt safe and secure throughout her childhood.

And before she knew it, she was there. Her house was on a street corner in a lower-middle-class neighborhood. The driveways and yards were mostly empty, but as the workday ended, people would start to trickle in from all over the city. Bikes, kickballs, and chalk sat abandoned on sidewalks, as if the children of the neighborhood had known something was wrong and ran home.

She parked on the street and gazed at the house. Red bricks, sagging gutters, blooming sunflowers, and a door freshly painted bright purple. Whoever lived here now was doing their best to make the place homey.

A clunky minivan was parked in the driveway. It looked empty. Invisible Dagger had been here for a while.

Annie turned off her car, sat in silence, and breathed. The engine ticked as it cooled, echoing her erratic heartbeat.

She wasn't scared. Nor did she feel particularly bold. Rather, her military intuition kicked in to prepare her for the upcoming battle. She kept her emotions on lockdown but allowed her instincts and training to flow through her body.

She didn't know what exactly waited for her inside that house. She was on her own—no directors or fellow soldiers to help her out. All she had was her own gut.

Before she could psych herself out, she got out of the car. A *ding-ding-ding* told her she had left the keys in the ignition, but she knew if she stopped and turned around, she might get back in the car and drive away.

Her boots clapped on the concrete as she approached the house. Birds chirped. Vehicles revved on adjacent roads. But she couldn't hear any of it. Her pulse thudded like a sledgehammer in her ears.

Again, she told herself it was just her instincts. She wasn't scared. She wasn't scared. She wasn't...

Using her left hand, she pulled her handgun from its holster on her hip. It felt foreign and clumsy in her non-dominant hand, but her shattered right wrist left no other option.

She moved to the blindingly purple front door and saw it was ajar just a crack. She nudged it open with her toe and crept inside.

Zeke had music blaring in his ears as he ran through a park in San Diego. The sky was clear, the temperature mild, and everywhere he looked, people were smiling. Picnics and outdoor games were in full swing. Families laughed together, couples looked at each other lovingly, and dogs frolicked through the lush grass.

For all intents and purposes, it was a perfect day.

Except he couldn't stop worrying about Annie. She had vanished, and she wasn't answering his calls. Whenever he called, the phone only rang a few times, implying that she actively rejected the call. That was more disconcerting than if she didn't answer at all.

But he tried not to worry. She was an adult who could take care of herself, even if she was injured. And pregnant. And alone.

He pushed his legs faster.

All at once, the music in his ears stopped and was replaced with a high-pitched buzz. An alarm of some kind, clawing for his attention.

He brought his momentum to a screeching halt and pulled his phone from his pocket. Instead of a song title, the screen displayed a bright red box that read:

BREAKING: Disgraced former captain Annie Kennedy is facing off with the domestic terrorist cell Invisible Dagger, which has acquired weapons of mass destruction. CLICK HERE NOW to watch LIVE.

Zeke's legs turned to spaghetti, and he nearly collapsed. He swiveled his head to look around the park—everyone in sight was looking at their phones as well. Some murmured to one another, some were shocked, some were excited to see this new spectacle. Whatever their attitudes, all tapped their screens to watch.

"Oh, Annie…" With a sweaty, trembling finger, Zeke selected the red box.

His phone's screen was filled with the image of a suburban home's living room. Two elderly men sitting in chairs were strapped back to back. The bald terrorist named Jody stood nearby.

In the lower corner of the screen, the word *LIVE* flashed.

Danny walked through the ground-floor lobby of Valkyrie Productions' office building, an extra-extra-*venti* frappe in his hand.

One of the TVs mounted to the wall started to blink. In fact, all of the TVs blinked, even though they were all set to different channels. A message popped up, bold and electrifying.

Danny blinked and rubbed his eyes. Was he reading it right?

The security guard at the front desk trilled. "No way," he chuckled. "Kennedy's at it again? I wonder if she'll choke on live TV." He hit a button on the master remote control, and all the television sets switched to a shot of a random house's living room.

"Holy Moses..." Danny dropped his coffee as he sprinted to the elevators. He needed to get to his office and figure out what was going on. The security guard yelled something about the mess, but as soon as Danny had seen Leigh Gambol and Richard Lightfoot duct taped to chairs, he'd stopped listening.

⁂

Annie's boots crunched on the old carpet as she moved through the foyer, gun extended, muscles tight. She kept her finger on the trigger, ready to blast anything she didn't like.

The walls were decorated with family photos and various adornments from cheap craft stores. A wedding picture here, an ornamental cross there...Evidence of people that Annie didn't know and never would. She hoped they weren't here to get in the way of her confrontation with Invisible Dagger.

Ahead was the kitchen, and a small bathroom was to her left. On her right, the space opened up into a living room. She took cover behind the wall of the foyer and popped her head around the corner to see what was waiting for her.

A couch. Shag carpet. Chairs. An old TV on a rickety stand. More photos and décor.

Her eyes kept scanning the material contents of the room to avoid seeing what was situated in the center of the carpet. Or rather, *who* was situated in the center of the carpet. Eventually, Annie had no choice but to look.

Richard Lightfoot and Leigh Gambol were fastened to chairs by silver tape, back to back. They didn't appear injured, but Gambol trembled as if he was about to keel over from a heart attack right then and there. Even Lightfoot's mischievous glint was gone, substituted with an expression of dread and defeat.

Neither Jody, Holland, nor Roderick were in sight. It would be best to get the hostages out of here and deal with the terrorists later.

She slithered into the room, rolling her feet onto the carpet, heel to toe, in an attempt to silence her steps. The house seemed frozen in time, utterly silent, more like a portrait than a home. She was afraid that the slightest noise would shatter the illusion and bring chaos raining down on them.

As she moved, she caught sight of the mantle, grimy from years of disuse. But ash and dust weren't alone atop it.

A suitcase sat open, filled with wires, circuitry, and other technology that Annie didn't know anything about. She recognized one thing, though—a large red button. A trigger that could turn the entire city into ash and dust.

One of the suitcase nukes. Right there, within twenty feet of her. A chill ran down her spine.

She swallowed the acidic lump in her throat and made her way to the two captives. She grabbed the tape binding Lightfoot's hands and tried to tear it apart.

Lightfoot snapped out of his limp stupor and stared at her in disbelief. She tore the tape off his mouth, and he immediately barked, "Kennedy? What're you doing here?"

"Who's that?" Gambol twisted in his chair to see what was going on. Apparently, the terrorists hadn't deemed him worthy of muzzling. "Is it time for *Wheel of Fortune?*"

"Kennedy," Lightfoot locked eyes with her, "these palookas are full-tilt insane. They've got nukes. You need to get outta here and come back with the whole cavalry."

"We don't have time for that," Annie hissed and strained against the duct tape.

"Well, make time!" Lightfoot snapped.

Then, a footstep creaked from within the house. Annie and Lightfoot froze, their senses trained on the sound. Gambol, on the other hand, gabbed on frantically. "I don't know where I am, Rick! Who is this woman?"

Click clack.

Annie recognized that sound. "Uh oh…"

So did Lightfoot. He shouted to her, "Get down!"

She spun around and dashed backward into the kitchen. She dove behind the counter just as a figure emerged from one of the bedrooms. A man of medium-build with a shaved head, wearing a baggy hoodie and wielding a military-grade assault rifle, locked and cocked and ready to fire.

The elevator to the top floor took centuries. Bland music filled the car as Danny creeped up and up and up…and all the while, his heart hammered and obscenities blared through his mind.

Why was Kennedy doing another live impromptu battle with Invisible Dagger? Winn had fired her—right? Danny hadn't been briefed on this battle, so he had no idea what the stakes were, and he hated that more than anything. He had no idea what was going on.

Finally, the elevator dinged, and he rocketed out toward his office. He burst through the door to find things just how he had left them—his chair, his desk, the blueprints and photos for his space battle, the massive window surveying the Pacific—except for one thing. A small portable TV sat on the desk, facing him. Its screen displayed the living room he had seen on the TVs downstairs.

Danny staggered toward the desk, as if in a nightmare. He gawked at the TV—it was decades old, and he definitely didn't own it. Someone had brought it in for a reason.

On the screen, Lightfoot and Gambol were screaming at someone. They both looked every second of their many, many years, so frail and timeworn. Just then, the terrorist named Jody entered the room with a terrifying machine gun. He snarled and opened fire on someone off-screen.

The shot changed to what Danny assumed was an adjoining room in the house—a kitchen, rather outdated in his opinion. Someone crouched behind the counter, hiding from Jody's wrath. Danny thought the woman looked familiar, but he couldn't quite make out who it was. Her eyes were bruised like a raccoon's, and she wore a plastic pane over her face.

Danny leaned in. "Kennedy? Is that you?" Her previous fight with Invisible Dagger had taken quite a toll.

Jody's bullets ripped the kitchen to shreds. Bits of plaster and wood exploded like confetti. The *rat-tat-tat* of the machine gun was so loud, it made the entire image pulse.

The sight of Annie Kennedy, beaten and bruised, cornered by such firepower, made Danny catch his breath. "Good Lord..." There was no way she was going to make it out alive.

A voice came from behind him. "It's good stuff, right?"

"This was you?" Danny turned, and those sharp eyes and sharp earrings glistened back at him in response.

The kitchen Annie had grown up in was destroyed right in front of her. The counter where she had eaten cereal was grated like cheese. The cabinets were shot full of holes. The fridge and light fixtures were utterly destroyed in a matter of seconds.

She briefly wondered where Invisible Dagger had gotten such a high-powered rifle, but it didn't ultimately matter. The reality was that if she didn't act fast, she didn't stand a chance.

She raised her left hand over the counter, fired a few haphazard shots of her own, and quickly returned to her cover. The bullets didn't come anywhere close to hitting Jody—she wasn't even looking, and she was using her non-dominant hand, after all—but they succeeded in making Jody stop shooting and take cover of his own. She heard him scrambling around the living room and settling somewhere on the far side, likely behind a couch.

Dust and plaster clogged her lungs and made breathing a chore. She ripped her face-guard off and tossed it out of sight—she needed every inch of vision she could get.

Jody called out to her. "You're gonna die today, Kennedy!"

General Lightfoot, still captive in the living room, replied on her behalf. "Oh, stuff it, you cross-eyed twit!"

"You're the twit, not me!" Jody's comebacks were as sophisticated as Annie had expected.

"Nuh-uh!" Lightfoot kept Jody busy for a few seconds with the *I know you are but what am I* game.

Annie slumped against the kitchen counter and caught her breath. She checked her gun's clip and huffed—there were only a few shots left. She'd wasted too many bullets shooting blindly.

Things weren't looking good. There was a nuke in play, with a big red button just waiting to be pressed, Jody had an assault rifle, and neither Rod nor Holland were anywhere to be found, which made her very uneasy.

She scanned the kitchen, looking for anything that she might be able to use to her advantage. A knife, a frying pan, an AK-47...

Instead, something tiny and nearly invisible caught her attention. She likely would have overlooked it if she hadn't been forced to stare at one before.

She squinted at the corner of the ceiling, not wanting to believe her eyes.

But she saw what she saw.

A small, portable camera. The kind Elena had used to capture Annie's earlier public action scenes.

Her blood froze.

Was this all a set-up by Elena? Had her former director positioned all these dominos? Annie getting fired, Invisible Dagger having these bombs, Lightfoot and Gambol being captured…Was it all Elena's doing?

And…

Her grip on the gun tightened until she was certain the metal would crack.

Was it *all* Elena's doing?

Each of Invisible Dagger's attacks—Boston, Baltimore, Nashville, and Milwaukee. All the innocent people they had murdered. Their online presence and fandom. Their merchandise and cultural impact.

They were effective showmen, and Elena was a great director.

Could Invisible Dagger be Elena's puppets? Was it possible that a person could be so cold and calculating so as to control a terrorist cell simply to create a spectacle?

Elena strolled into Danny's office as he stood immobilized by his desk. "What is this, Winn?" He felt lost, which was an emotion he didn't relate to and therefore despised. "What's going on?"

"History. I thought you'd see that."

He glanced at the TV on his desk—Kennedy was now glaring directly into the camera, her eyes aflame with indignation. He exhaled as he sized Elena up, truly seeing her the first time. "Are you Invisible Dagger?"

She didn't answer immediately, so, rather than sit with the horror of his accusation, Danny filled the silence.

"But that's not possible. They've killed people. Thousands of innocent lives."

She walked past him and stared out the window. White waves dotted the dark blue ocean, like sheep on an azure landscape. She was quiet for a moment longer, then spoke. "Have you ever killed someone, Mr. Carr? I recommend everyone do it at least once in their lives. It's transformative, turns you into your truest self."

Danny's head swam, and he set a hand on his desk to keep from falling. "Innocent people, Winn…"

In response, she scoffed and locked eyes with him. "Psshh. Those who Invisible Dagger killed were just as innocent as the millions upon millions of quote-unquote 'soldiers' we kill every year. Audiences roar with applause whenever someone dies in an arena—it's not fundamentally different when it happens in the streets of Nashville or Milwaukee." She nodded toward the TV. "Or Wichita. And I guarantee you, the little escapade happening on that screen is getting better viewership than any battle in an arena ever did or ever will."

Danny shook his head. "So Leigh Gambol and General Lightfoot are props in all this? And the whole city of Wichita? Or is that suitcase nuke just a prop too?"

"Nope." Elena reached into her pocket and pulled out a switch with a red button. "It's very, very real."

He instinctively reared back. "Good Lord, Winn!" Cold sweat beaded his forehead. "Put that down before someone gets hurt."

She arched an eyebrow at him. "Really?" She tickled the button with her thumb.

Danny tried to slow his galloping heartrate as his paradigm of the world crumbled around him. He had believed he was in charge of the Army of Liberty, Annie Kennedy, and Elena Winn. It turned out the org chart had been reversed all along.

"How does this help anyone, huh?" he asked. "People are gonna find out the truth about all this, and then they're gonna try to emulate it. Every war enterprise in the world will have their own pet terrorist cell, and it'll be chaos."

"No one will find out," she said as if speaking to an ignorant child. "You didn't, until I told you. And even if someone does find out...They won't be a problem for long."

Danny raked his hand through his hair. "This is insane. On the field and in stadiums, we can control things. Out in the world, we're worthless."

Elena laughed. "You think you can control *everything* that happens in a battle stadium? Tell that to Ranger Monroe. And you say a director is worthless out in the world?" She held the trigger aloft. "Tell that to me."

Control. A piece of the puzzle fell into place in Danny's head.

"When Kennedy froze on the battlefield," he said as the realization came to him, "and was about to be killed by Tremaine Dodson, you intervened and set off those mines...And when Kennedy was in the helicopter, about to be killed by Jody, you opened that hatch and dropped her into Lake Michigan."

She beamed with pride. "On the field and in the real world, I always have my finger on the button."

Jasmine watched the TV in rapt horror. Ravi had been wrong—somehow, Valkyrie had known about Invisible Dagger's whereabouts. And the nukes. Somehow, someone somewhere had known about the terrorists having weapons of mass destruction, and instead of stopping them or warning the city, they had set up cameras.

She dialed Ravi's number, her hand trembling as she pressed the phone against her face. Finally, he answered.

"Boss! You won't believe the footage I'm getting. The bald guy is shooting at Kennedy. And one of the generals and the Valk president are tied up. It's crazy—"

"Ravi!" she screamed and cut him off. "Listen to me *right now*. Get away from there. You'll get killed! And it's pointless—there are already cameras set up in the house. The whole thing is playing live on TV. Your footage won't be exclusive anymore."

Ravi paused. In the background of his call, Jasmine could hear Jody bellowing insults at General Lightfoot. She gasped—Ravi was *that* close to the action. He was inches away from getting shot. Or blown up.

"Sorry, boss." His voice was low, disheartened, his good-humored manner slipping for the first time. "I can't leave now. You'll see—I'll make you proud."

"Ravi!"

But he had already hung up. She hurled her phone against the wall, allowing tears of fury and despair to fall from her eyes.

"Shut up, old man!" Jody was still trading barbs with Lightfoot.

"No, *you* shut up!"

Annie glowered at the camera affixed to the ceiling. She couldn't believe it. Here she was, risking her life to stop these villains and save the day...all for Elena's directorial career.

But even she had to admit, it was brilliant—as long as no one ever connected Elena with Invisible Dagger, that is.

Her gaze flickered toward the front door. It was within sight, not too far away. While Jody was busy with Lightfoot, Annie could sprint out of there. She'd be able to recruit back-up to save the two hostages, tell the world about Elena's treachery, and live to fight another day.

Or not fight. She could simply drop her gun and leave. Another life awaited her on the other side of that door. She could be a high school coach, a pro athlete, a nurse, a stay-at-home mom...anything. If she lived through today, the possibilities were limitless.

But the bomb. Lightfoot and Gambol. If Annie ran, Invisible Dagger wouldn't allow the hostages to live long enough to be rescued, not to mention all of Wichita.

And...

She glared again at the camera.

The world was watching. Zeke, Danny Carr, and everyone she knew were all watching. Most of all, *Elena* was watching.

Annie readied her gun. She wouldn't freeze again in the middle of a battle. She wouldn't retreat. She wouldn't fail.

Because, by God, she was *Captain* Annie Kennedy.

She screamed at Jody from behind the counter. "Hey, barf-breath! You gonna keep fiddling with grandpa, or are we gonna do this?"

Jody roared, "I don't fiddle with grandpas!" A moment later, the machine gunfire continued. A hurricane of bullets chewed up the kitchen walls and spat them out in the form of rubble. As Annie was covered in debris and dust, she waited. She waited for the telltale sound that always accompanies an immature man with an automatic weapon.

A hollow *click*.

The gunfire stopped, and Annie vaulted the counter and stormed forward. Jody stood in the living room, fumbling as he tried to quickly reload his empty rifle. He saw her charging straight at him and let out a yelp.

She raised the gun in her non-injured hand and pulled the trigger until her own weapon made a similar *click* sound. Empty.

None of her three bullets hit their primary target, which was Jody's bald head, but Annie had expected that. Two buried themselves in the plaster wall, but one of them found a new home in Jody's forearm. He screeched in anguish as the shot fragmented his bones, and he dropped the rifle.

As she ran at him, she chucked her handgun at his face, and the metal smashed into his nose. He staggered backward and winced, "You little bi—"

She threw a punch at him with her good left hand. He raised his uninjured arm to block the strike, but she had anticipated that. She balled her plastered right hand into a fist, cocked it back, and socked it into his nose.

Agony ran through her broken wrist, throughout her body, and practically blinded her. She might have screamed, but she wasn't sure. When she saw blood streaming down Jody's face, though, in spite of everything, she felt good. Really, really good.

She released a primal yell and didn't let up.

Danny faced Elena Winn, feeling like an amateur matador in the ring with the cleverest bull in the world. He couldn't stop stealing glances at the trigger in her hand. "So where do we go from here?"

She smiled. "How'd you like to be president of Valkyrie Productions?"

Danny saw what she was getting at—once the bomb went off, and General Lightfoot and Gambol were gone, that job would be newly vacant.

He stammered in shock. "And that'll make you...what? General of the Army of Liberty?"

"Nah. I'll stick to directing. That's what I'm good at. But things will definitely change around here. Arena battles will be good for placating the masses, but this," she again pointed at the TV, "is the future."

"Well..." Danny clucked his tongue. He had run out of things to say. He felt drained, exhausted, dejected. "You're sucking the life out of me, twiddling with that button. I can't talk you out of pushing it, so just push it." He pinched the bridge of his nose, trying to stave off the monster of a migraine he felt coming on.

"I'm not going to push this button, Mr. Carr." She set the trigger on Danny's desk and sauntered away from it. "You are."

Danny stared at the big red button. And it stared back at him. "Are you insane?"

She avoided the question. "I've already killed people in my life. Like I said, I think everyone should experience it, at least once. With a single push of a button, you could experience it a million times over."

He gaped at Elena. "How...How could you possibly think I would do this?" Even as the words fell from his mouth, his feet brought him closer to the desk.

"This could be your masterpiece, Danny. Your *Mona Lisa*, your *Hamlet*, your *La Bohème!*" Her words were precision strikes, impassioned, vigorous, enthusiastic. She had transformed from a clever bull to a shrewd merchant hawking her wares. "Valkyrie has told a splendid story with Annie Kennedy. A nurse, coming up from the bottom to become captain of the Army of Liberty. She replaced Ranger Monroe and took the world by storm. But she hit a few stumbling blocks and got beaten to a pulp, so she quietly retired. She's had agony and ecstasy, peaks and valleys, high victories and low defeats. And she's a *mother*. You can't get any better than that!"

Danny loomed over the button. On the TV next to the trigger, Annie was in a brutal fistfight with Jody. Both were getting in good hits. Blood and sweat flew all over the living room, like they were heavyweight champions slugging it out.

Elena kept pushing. "This is the best ending imaginable, Danny. In an effort to redeem herself and save her general and president, she went rogue and got back in the game. She risked it all, facing this wicked terrorist cell all on her own, coming so close to victory, she could taste it. The whole world watching could taste it. But..." She nudged the button closer to Danny. "But she fell just short. She failed, at no fault of her own. History will lionize her. The world will adore her. And you'll be immortalized as Annie Kennedy's advocate and patron."

And just like that, the switch was in Danny's hand. He expected his finger to tremble as it hovered over the button, or for sweat to trickle down his spine. But he was as solid as a marble statue.

Jody landed a punch squarely on one of Annie's black eyes, but she didn't feel a thing. Her entire body was a scab, numbed by pain. As soon as this was over, she would have time to cry and heave, but for now, she had to keep fighting.

"Don't stop!" Lightfoot called out encouragement from the sidelines as he continued to struggle against his bindings. "He's on the ropes, wear him out!"

"I said..." Jody grit his teeth. "Shut up, old man!" He struck the side of Annie's face, and while she was occupied, he kicked her feet out from under her. She landed hard on her back, the air rushing out of her lungs and leaving her gasping.

Jody towered over her, a vision from a horrific mirage. Blood seeped from his mouth and nose, staining his hoodie. He gnashed his teeth like a feral wolverine as he stepped closer to put his heel on her throat.

She panted and glared at him. "You never—"

He growled, "You don't get any last words, lady."

She almost smiled at him. Almost. Using the last of her strength, she lashed out and kicked Jody right in the sack between his spread legs. He squealed, and she rolled to her feet.

"You never learn, do you?" She snatched up the rifle he had dropped, held it like a baseball bat, and walloped his bald head with it. He crumpled to the floor and stopped moving.

"Yes! Ha ha!" Lightfoot cheered. "That's *my* captain!"

Annie wiped blood from her jaw and stared into the tiny camera fastened to the living room ceiling. "And scene." She bowed.

Elena nodded as Danny's forefinger lowered toward the button. "In a hundred years, scholars will still be talking about the tragedies of Oedipus Rex, King Lear, and Annie Kennedy. You can't pass this up."

With his finger an inch away, Danny hesitated. "It's a *nuke*, Winn. Millions dead. Fallout for years. Global implications..."

Her eyes flashed. "If you don't push that button now, another war executive will tomorrow. Well, more like within an hour, if I'm being honest. Or what about your assistant, Suzanne? She has a killer instinct. If you don't do this, I bet she will."

He rankled.

No one outflanked Danny Carr.

So he pushed the button.

Beep beep beep.

Annie's ears perked up at the shrill digital alarm. She scanned the room until...

She saw it. The suitcase on the mantle. The red button was flashing and bleeping.

Gambol twitched against the sound. "What's that horrible chirping?"

Lightfoot's mouth fell open. "Oh God..."

The beeping got faster and faster.

It was seconds from blowing.

Annie blanched. No one had pressed the button. She had stopped the terrorists and saved the day. She had won. It was over.

But apparently not.

Terror flooded her veins, along with regret, panic, and a thousand other emotions. She lunged toward the bomb, hands outstretched.

"NO!"

The button stopped beeping.

And everything went white.

Jasmine blinked. What had happened?

The feed had suddenly cut. An error message popped up on the screen, saying something vague about *technical difficulties*.

She bounded to the television and slapped its side, even though she knew that wouldn't help. She shook the set and screamed at it. Screamed until her throat was sore.

"Turn back on!" She hit the TV with each word. "Turn on, you bloody useless box of no-good, stupid junk!"

The bomb had been beeping. Kennedy had yelled. And then the feed had cut out.

She didn't want to believe it. There was no possible way that what she was imagining was what had actually happened. That's madness. Lunacy. Unthinkable.

"Turn. On. Now!"

The TV screen flickered back to life. Jasmine jerked backward and wiped her watery eyes to get a good look at the feed. She hoped to see the living room in one piece, Annie Kennedy standing over the defeated terrorist, the two hostages alive and well, and Ravi cheering through the window.

But none of that was what she saw. Instead of the live feed, the national news popped up. A harried anchor gawped at the camera, trying and failing to read the teleprompter in a level voice. "The live feed of Annie Kennedy confronting Invisible Dagger has been interrupted. If you're just joining us, the disgraced former captain of the Army of Liberty was facing the wildly popular domestic terrorist cell in Wichita, Kansas, but we don't know the outcome..." Someone off-screen whispered to the anchor, who recoiled. "Are you serious? You're joking, right?"

The screen changed shots. The bottom corner read, "*Live – Stillwater, Oklahoma.*"

Jasmine brought her mental map of the U.S. to mind and guessed that Stillwater was about a hundred miles from Wichita.

Then, all thoughts evaporated from her mind. She couldn't think, she couldn't speak, she couldn't breathe. She withered to the floor and bawled.

A monstrous mushroom cloud plumed above the horizon.

Wichita was gone, along with millions upon millions of people all around it.

Danny removed his finger from the depressed button and turned off the TV on his desk. He didn't want to see the news coverage of the mushroom cloud. This was all the pundits and so-called experts would talk about for years, and he was already tired of it.

So tired.

Elena patted his shoulder as she walked toward the door. "Congrats. You just made history." She leered at him. "Leave the details to me. But you might want to prepare a few remarks for Gambol's funeral and your promotion." Her footfalls echoed in Danny's skull long after she was gone.

The world was quiet. He sat behind his desk—his drawbridge. The border of his domain. He reached into the bottom drawer and pulled out a sealed bottle of scotch he had been saving for years. He'd intended to share it with Suzanne and his other coworkers after closing the biggest deal of his career—what that deal was, he didn't know, but he'd believed he would feel when the time was right to open it.

That day, Danny drank alone, straight from the bottle, knowing he wouldn't stop until it was gone.

Days passed. For longer than Jasmine wanted to admit (least of all to herself), she'd laid on that motel room floor and wailed. She cried until she had run out of tears, and then, she had screamed and moaned.

She couldn't quite name her immediate grief. It was a deadly mixture of the loss of Ravi, a sense of failure at the fact that she hadn't stopped the bomb, and the cosmic dread that the world had changed forever...for the worse.

But as heavy as the grief was, and as much as she didn't want to, she had eventually stood up. Her eyes burned, her legs had turned to jelly, and her head ached like never before, but she stood up and got to work.

At the last second, as she left the motel, she had snatched Ravi's laptop from his dresser. Over the next several days, as she hitchhiked and bussed her way to San Diego, she'd kept herself glued to that laptop.

Something nagged at her—a hangnail in her mind. Finally, while waiting for a bus in middle-of-nowhere Arizona, she realized what it was.

Roderick. The last remaining member of Invisible Dagger. Where was he?

She reached a decision without realizing it.

Using Ravi's technological methods, she would find him. And she would *get* him.

As she trekked westward, she couldn't ignore the cloud that cloaked the nation—and not just the literal mushroom cloud. A crippling, dreary haze of despair had moved in. People walked slowly, looking over their shoulders and glaring at their neighbors. Cops and soldiers stood on street corners, pointing their handguns at passersby. When the handguns didn't make people scared enough, rifles, grenades, and tanks were brought in. Supermarkets were cleared out, along with ammo stores. Large crowds were tinged with suspicion and fear. Every city seemed to be asking itself, "*What next?*"

As impossible as it was, Jasmine wanted to comfort every person she saw. She yearned to wrap them in a warm embrace and assure them everything was going to be okay. And that wouldn't be a lie, because she would make sure of it. She was going to track down Roderick and send the full might of the Army of Liberty after him.

Once he was wiped out, stomped like the cretinous bug he was, things would get better. The threat would be gone, and the world could begin to rebuild.

While in a taxi passing through mid-California, she found him. She knew where Roderick was headed.

She almost let out a whoop, but she didn't want to alarm the driver. But she celebrated on the inside. She had used Ravi's method of tech tracking to locate the final terrorist as he drove across the country. Her friend would've been proud of her.

At long last, several days after the fateful bombing of Wichita, she had finally made it to the Valkyrie building in San Diego. She finagled her way past the security guard in the lobby. His face was shell-shocked, droopy and ashen, seemingly afflicted with PTSD in the present moment.

And yet, he was watching TV footage of the nuclear explosion and fall-out. Spectatorship lived on.

He waved her through without peeling his eyes from the screen.

On board the elevator, she stabbed the button for the top floor—surely, that was where those with effective power would be. As she traveled up and up and up, she adjusted Ravi's laptop under her arm. She was armed with the truth, and she was itching to unsheathe it and do some damage.

Ravi had been right when he said she'd come a long way from being a history professor interviewed on public access TV. Now, instead of just talking about war and its effects on people, she was out in the world, truly making a difference.

Alone in the elevator, she muttered to herself, "What happens after the heroics...? What happens after the tragedy...?"

If she had anything to say about it, this story was going to have a happy ending.

Ding. The doors slid open, and she emerged in the halls of power. It was strangely quiet, like an ancient ruin rather than a bustling enterprise.

No matter. There had to be someone of importance here.

Jasmine marched down the hallway, toward the large office at its terminus. She burst into the room and squinted against the sun streaming through the wall-sized window. The Pacific churned and roiled far below—even the oceans were apprehensive these days.

A desk sat before the window, and someone sat at its chair, but Jasmine could only see a silhouette against the sun. "H-Hello?"

The figure rose from the chair, bathed in sunlight like an Egyptian god, and walked forward to meet Jasmine. It was a woman, slender and frankly unassuming. She held out her hands. "Yes, hi, hi. My apologies, I just moved into this office, and I don't have a secretary yet. I didn't know I had a meeting on the books. What can I do for you?"

"Um..." Jasmine swallowed. For all her grand plans, she suddenly realized she hadn't planned what she was going to say. "This may sound odd, but who are you?"

The woman sized up Jasmine for a moment, then smirked. "I'm Elena Winn, the executive director of Valkyrie Productions. And you are?"

"Jasmine Creedy, investigative journalist."

Elena clicked her tongue as her smile grew. "Sounds like my day just got far more interesting. Sit with me." She led Jasmine to a nearby table, which was overflowing with folders and stray paperwork, and they sat across from one another. Elena crossed her legs and leaned back, as confident as could be. Jasmine gingerly laid Ravi's laptop on the table, next to a stack of papers, and kept one hand on it for safe keeping.

The two sat in silence for a few beats. Elena seemed to be understanding Jasmine more and more each second without them even opening their mouths. Jasmine shifted uncomfortably. At first, Ms. Winn had appeared rather non-threatening, but now, as she absorbed Jasmine with her fox-like eyes, she was the most terrifying person on the planet.

Jasmine began. "Ms. Winn, I started on the path that led me here because I wanted my own streaming show. It sounds ridiculous, but it's the truth. Along the way, however, my..." She started to say *cameraman*, but corrected herself. "...My partner Ravi Stockett and I discovered that Invisible Dagger's destructive reach far exceeded previous expectations. They started by knocking out power grids and blowing up empty factories, but their worst potential reared its ugly head."

She felt tears welling up behind her eyes, but she refused to allow them to fall. She pressed on, feeling like she was back on public access TV, giving an expository interview for an unseen audience.

"Somehow, Invisible Dagger commandeered two suitcase nuclear devices from a Valkyrie silo. A few days ago, one was activated in Wichita, which leaves one in the wind. Well...I've found it."

Elena arched a brow but didn't say anything.

"That is to say," Jasmine stammered and continued, "I know where it's going. Using a tracking system created by Ravi, I believe I have located Roderick, the final member of the cell." She took a breath and laid out her facts. "Over the past few days, ever since Wichita, a blue Lamborghini has been traveling northeast. A very conspicuous vehicle in the Midwest, for many reasons, but most notably because it belonged to Mr. Salvatore Caracas, a Valkyrie recruiter who was executed by Invisible Dagger on livestream. The blue car was even in the background of that very video. One can easily conclude that Invisible Dagger took that car after killing Mr. Caracas and used it in addition to their traditional red minivan. Now..." She prepared to lob the harpoon. "Judging by the trajectory of Mr. Caracas's car, the assumption that Roderick is the person driving it, and the fact that Invisible Dagger just bombed Annie Kennedy's hometown... Ms. Winn, it's clear that Roderick is planning on detonating another nuke in Ranger Monroe's birthplace: West Amana, Iowa."

The room vibrated at her bombshell revelation.

Elena's first question was: "And where is Mr. Stockett?"

Jasmine answered without averting her gaze. "He was in Wichita." She pressed on. "Ms. Winn, I'm not sure why Roderick is taking so long to travel to Iowa. He should be there by now, but he's taking his time for some reason. Maybe he's nervous. Maybe he stopped by some moronic gift shops on the way. I don't know, and I frankly don't care. All that matters is that the bomb hasn't gone off yet. Thanks to Ravi, we have a way to find him and prevent another tragedy."

"Mmm." Elena tapped her temple with a fingernail. "Have you told anyone else about this theory?"

An icy chill ran through Jasmine's bones. That wasn't the sort of question she had wanted to hear.

Elena caught Jasmine's reaction and leaned forward. "Ms. Creedy, I'm going to make you one offer, and I strongly suggest you take it." She reached across the table and dragged a folder toward her. She adjusted the papers within, then locked eyes with Jasmine. She didn't need to threaten her with physical violence to make her intentions clear. "How would you like to be the Army of Liberty's exclusive war correspondent?"

Jasmine was speechless. Her hand tremored on top of Ravi's laptop. She could barely form a cogent thought. She had entered this office prepared to sic the dogs on Invisible Dagger, and now she was being pressured to never speak of her findings. Those words had never been said, but Elena's sharp eyes did all the talking.

Elena went on. "You'll travel in lockstep with the world's premier army. Five-star hotels. Exotic locales. Hunky men tripping over each other to win your favor. All the glitz, glam, fame, and fortune you could ever want."

As she spoke, she slowly, inch by inch, pulled the laptop out of Jasmine's loose grip and replaced it with the folder.

The next thing Jasmine knew, Elena stood up and tucked the laptop under her arm. "It's an honor to have you aboard, Ms. Creedy. I know you'll do wonderful things for Valkyrie." She gestured to the folder in Jasmine's hand. "Better read up." She strode across the office back to her desk.

Jasmine felt hollow. Intangible, like a ghost. An ember of anger burned deep down in her gut. Anger on behalf of the millions of had been deceived. On behalf of the thousands who had been killed. And on behalf of Ravi, her dear friend whom she had known for far too brief a time. But that glimmer of anger was overshadowed by sheer terror.

The battle was over, and she'd lost. Elena was the overlord of this new, post-Wichita world.

So...It turned out *this* was what happened after the heroics.

She saw no choice other than to open the folder and see what she was going to report. After skimming the first few lines, her jaw dropped open. She gasped at Elena in shock. "This says Roderick is the nephew of President Ahmar of the State of Palestine! Is this true?"

Elena set the laptop in a desk drawer, slid it shut, and locked it tight. "Not yet. Not until our new war correspondent reports it."

At that moment, Jasmine saw it all. A link between Invisible Dagger and a foreign nation (a foreign nation with an army conveniently under the purview of Valkyrie Productions). A scapegoat for the bombing of Wichita...and the forthcoming bombing of rural Iowa. Tens of millions of deaths, untold grief and destruction, all laid at the feet of someone else. The first real war in decades was on its way—must-see TV, a box office bonanza, the most-watched event of all time.

And Elena Winn was its mastermind. Once the sprawling war between the Army of Liberty and Palestine was complete, Jasmine had no doubt another tragedy would pop up, prompting more war and even higher viewership.

"Best hop to it, Ms. Creedy." Elena slunk back into the sunlight, once again becoming a godlike silhouette.

Jasmine hugged the folder full of lies—lies that she would turn into truths—to her chest. She stood, took a shuddering breath, and shambled out of the office, into her new life.

Danny's new office was even bigger than his previous one. Made sense—it had belonged to Leigh Gambol. President of the enterprise.

President Daniel Carr. The head of Valkyrie Productions. The big boss, the Executive executive.

He was still on the top floor, but the ceilings were higher, the carpet thicker, and the colors richer. The office had no window, but instead, there was a grand fireplace, a billiards table, a diamond chandelier, and a rifle belonging to George Washington mounted on the wall. He felt like he was in a womb, warm and closed off from the rest of the world.

The instant he had moved in, he'd had a bar installed. He didn't intend on spending a minute as president of the enterprise sober.

Suzanne clomped in, clutching a binder. She looked around and whistled. "I'm still getting used to this place. Swanky."

Danny took a sip of whiskey as he lounged on a leather sofa. Never before had he wished for Suzanne to leave him alone, but the dull throb behind his eyes was putting him in a foul mood. Without raising his head from the cushion, he snapped, "What is it, Suze?"

She bristled and plopped the binder on his desk. "From Winn. She says it's a summary of next steps." She swiveled and left the office, refusing to put up with his attitude.

Ever since Elena had handed Danny that godforsaken button, Danny had been too jittery to make any decisions a president would typically make. Currently, Elena was arranging some sort of game-changing war in Palestine, allowing Danny in the loop only to sign the necessary documents.

All of this meant that Suzanne's passion project of a Palestinian sneak attack on a Russian city was "indefinitely put on hold" (which was industry talk for "dumped in a trash can"). She was unspeakably bitter toward Danny, and he doubted their relationship would ever be back to the way it was before.

Danny groaned. The binder was pretty thick to be a summary. He lurched off the sofa and padded over to the desk. His new drawbridge... except he felt like an invader, not the rightful ruler.

He downed his whiskey as he opened the binder.

A house key sat on top, a red velvet bow knotted around it. Attached to the key was a handwritten note: *"Enjoy your new house. E. Winn."* An address was printed underneath.

Danny scrunched his forehead in confusion. Winn gifting him a house? Why?

Then, he recognized the address. It was on Coronado Island.

Salvatore Caracas's mansion.

Winn had been the one to outbid him at the last second. She had paid triple the asking price...and was now *giving* him the key.

He clutched the key in his fist until its teeth bit into his palm. He desperately wanted to reject the taunt—throw the key in the fireplace, toss it in the ocean, drop it down a garbage disposal.

But he couldn't. He wanted the house.

And he was afraid of what Winn would do if he crossed her. So he pocketed the key, reached into a desk drawer, and withdrew a bottle of whiskey. He was never more than a few steps away from booze while he was in his office.

His domain. It struck him that, now that Winn had sunk her talons into the house where he lived and slept, this office was the last place he could control.

So he poured a hefty amount into his glass and kept drinking.

Bzzzz. Bzzzz.

His phone buzzed in his pocket. The last thing he wanted at that moment was to gab, argue, or schmooze, but he yanked it out and checked the caller ID. A name stared back at him that he had thought he'd never see. His heartrate spiked, and he answered.

"Hey, son."

The voice on the other line wavered. Finally, it said, "Hi, Danny."

Yep, it was Zechariah alright. For the last several years, he'd refused to call Danny "father" or "dad."

"What, uh..." Danny set his drink aside. "What can I do for you? Need anything?"

"No, I don't need anything." His son sounded lower than dirt. Despondent. On the verge of a tar pit of total depression.

Danny said, "Okay then. What's up? How's your time in the Army of Liberty going?"

"I'm not in an army anymore."

"R-Really?" Danny stammered. Not because he was surprised, per se, but because he hadn't known this already. "Let me meet you somewhere for dinner. We can talk about whatever's on your—"

Zechariah cut him off. "No, I just have something to tell you." His voice hitched as if he wanted to sob but had no more tears to contribute. "Ever since Mom...Well, ever since then—"

Danny jumped in. "I know that was tough. I could barely see straight for months after she died."

"I didn't call to talk about how hard her death was on you." Zechariah's tone was still shaky and dejected, but he may as well have screamed the words.

Danny didn't have a response. Not a good one, anyway.

"But woe is you, right?" Zechariah cleared his throat. "So. Since Mom, I haven't had a reason to talk to you. But now...I just...There's something you have the right to know."

Danny braced himself and, for the first time in his long-reaching memory, let someone else talk without trying to gain the upper-hand.

"I..." Zechariah heaved a sigh as heavy as Sisyphus's boulder. "I was in love with Annie Kennedy. The captain who...who was in Wichita. She fought Invisible Dagger...which you know. Of course. But..."

The line crackled with silence. It lasted a full minute, maybe even longer. Danny fought every urge in his nature, but he didn't say a word. He just waited for his son to talk.

Finally, Zechariah continued. "But she was pregnant. I mean...She was pregnant with our child. My child." He paused. "I was the dad."

At first, Danny didn't react. He couldn't, because there was no way what his son had said was true.

But after a moment, his hand began to shake. He could barely hold onto the phone.

"Umm..." He forced words past the cactus in his throat. "I-I'm sorry, son. We'll talk more, okay? Gotta go." He hung up before Zechariah could respond.

The world pulsed around him. Bile churned in his gut, and he felt like he was close to blacking out.

He had pushed the button.

He had murdered untold millions of people, including his own grandchild.

Because...Because...All of a sudden, he couldn't think of a single good reason.

Danny Carr set his face in his hands and wept.

www.ingramcontent.com/pod-product-compliance
Lightning Source LLC
Chambersburg PA
CBHW030633030726
47497CB00006B/1763